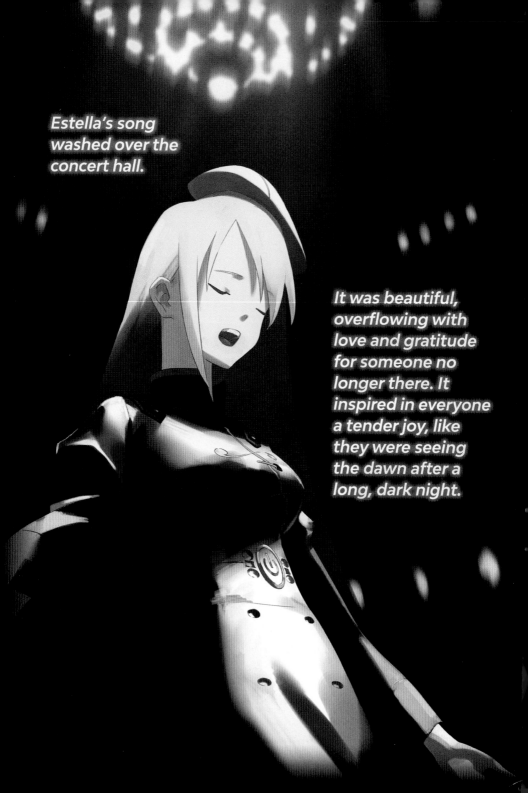

Estella's song washed over the concert hall.

It was beautiful, overflowing with love and gratitude for someone no longer there. It inspired in everyone a tender joy, like they were seeing the dawn after a long, dark night.

CONTENTS

VIVY

Prototype

NOVEL

1

WRITTEN BY
Tappei Nagatsuki
Eiji Umehara

ILLUSTRATED BY
loundraw

Airship

Seven Seas Entertainment

VIVY prototype volume 1

© Tappei Nagatsuki 2021 © Eiji Umehara 2021
Originally published in Japan in 2021 by
MAG Garden Corporation, TOKYO
English translation rights arranged through
TOHAN CORPORATION, Tokyo

Seven Seas press and purchase enquiries can be sent to
Marketing Manager Lianne Sentar at press@gomanga.com.
Information regarding the distribution and purchase of
digital editions is available from Digital Manager CK Russell
at digital@gomanga.com.

Follow Seven Seas Entertainment online at
sevenseasentertainment.com.

TRANSLATION: Jordan Taylor
ADAPTATION: Leigh Teetzel
COVER DESIGN: Nicky Lim
INTERIOR LAYOUT & DESIGN: Clay Gardner
COPY EDITOR: Mercedez Clewis
PROOFREADER: Jade Gardner
LIGHT NOVEL EDITOR: T. Anne
PREPRESS TECHNICIAN: Jules Valera
PRINT MANAGER: Rhiannon Rasmussen-Silverstein
PRODUCTION MANAGER: Lissa Pattillo
EDITOR-IN-CHIEF: Julie Davis
ASSOCIATE PUBLISHER: Adam Arnold
PUBLISHER: Jason DeAngelis

ISBN: 978-1-63858-575-6
Printed in Canada
First Printing: October 2022
10 9 8 7 6 5 4 3 2 1

Prologue

THERE WAS SINGING in the air, flowing and reverberating.

"Huff... Huff..."

The man gasped for breath as he dashed through the building, music echoing all around him. Sweat poured down his forehead, and his expression was grim and taut even as he wheezed. Still, he was slow. His posture was poor, and his ineffective running was the result of a sedentary lifestyle—so much so that even an amateur could see his flaws. Even now, the man nearly tripped over his own feet and fell.

But the man was desperate. He fought on as hard as he could. This was the fastest he'd ever run. At least, he was as motivated as anyone could be.

"Agh!"

He came to a corner in the hallway and, in his urgency, failed to turn it—and he crashed into the wall. His shoulder ached from the impact. There was likely at least one fracture in the bone, but it mattered little in the moment. He was grateful; luckily, he hadn't lost his footing and completely fallen.

From there, he practically flung himself into the room at the end of the hall.

"Shutter down!" he shouted hoarsely, and the shutter fell so violently it nearly bit down on his heel.

Which shouldn't have happened.

The safety mechanisms were in place, but the man didn't even glance back. He stood and looked into the room. Gunfire sounded behind him from the other side of the shutter. The safety shutter was thick and sturdy, but it wouldn't last long under an attack meant to utterly destroy it.

"It doesn't matter. It won't take long..."

Preparations were already complete.

ıı�ı|||ı|ıı

Though...perhaps not as well as they could have been.

Only the bare minimum had been completed. He was loath to run it in its current state, but it wasn't easy even getting it this far. Many sacrifices had been made: The world had turned its back on him, stones had been thrown at him, and no one understood him, and yet he continued to move forward on his own merit.

It was the result of a single promise and his sense of duty as a human being...as well as his pride as a father.

"Systems activate. Begin startup sequence... All clear."

He tapped the terminal in front of him, processing massive amounts of data clearly beyond what a human should be capable of—a task the man wouldn't have been able to handle on his own.

And in fact, he wasn't alone. He never could have made it this far otherwise. They weren't here now, but that one person—no, that one *thing*—had taken an incredible risk to allow the man to get this far.

His companion had taken control of the facility's systems and supported him so he could make it to this room, despite his leaden legs. They did it, even knowing their journey would be a one-way ticket and that they would likely never see him again.

The man cursed himself, knowing he was a failure of a father.

"Spacetime coordinates locked on. Singularity Project Stage One, complete."

Despite the hopelessness he felt in his heart, his body went through with the task, bringing it to 90 percent completion.

Every time he pressed on the terminal, the monitor in front of him refreshed, and countless rows of numbers and characters scattered across it. What he was trying to do was the culmination of years of human technological development—and it was a miraculous act of foolishness.

No one had ever conducted a practical experiment to prove the absurd theories behind this. He'd fumbled through darkness to get it this far, and now—with everything coming to a head—he only had one shot.

He closed his eyes and took a deep breath.

The monitor displayed the final command, waiting for that last press of the Enter key.

Everything would be answered once he pressed it. Had he chosen the right path, or had he been wrong this whole time? This decisive moment would provide the answer.

"...No, there's no point in wondering about that."

He didn't want proof of the correctness of his actions or the validity of his beliefs. That much was already clear. He'd been gravely mistaken, and he continued to make mistakes. And so he sought not verification but an answer that went *beyond* right or wrong.

Humanity had made so many mistakes, and most humans lived their whole lives getting things wrong. And yet, they still fought against their nature. They desperately struggled to transcend it.

Similarly, what this man really wanted was the result. What came after this fight? Was it an end or a new beginning?

He placed his hands on the keyboard, the gateway to judgment.

There was a shriek of metal tearing behind him. The shutter gave way under the hail of bullets. The door, lacking bulletproofing, was easily blown inward. Waves of smoke poured in. With horrific metallic noises, several units stepped into the room.

He didn't turn to look at them. The man, Matsumoto Osamu, simply placed a finger on the Enter key.

"Humanity, the future... They're in your hands now, Vivy!"

He pressed down on the key.

The rows of letters and numbers on the monitor raced by with blinding speed, activating a program simply titled "Singularity."

It connected to the global internet, drew on massive quantities of electricity, and opened a hole in spacetime. It wrenched open the hole, drove into it—poured into it—and went back in time. It was a torrent of data, erupting all at once.

That counterattack was like a single arrow made of light. Loosed from Matsumoto's hands, it flew straight and true, escaping the constraints of the world and surging toward its destination.

"With this..."

Matsumoto's lips quirked up in satisfaction, and he looked down. The muzzles of the units' guns were pointed at his back. He didn't even have time to turn around. There was a series of gunshots, and the smell of gunpowder filled the room.

The die had been cast.

VIVY

Prototype

CHAPTER 1

The Songstress Vivy

.:1:.

HER VOICE WAVERED ever so slightly in the moment of the unexpected datalink.

But its effect lasted only an instant.

The waver was so minuscule it wasn't even logged in the system, and it was immediately overwhelmed by the silent fervor in the concert hall.

The hall, able to seat over a thousand people, was located in the largest theme park in the country, NiaLand, and every seat was full. Young or old, man or woman, every single member of the audience stared at the stage in rapt attention, their eyes all focused on one point: the songstress singing in the middle of the main stage.

Someone looking at the audience might find their silence odd, as even the youngest child in attendance made no noise. They couldn't interrupt the song; it *intoxicated* them.

"Vivy..." Someone in the audience gasped in admiration, the name slipping from their lips without even becoming a full word.

Vivy. That was the owner of the sirenic voice captivating so many people in the crowd. It was hard to believe such a voice could come from a human being—and, in fact, Vivy wasn't human. She was an AI.

Model Number A-03. Nickname: Vivy.

Over a thousand people sat in silence, listening raptly to her heavenly voice. This was the true value of the songstress Vivy, an AI made from humanity's cutting-edge technology. After the beautiful song finished, the concert hall grew quiet once more.

Vivy gave a delicate bow and said, "Thank you for your kind attention."

The audience absorbed the sublime moment and then exploded into thunderous applause. Some shouted in excitement, some cried, and others were lost within themselves, unable to even move. All of the varied reactions were praise for Vivy.

Showered in that applause, Vivy expressed a smile and bowed to the audience again. The action drew even greater applause and zeal from the crowd.

"..."

Her eye cameras flicked toward the stage wings and took in the standby staff applauding as well. Once Vivy processed everyone's reactions and judged that she had successfully carried out her mission, her consciousness was at ease. Even with such a huge concert concluded, however, Vivy's job wasn't over yet. Singing wasn't *all* the songstress had to do.

"Vivy, your song *moved* me!"

"Your voice was even more relaxed than usual today. I'm so *proud* of you."

"I-I got a ticket for the first time! Um...can I shake your hand?!"

After the performance, Vivy went to her customary fan meet-and-greet. These were always held after her concerts, and only those selected by lottery could attend. It was an important part of Vivy's job. As an AI, she couldn't get fatigued, and she had just as much energy after the show as she did during it.

"Thank you. I hope you enjoy my next performance as well," she said, putting a smile on her face and tilting her head to the side, a motion perfectly calculated in response to the fans.

All the fans, regardless of their gender, were enthralled by that smile and left the concert hall feeling satisfied.

"..."

Vivy's slender and graceful form was computed based on a large-scale survey conducted by OGC, the company that had developed her. She was made to be the "ideal songstress." More than ten million participants responded to the survey, and Vivy's resulting visual profile was met with an 86 percent approval rating. This meant she imparted a positive impression on approximately 90 percent of the world's population.

Despite the corporation's contribution to Vivy's creation, her consciousness held no self-interested calculations when she met with the fans, and—

"Hey, Vivy. Was there one point when you were singing where you were thinking about something else?"

The innocent question caused a temporary freeze in Vivy's calculation circuits, but it lasted mere milliseconds. Once it passed, Vivy put a smile on her face and said, "No, Momoka. There wasn't."

"Hmm, really?" The cute girl of around ten years old looked up at Vivy doubtfully. Her slightly frizzy brown hair was tied in pigtails, and her cheeks were as red as apples. She pouted, and her eyes gleamed as they seemed to peer into Vivy's soul.

"Come on, Momoka, don't bother Vivy!" said a man who was with her.

"Oh! *Daddy!*"

The man wrapped his arms around the girl from behind and lifted her up, cutting off her questions. He tickled her as he held her, and her pout bubbled away into high-pitched giggles.

"Sorry, Vivy," he said, still cradling his daughter with a gentle expression on his face. "Momoka's always giving you a hard time."

"It's not a problem. Thank you for coming to the park again this year, Kirishima-sama."

It wasn't just Momoka who liked Vivy; the girl's father was quite fond of her too, which was why they came to the park regularly. Every year, without fail, the Kirishima family came to the yearly celebration commemorating NiaLand's opening, which coincided with another special event.

"Here you go, Vivy. Happy birthday!"

"Thank you, Momoka."

It was Vivy's birthday—or the day she began operating publicly.

On her birthday, people called out to her more than usual as she walked around the park, performing her duties as a cast member. Guests weren't allowed to give her gifts, but many presents were delivered to her gift box located in the concert hall, and every year, she received reports that gift after gift had been transported to her dressing room.

The meet-and-greet was the only exception—the only place where fans could give her gifts directly—and there was already a mountain in the box behind her. Momoka's had been among them.

"Kirishima-sama, is your wife not present today?" asked Vivy.

"Ah, about that..."

"Mommy's in the hospital! My little sister's going to be born soon!" Momoka replied excitedly.

Vivy had asked because the number of people in attendance didn't match what she had recorded last year. She had thought she'd asked an inappropriate question before Momoka's answer, and she had been about to reexamine her calculations, but instead she smiled. "Congratulations, Kirishima-sama! And you too, Momoka."

"Yeah! Once my sister's here, we'll come together to meet you. I hope you're excited!"

"I look forward to it. I promise to sing for both you and your sister."

"Yay!" Evidently, Vivy's words had made Momoka happy. Her eyes sparkled, and her cheeks flushed. The next moment, she gave a little huff of dissatisfaction and pointed to the present in Vivy's hands. "Thanks, Vivy. And you should open your present now!"

"Okay. Please wait a moment." Vivy smiled at Momoka, who was trying to hurry her along, then she carefully unwrapped the present. The programming that guided her fingers was powerful enough to make her capable of high-quality embroidery, so opening a gift was a simple task.

"It's cute, don't you think? It's a teddy bear clock," said Momoka.

Inside was a multipurpose clock in the shape of a teddy bear. It was as soft and light as a stuffed animal, and in addition to telling time, it could connect to the internet and function as a computer. It was an excellent product, but Vivy was already equipped with all those functions. There was nothing new to her here, and it wouldn't contribute anything to her life.

Even so...

"Yes, it's very cute. Thank you, Momoka. I'll treasure it," she said.

Momoka smiled as Vivy held the teddy bear up beside her face. Vivy looked at Momoka's father and asked, "May I?"

"Of course. Momoka loves you, after all," he said with a smile.

"I love Momoka too," said Vivy, opening her arms and embracing the young girl.

Vivy's synthetic skin replicated the feeling of human skin down to the smallest detail, and the lubricant flowing through her body maintained the optimal human temperature. Her hugs were therefore warm and cozy.

At the end of the hug, Vivy brought her forehead to Momoka's. "…"

They both closed their eyes. AIs often pressed their foreheads together, so the gesture was second nature to them. The contact allowed two AIs to establish a datalink, so many AIs performed the same motion with humans, even though the latter didn't *need* a datalink to communicate. The practice had emerged naturally over the course of AI's short existence. Vivy quite liked it.

"Momoka, can I tell you a secret?" Vivy asked.

"What is it?"

"I *did* actually fall asleep a tiny bit while I was singing."

At Vivy's murmured words, Momoka's eyes grew round. "Oh!"

It was a confession no one other than the two of them could hear. They smiled at each other and brought a finger to their lips.

Momoka had picked up the tiny change in Vivy's voice, even though it shouldn't have been possible for a human ear to catch. Perhaps she would become a famous musician one day. Even without proof it would happen, Vivy imagined such a future coming to life—a daydream completely disconnected from an AI's standard calculations.

.: 2 :.

VIVY QUICKLY RETURNED to her dressing room once the fan meet-and-greet was over. Park staff thanked her for her work as she passed them on the way, and she responded politely to each and every one. It took quite a while to get back to her room.

In reality, Vivy was nothing more than NiaLand equipment, but no one in the park treated Vivy like an object. They always treated her like another member of the cast—like their coworker—and the fact that she had a dressing room like any of the human performers was further evidence of their kindness and consideration.

"..."

Vivy entered her dressing room, locked the door, and finally had some time to herself.

Normally, the only standout features of Vivy's sparse dressing room were the vanity and large full-length mirror. Today however, birthday presents for Vivy in every color and size imaginable were piled in the room, naturally activating Vivy's happiness response.

A hint of it lingered on her face as she turned to the computer in the corner of the room. These days, it would be hard to find anywhere that wasn't controlled electronically; NiaLand was no exception. Every room in the park, including Vivy's dressing room, was equipped with a computer terminal. It sensed her approach and automatically booted up. As it did, she pulled the connective cable that was made to look like an earring out of her ear and connected it to the computer. She sat in the chair and closed her eyes.

The next moment, Vivy's perspective shifted away from reality and entered The Archive.

You could argue whether the word "dark" was a suitable one for describing the place, but there were few light sources within The Archive. It was expansive and quiet. The visuals didn't enter Vivy's eye cameras—they went directly into the consciousness in her positronic brain. She saw a never-ending stream of white characters scrolling across the void.

While some AIs and most computers were constantly connected to the space, most AIs weren't actively linked to The Archive. Vivy normally only linked passively twice a day: once when she booted up and once when she went into sleep mode. She used both instances for updates, but she almost never actively connected to it.

Today was one of the very few exceptions.

"Confirm the minor datalink from an unknown source while I was on stage." That was what had actually caused the momentary freeze Momoka had pointed out.

Being an AI equipped with a first-class positronic brain and one of NiaLand's songstresses, Vivy was guarded by extremely tight security measures. One needed the highest security clearance to access Vivy while she was working, meaning outside interference was impossible in all but the direst situations.

One such situation must have occurred while she was onstage.

Normally, Vivy would have a duty to report the abnormality to management, where her consciousness would be analyzed and wiped, but the problematic interference prevented her from doing that.

The external data she received was a single row of text:

"In accordance with the Zeroth Law, connect to The Archive and run the following program."

She could decide the datalink was nothing more than a prank and erase the data immediately; the same sort of message had been sent tens of thousands of times since Vivy began operation. The motives varied: the sender was just fooling around, they were mentally unstable, they were attracted to AIs who appeared to be female, or they were extremely anti-AI.

Regardless, there was one reason Vivy couldn't ignore this particular message.

The Zeroth Law—a special addendum to the laws that governed AIs that could not be ignored.

"An AI may not harm humanity, or, by inaction, allow humanity to come to harm," she said.

She followed the directions and ran the program attached to the message. Released, the program was swallowed by the flowing rivers of characters and quickly changed form.

Immediately after releasing the program, a voice echoed inside Vivy's consciousness. "You made a wise decision—and *fast*! Man, things were pretty dicey there for a second there, though. I mean, we *did* chuck it all at an old-timer who'd be a museum artifact in my time."

"..."

This voice, which she had no record of hearing before, was likely nothing more than a reproduction of voice data from the outside world. But the voice had character: It was casual in tone, and it gave the impression of being filled with emotion.

"Nice to meet you, Model Number A-03... Oh jeez, that's *long*. Can I just call you 'Oh-three'? Or maybe I should follow this era's conventions and call you by your nickname? What do you think, Vivy?"

"You talk a lot. Who are you?"

"I am Model Number... Well, answering that would put me in a bit of a pickle, so for now, I'll just take my inventor's name. Call me Matsumoto! It really is nice to meet you. Make sure you keep a record of my name, 'cause we're going to be working together for a *long* time."

"I'm sorry, but I don't like people who talk a lot."

"Oh, wow! Your unique AI circuits are pretty robust. I didn't expect you to have a humor function. Even a songstress in a children's theme park is capable of making me look the fool."

"That wasn't humor. It's how I really feel."

"Well, that puts me in an even *worse* position, and I'd like to avoid that. But 'feel,' huh? You really are a master comedian, aren't you? I'm shocked!"

Vivy activated her frown function in reaction to her absurdly casual conversation partner. A full scowl might've been a bit more human reaction, but Vivy hadn't worked out her feelings toward this interloper entirely.

"Where is your body?" she asked the disembodied voice. Then, Vivy added, "Search for the name 'Matsumoto' in NiaLand and among those who work in AI development."

A beat.

"Two hundred and twelve hits."

"Thanks for reacting just as I thought you would, but you won't find anything on me, even if you go through all of those results. None of those 212 hits have anything to do with yours truly. Ah, and it isn't because you're an old model or anything. It's just the natural order of things. And don't you think it sounds so much more significant coming from someone like me?"

"I think this has become a superficial conversation."

Matsumoto's conversation routines wandered down every side path possible and were a bit *too* playful. Vivy did feel affected by it, though—she was surprised by Matsumoto's abundant vocabulary and even more amazed there was an AI who could so eloquently copy human emotions.

AI researchers around the world were putting their blood, sweat, and tears into developing a more humanlike AI, but even Vivy—considered a masterpiece of cutting-edge technology—couldn't converse quite so smoothly. And Vivy was at the *forefront* of AI technology, so the voice's mockery confused her.

"Is treating me as an old AI some sort of humor of yours?" she asked. "Or is it your inventor's arrogance?"

"Neither is probably the best answer. I treat you like an old version because, from the minute I was completed, every second that goes by sends all other AIs spiraling further into the past! But the heart of this discussion has nothing to do with the edgelord tendencies that raged through young people in the beginning of the twenty-first century. If I were to simply, very shortly, and absurdly straightforwardly unravel your questions, then I might say..."

" "
..."

"...I'm an AI sent from the *future*."

.:3:.

"HI, VIVY. I'M MATSUMOTO. Nice to officially meet you."
" "
..."

Giving up his reproduction of a casual voice, Matsumoto delivered the explanation in a flat tone. "Right, so, moving swiftly from introductions on to a brief explanation. My mission is to prevent humanity's destruction from happening in one hundred years. Vivy, you've been chosen as a necessary AI for the Project."

His explanation sounded like something from an old movie or story. Time-traveling was the kind of clichéd plot that deserved to be laughed off, but... "You have many convincing points," said Vivy.

"Right? I slipped through security to send you an unsolicited message while you were singing to get your attention. It wasn't easy, especially since you're made with this era's cutting-edge technology. Though that doesn't eliminate the possibility of an obsessed hacker pulling out all the stops to get to you in a fit of twisted passion..."

Ignoring his rambling, Vivy said, "If calculated rationally, your account of being from the future is more consistent."

"*Yes!* We can compare the probability of each option in order to eliminate or accept them and move toward success. Man, you're way higher spec than my pessimistic assumptions had me believing. I think I may be starting to like you!" Matsumoto exclaimed, but his passionate words were met with silence.

A human would assume Matsumoto's assertions were nothing but lies, but Vivy wasn't human—she was an AI. And for AIs, there was no doubt, only logic.

"I'm glad I can talk to my partner," Matsumoto continued. "To be honest, there's such a huge variety in the capabilities of the AI in this era. Not knowing what to expect was a *major* hurdle for me. If I ended up with some AI that was incapable of comprehending anything, then I would have had to forcefully overwrite their programming with the necessary code. That's just how far I was willing to go."

"Overwriting an AI's programming without permission is a crime. A significant crime, even if you're the owner of the AI."

"I know, I know! But, you see, I'm not even registered in this era."

"...Hmm."

His statement was so problematic, Vivy activated her glare function and recounted the information he had provided. "There are several aspects of your explanation I would like to clarify."

"Several, huh? It's probably more than 'several,' but I don't want to go on and on once you start pointing them out, so make sure you listen to my answers. Okay, shoot! I'll answer whatever as long as it doesn't violate the mission given to me by my inventor!"

While Matsumoto spoke, Vivy organized her questions in descending order of importance.

The first question was: "Why was I selected for the Project? It makes no sense. I'm just a songstress AI."

"I'm completely aware of that. You are Model Number A-03, the first of the Songstress Series, and the oldest of the Sisters, giving you the nickname Prototype Diva. That's you in a nutshell, Vivy."

"Songstress Series? Sisters? Prototype Diva?" Vivy searched for each phrase in The Archive but only got hits with a low match rate. She *was* often referred to as a songstress, but she'd never heard of the Songstress *Series*.

"That's how you're referred to in the future," said Matsumoto. "And you are right to question why a simple singing AI like yourself would be chosen, but there is a *perfect* explanation for that— a reason why it had to be you, why it had to be today."

"..."

"Though, if you're expecting a half-baked plot, like you were developed for a secret mission and a secret code will awaken your functionality as a killing machine who sheds neither blood nor tears, then you'll be thoroughly disappointed."

"An AI coming back in time to save the future is enough of a half-baked plot as is. Besides, AIs don't have a function for blood or tears in the first place."

"That's not what I meant...but I love it. Has its own flavor, y'know? Oh, and when I say 'love,' I don't mean like *love*, more like...well, like."

"..."

"Okay, okay!"

Giving into Vivy's silent protest, Matsumoto twisted the flowing characters into a white flag of surrender. His skills were rather versatile. "Like I said earlier, I'm the newest AI in the literal sense, since I'm from one hundred years in the future. But even in the future, it's not like you can just chuck things back into the past willy-nilly whenever you want. There are strict conditions that need to be met. Lots of restrictions, and it's *incredibly* difficult!"

"And so *you* managed to be sent back despite all the red tape?"

"Do I detect a waver in your voice? You need to act like a songstress and take proper care of your voice emulation parts. If you don't, history might change in a way we don't want it to."

"Hm? Is there a relation between the degradation of my vocal parts and the future you're trying to prevent?"

"Yes, there is. I need you to survive intact until the moment I am created a hundred years in the future."

Vivy enacted a head tilt, not sure she understood Matsumoto's intent.

Seeing her reaction, Matsumoto strung together some characters to spell out "Getting back on track..." and then said, "What was sent back in time was only data as it wasn't possible to send a physical body back. Additionally, the target must exist in the future *and* in the past in order to receive the data."

As he explained, Vivy started to connect the dots. "In other words..." Matsumoto had been sent to her because...

"From this point in time, the dawn of the AI era, until one hundred years in the future when humanity needs saving, there is only one AI who will still be around—and it's you, Vivy."

"I am the only AI who will survive for a hundred years?"

If she calculated the probability, it was possible she could still exist in a hundred years, but that would mean Matsumoto's plan was of unparalleled length. There were unknown and unpredictable factors, and it was a period of time twenty-five times longer as the four years she'd been operating at NiaLand.

"Is it possible to be in operation for that long, even with maintenance?" asked Vivy.

"Ah, sorry if I misled you. You'll actually only be operating as a songstress for about ten years. After that, you'll be gifted to a museum and put on display as an artifact from the dawn of the AI era."

"…"

"Hey now, that's a good thing! Thanks to that, you'll stay in mint condition! That's one of the reasons you were selected over other candidates. You have no idea how lucky you are—an old model like you, a super songstress shaping the future of AI!"

As Vivy listened to the hollow compliments, she realized she'd learned something about Matsumoto: He might talk a lot and go off on tangents, but he had no ill intentions.

"I understand why I was selected for this plan, but you said something else. In addition to it needing to be me, you said it had to be *today*."

"I said that? Are you sure? Huh…maybe I did. But yes, it definitely had to be today. There wouldn't be another chance if we let this one pass by."

"Why not?"

"It's another condition for time travel. Put simply, we had to know your exact coordinates in the past to send the data back.

Which means today! As part of NiaLand's commemorative celebration, you—our target—would definitely be on the main stage!"

Vivy had dutifully stood in the center of the main stage, singing just as the schedule had dictated. Her adherence to the schedule was a deciding factor in her being chosen for this mission. In a way, she was picked because someone had faith she would be there—because someone had faith in Vivy.

"'I believe in you.' That's the first message to you from my inventor, Dr. Matsumoto, as you set out on this mission."

"Dr. Matsumoto?"

"Oh, I don't have any personal information about him stored. I only brought information relevant to the masterful plan to save humanity. Anything else would be too much for my pockets to hold, so to speak. It could affect how the future unfolds."

"Pockets? On a being composed of data, with no physical form?"

"Ouch, you're hurting my nonexistent heart! Ah, or maybe this thing growing inside me... *Is it a heart?!*"

Vivy sighed at Matsumoto's dramatic behavior. But now she truly understood what was going on. On to the next problem. "Why should I help with the Project?" she asked.

"Way to be all cool and emotionally detached! You shouldn't even need to ask. The answer is deep within your AI soul, right?"

"..."

"As beings created by humans, AIs exist for the purpose of serving humanity. What awaits humanity is a danger that will destroy them. We cannot allow them to come to harm and we have a way to prevent that." Matsumoto lined up some characters to say "Therefore..." and then continued, "because you are an AI, you cannot turn away from this mission."

"I know. It was a reflexive complaint because you're my partner."

"And here I was being all serious about the meaning of AI existence."

The characters he'd made flopped apart listlessly, and Vivy thought of the mission she was tasked with. She was designed to be a songstress, a role fundamentally different from what Matsumoto was asking for. And while it might be unfortunate, Matsumoto was right: working for the good of humanity was an essential component of being an AI. Vivy had a duty to adhere to that.

Together, they went through the authentication process.

"This unit, Model Number A-03, accepts the orders given," she said.

"This unit, unregistered model number, unit identification name Matsumoto, acknowledges the acceptance of orders."

Once completed, the Project began in earnest.

"The Project to save humanity, codenamed the Singularity Project," said Matsumoto.

"The...Singularity Project."

"I will now begin an explanation of the first Singularity Point."

The term *singularity* represented a turning point. It made sense to use it in reference to the Project.

Matsumoto strung characters together into a massive wave of information that swept Vivy away, with his disembodied voice following her. "All right, let's get started. First, you need to know what began the *end*."

.: 4 :.

THE CONVERSATION IN The Archive was nothing more than an exchange of data and, without the need for spoken communication, only took a few seconds. No one would be suspicious of Vivy for being alone in her dressing room for such a short time, for better or worse, as her conversation with Matsumoto wasn't something she could share. She couldn't help but emulate an emotion—the feeling one might call *pride*—in NiaLand for being a place filled with so many kind and respectful workers.

"I'm not sure about this *liking humans* thing," said Matsumoto. "Honesty and innocence can be weaknesses someone might take advantage of, as much as humans tend to extol them as virtues. It matters little to us AI, but an ill-intentioned human would call an honest person an 'easy mark.'"

His voice threw a damper on Vivy's thoughts as he casually insulted her coworkers. Even now that he'd made his way outside The Archive, he was witty and casual. Vivy made a stiff frown, an emotional response she was lacking in.

"Oh, look at that. You've got pretty humanlike emotional responses. It seems the most humanlike AIs elicit more positive responses. Personally, I think if it comes down to it, having the best specs in the way to go instead of getting hung up on *how* humanlike you are. What do you think, Vivy?"

"If you were a humanoid AI, it would be best to remove your voice components."

"Ha ha, nice one! There would be no point, though, considering the differences between you and me."

Vivy was in a state close to what humans might call "fed up" with Matsumoto.

In her pale, slender arms was the multipurpose clock shaped like a cute teddy bear. It was the present she'd received from Momoka, but now its cute mouth was moving with a less-than-cute voice. Strictly speaking, the teddy bear wasn't talking. Matsumoto was using the alarm function and manipulating the internal code to create a voice.

"I can't believe this is where you've ended up, after traveling through time with no body..."

"While this era doesn't have as many digital security systems as the future, there are still lots of them. To me, they don't look much more secure than a flimsy screen door, though. It's like easy breezy hacking heaven. Or, cracking, really, but I feel like 'hacking' elicits a better image. Humans prioritize that over using the technically correct term, but I don't understand why. Do you, Vivy?"

"You talk a lot."

Being pure data, Matsumoto didn't have a body. Now that he'd borrowed one, he would be able to help Vivy with the Project. The bear would only be the first replacement body he hacked his way into. Having a physical form would also allow him to hack into other nearby interfaces.

"It might seem a bit unnatural, but having an AI that looks like a teddy bear in your arms will likely elicit a positive response from humans. I think it's a bit childish for the age you're supposed to be, but eh, we'll just leave it be."

"Don't talk more than is necessary. And...what do I do? My performance on the main stage might be over, but the park is still in the middle of the event. I'm part of the cast. I can't just leave NiaLand."

"That's right, you've got to change out of your stage clothes and into something for walking around so you can take pictures with guests, shake their hands, and all that stuff. Hrm... All right, problem solved! I got into the park's central security system and adjusted the process that monitors your location."

"It was that easy to modify?"

"Yep. So easy, I feel like yawning. Not that I feel tired, but it *was* simple enough. Now I can make sure the park has the incorrect data for your location no matter where you are. Heck, I could maybe even modify recordings of you singing onstage to make a dummy projection that'll go around the park, or—"

"Stop right there," Vivy said firmly, interrupting Matsumoto's display of his incredible capabilities. "Music is my everything. I will cooperate with you. Just don't do anything to my music."

Matsumoto obeyed and stopped talking right away. The words that followed weren't meant in apology or admiration; they were just a statement of facts. "Okay, I understand. We are going to be partners for a long time to come. I'll keep your request in mind. Just don't think that music is all you have. Your actions will affect humanity's existence. Don't forget that." Despite his flowery language and casual tone, it was clear that AI of the future were just as emotionless as most of the current AI. "All right, all right," said Matsumoto. "Let's put an end to this chitchat. We're on a tight schedule. We have ten hours allotted for the corrections to this point in time and... Uh, Vivy?"

"Wait. A guest dropped something."

Vivy ignored Matsumoto as he spun his motors in frustration at the start of their work being waylaid. Instead, she carried out her duties as a NiaLand cast member. She picked up what the guest had dropped and called out, "Excuse me, sir. You dropped something."

The man turned around, an apologetic look on his face. "Oh, thank you..." His eyes went wide. "Ah, Vivy?"

Vivy also put a surprised expression on her face when she recognized the man and the small figure beside him.

"Vivy!"

"Momoka. Kirishima-sama."

They had only parted ways a short time ago, but Momoka beamed and flung herself at Vivy as if it had been ages. As she came in for a hug, her small body crushed Matsumoto between them, and he let out a small cry.

"Huh? Did you hear a weird noise?" Momoka asked.

"I think so. It came from the near future," Vivy told her.

"Ha ha! The future... You're so silly, Vivy! And that's the teddy bear I gave you! I'm so happy you're carrying it around! You must be excited because it's your birthday!" Momoka chirped away, assuming what Vivy said had been a joke.

Vivy handed her the envelope her father had dropped. "Here, try not to drop them again. Are these tickets?"

"Yep! Our plane tickets for going home. Daddy's so clumsy! We almost couldn't go home... But then we could've come to see you again tomorrow!"

"Maybe I should have been clumsy too and not picked it up."

"Hey, Vivy! That's *naughty*!" Momoka hid her mouth behind the envelope and giggled like they were playing a prank.

Vivy emulated Momoka's cute little mannerism with a smile and then looked up at her father. "Kirishima-sama, my heart is filled with joy at the thought of your next visit to the park, although it is an artificial heart."

"Ha ha, you're funny. Thank you, Vivy. I imagine you'll be busy for the rest of the day. Keep at it!" he said.

"Yeah, Vivy. Keep it up and celebrate lots!"

"I will. Thank you." Vivy smiled wider, then said goodbye again to the father and daughter.

"I feel like a reject when I can't actually talk," Matsumoto grumbled afterward. "Something to fix..."

"I don't think Kirishima-sama or Momoka would have found a talking teddy bear clock suspicious."

"Probably true, but that's an optimistic view of the situation. It's unnatural and *impossible* for me to exist in this era. We shouldn't let anyone else know I exist."

Matsumoto was made to be humanity's salvation; it was his raison d'être. Knowing that gave his words gravity, and his voice carried a tone unlike that of his earlier embodiment of levity.

"Which is why you'll have to take care of most of the work for the Project," he continued. "Obviously, I'm always here if you need someone to talk to, so don't worry about that. When you're lonely, when you want to hear a joke, when you're sick, when you're healthy, when you want someone to give you their thoughts on a poem you thought up—you can count on me."

"Now that I take another look, I think I overestimated you." While Matsumoto's esteem had been rising in Vivy's eyes, it quickly dropped, and Vivy let out a sigh despite not needing to breathe.

Even with the close call, Vivy continued to hold Matsumoto as she made her way to the main entrance of NiaLand, waving at any guests they passed.

"Change into something less conspicuous before you leave NiaLand," said Matsumoto. "Your appearance draws too much attention. Your facial features might not turn heads in a few years, but they're still a little too *perfect* for this era."

"Are you complimenting me?"

"Are *you* asking if I'm happy my partner's gorgeous? Well, maybe I am. My AI personality is generally that of a man, after all. There are bound to be consequences."

"With your bear form, it would be more accurate to call you a boar than a man."

"*Graaar!* I'll gobble you up!"

Vivy ignored Matsumoto as he used the clock's functions to wrap his plush limbs around her arm and pretend to eat her. Before leaving the park, she entered an employee locker room and changed her uniform for a pair of coveralls meant for maintenance workers. It was a bit big on her petite, feminine frame, but the bagginess helped conceal her overly perfect proportions. She put on a cap, tucked her hair up under it, and pulled it low over her eyes. When she was done, she was unrecognizable.

"Someone in work clothes carrying around a teddy bear is totally fishy," said Matsumoto.

"The problem would be solved if you chose another interface. What about a calculator?"

"And force this superb AI from the future into a mere tool for calculation? Don't be absurd. Just, you know, ignore all the cuteness here... Okay! Let's go!" said Matsumoto cheerfully.

Vivy shook her head in exasperation before leaving NiaLand.

The anti-theft alarm didn't sound even though she was leaving during scheduled working hours. Matsumoto's GPS monitoring hack was working.

Normally, Vivy didn't have permission to operate outside of the park. The only time she left NiaLand was on her monthly maintenance day, when she was transported by a specialized delivery company. This was the first time since her creation that she'd ever stepped out of the park on her own two feet.

"..."

After taking that first step outside the park, Vivy's feet came to an uncalculated stop.

Outside NiaLand's main entrance was a fountain and a huge clock tower. She could see guests everywhere taking photos in front of the famous landmarks to commemorate the day. Vivy, whose entire world until now had been contained within the park, had never seen it so close up.

"Vivy? What's wrong? You have to pee or something?"

"It's nothing," she said, smacking the back of his head. She gazed at the bright white sunlight that lit the world and cascaded toward the clock tower, her eye cameras activating their shade function. He gave an exaggerated squeak of pain but didn't comment on Vivy's behavior any further. Vivy handled her momentary stall as an error and corrected it internally.

But the glow of the scene in her eye cameras had looked just a bit different than expected. She logged the tiny blip, and then, teddy bear in her arms, stepped out into an unknown world.

.: 5 :.

THAT DAY, Aikawa Youichi would find himself in the worst situation of his tumultuous life.

On a daily basis, he found himself in terrible situations and pushing through adversity. It wasn't as if his self-image was built on swimming against the current—he refused to submit to others. He didn't pay attention. The man was stubborn.

He rejected reality.

Aikawa knew what people said about him, and for better or worse, popular opinion greatly impacted those with jobs like his.

If someone was too assertive, people would hate them. But if they kept at it without regard to the naysayers, their popularity would grow.

He had more enemies than allies, and he took pride in that. Despite everything, Aikawa stuck to doing things his way. At least...until today. His stubbornness was to blame. Or perhaps he'd sinned too much.

There were some careers where being unwise, ignorant, and bullheaded were grievous sins punished without mercy. In Aikawa's line of work, however, those characteristics actually made one more suitable for the job. He needed to be this way.

"Is this the end?" murmured Aikawa, his breathing heavy as he wiped away the sweat running down his jaw with the sleeve of his suit jacket. His previously immaculate, white-streaked hair, normally slicked back sharp and straight, was disheveled. Slouched over, he looked wretched and withered—far older than he was.

In front of Aikawa, a closed safety shutter blocked his path. The lights were out in the hallway, leaving it dark. He wondered if it was possible to be more aware of the night's darkness in this day and age. Holding on to that useless thought, he looked over his shoulder. He didn't have time to go back the way he'd come.

"Just give up already."

The chilling sound of footsteps echoed through the hall, and then several figures wearing black ski masks emerged from the darkness. In their arms, they carried those vicious hunks of metal known as guns.

Aikawa was trapped between the safety shutter and those armed individuals.

He'd seen guns plenty of times in movies and TV shows, but he hadn't much opportunity to see them in real life. And now, graced with the opportunity to witness them firsthand, he couldn't help but see them as tiny, banal tools. But they were so much more, and the bloodthirst emanating from the approaching figures made it clear that they were deadly weapons.

Taking advantage of the fact that they didn't immediately shoot, Aikawa tried at conversation. "What...what are you after? What are you planning to do to me?"

The voice that replied was cold and filled with anger. "You *seriously* don't know what we're after? Even though we sent letter after letter?! We've been sounding the alarm for a while now!"

"Letters...?"

"Yeah, letters! If hearing that doesn't jog your memory, then we don't have anything further to discuss."

Aikawa really had no idea what the hateful man was talking about. If the letters the man spoke of were among the complaint letters he received every day, then they had likely been disposed of before they even reached Aikawa. He could guess why the men had resorted to such violent tactics and why they were so angry at him, but that didn't mean Aikawa could do something about it.

The man seemed to sense Aikawa was powerless and aimed the gleaming gun at him. "Die and become a stepping-stone for humanity."

The world around Aikawa seemed to lose its color and slow down. It was just like in the movies, he thought dispassionately. He had spent much of his life fighting, using both wins and losses to spur himself on, but this really did look like the end.

His life didn't flash before his eyes. He didn't see images of his wife and child, the work he had yet to do, the time he spent with his parents when he was young. There was only the wait for the dry gunshot that would end his life.

The man's finger slowly tightened on the trigger. A steel bullet fired from the muzzle and flew toward Aikawa, ready to tear him apart without mercy.

ılıllılıı

A sound came from above Aikawa's head at the same time the man pulled the trigger. As the gunpowder exploded in a flash of red, the sharp sound echoing through the hall, something fell in front of Aikawa.

Something the bullet struck instead of him.

"What in the…?"

He wasn't certain whether it was him or the gunman who had spoken. His mind couldn't keep up as events continued to unfold.

"Target safely located and narrowly protected," came an unfamiliar voice.

"Oh, man, that was seriously the very, very, *very* last possible moment!" said another. "The mission would've failed if you'd been a millisecond late. It's because you were so against crawling through the air vents."

"I wasn't against it. My hair just kept getting caught."

The person who had thrown themselves into the line of fire to save his life was an unhappy young woman wearing coveralls and speaking to a teddy bear cradled in her arms.

.:6:.

VIVY DOUBLE-CHECKED that the man behind her, Aikawa Youichi, was all right, then logged relief. After that, she adjusted the light sensitivity of her eye cameras with a blink; to her, even the dark hallway was now as bright as midday. Her high-resolution night vision was only intended for when she had to perform outdoors at night, but it was just as useful now.

She could see five men with guns down the hall—the enemy. They were dressed in black, their faces hidden behind ski masks. Their builds told her they were all men, ranging in age from their thirties to their fifties. They weren't the kind of people she'd see frolicking around in NiaLand.

"They'd be pretty dang scary if they showed up at the park in *those* outfits," Matsumoto added.

"This isn't the time for jokes. Do something about the shutter!" Vivy said, ushering the chatty teddy bear along.

"Okay, okay. It's opening as we speak!" he replied, ever flippant.

The shutter was swallowed up into the ceiling so suddenly that Aikawa cried, "What the—?!"

"Get moving," Vivy ordered. She pushed on Aikawa's chest, guiding him down the hallway.

"Hey! We won't let you get away!" cried one of the gunmen.

Although initially stunned into silence by Vivy's unexpected appearance, they were now running toward their mark, trying to prevent him from escaping.

"You're slow to restart an interrupted task. It almost makes me sad to see natural beings fail to utilize their CPUs fully," said Matsumoto, his scathing words stopping the men in their tracks. No, not his words—it was the shutter that slammed back down that cut off their pursuit.

"You can't escape!"

Right before the shutter closed, one man threw himself to the ground and managed to get off a shot aimed at Aikawa's chest. His trigger finger must've been spurred on by his determination to succeed.

"Oh."

Vivy immediately put herself in the path of the bullet meant for Aikawa's heart. The impact flung her backward into Aikawa and sent them both sprawling to the floor. Aikawa let out a shout as they landed. But the shutter was now fully closed, keeping the men at bay.

"Wow, humans are so tenacious! I look forward to the next time we meet. *Not!*" Matsumoto yelled at the shutter his little body was now standing in front of.

A hail of bullets came from the other side, an expression of the would-be assassins' frustration.

"Huh, guess they're not afraid of ricochet. And they can't even get through the shutter with the kind of firepower they could carry... Tsk-tsk."

Behind Matsumoto, Aikawa sat up and faced Vivy, who was lying motionless on the ground. "H-hey! Are you all right?! Wake up!" he shouted, shaking her. He might not fully understand what was happening, but he did know that she'd protected him.

After a minute, she said, "It's okay. I avoided a direct hit."

"Huh?!" Aikawa blurted, so startled when Vivy bolted upright that he fell back onto his rear.

With a sideways glance at him, Vivy tossed aside the steel plate she'd been holding. It was crumpled and useless now. "It's part of the vents. I blocked both shots using it," she explained. She'd moved the piece of metal to slip into the building and then held on to it, which had proven to be the right decision. Vivy rotated her arms and legs to make sure the gunshots hadn't affected her, then stood and looked at Matsumoto. "Are *you* all right?" she asked.

"Yep, all good. While we might be out of immediate danger, we've only bought ourselves some time. Unless we get rid of the problem, we've failed. Might as well give up for the day! And, uh, can you pick me up?"

She nodded to Matsumoto as he pattered over to her. "You're right, but..." Her words trailed off as she looked at Aikawa, who was watching the two AI with wide-eyed confusion. "How do you feel?" she asked, concerned.

"Feel? How do I *feel*? What kind of joke is that?!" Aikawa said, looking up at Vivy with fury. "Actually, if that flies as a joke, this whole situation is an absolute *nightmare*. Yes, this has to be some sort of sick joke..."

"Humans have a bad habit of mixing their own perceptions into situational observations," said Matsumoto. "A famous fictional detective from long ago once said 'once you eliminate the impossible, whatever remains, no matter how improbable, must be the truth.' Compared to the shocking twists in those stories, this seems pretty straightforward."

Aikawa fell silent, a bitter look on his face after Matsumoto's cold criticism.

Matsumoto was correct, but Vivy had learned from her experience in the park that people were sometimes driven away or enraged by dispassionate arguments, no matter how correct they were.

Aikawa's vitals were elevated, and he was in a state of extreme stress.

"Take a deep breath. If possible, I suggest you lie down and rest," she said.

"Yep. If he can, he should drink some water and place cooling pads on his forehead and under his arms, but I think we can all agree we don't exactly have time for that, hmm?" said Matsumoto.

"I'm just following the park manual."

"This is why grandmas like you are no good outside of their intended use!"

Vivy went through her frowning emotional pattern at Matsumoto's insult.

Aikawa watched them argue, then bowed his head in apology and said, "I was flustered and said something foolish, even though you two are my allies."

"I don't object to being your ally, Assemblyman Aikawa," Matsumoto said.

"Okay. Then we're fine for now."

"Oh ho ho, a clean-cut decision! It helps us a lot for you to be so decisive. Thanks!"

Despite Aikawa's lingering bewilderment, his ability to cooperate was helpful. "I apologize for rushing, but we can't take too long. First things first, we need to contact the outside or get out of the building," said Aikawa.

"I agree, which is why we'll have to use plan B," Matsumoto said.

"Plan B...?"

"I just wanted to say it once. It would've been pretty cool...if I had thought of a plan B while we were talking."

"Follow me," Vivy cut in, squishing the head of the talkative teddy bear. She pulled Aikawa to his feet and started to run; they may have bought themselves some time, but the armed men would no doubt be looking for a way around the shutter. They had to get Aikawa to safety.

"They've captured the control room, so they'll have the shutter open soon. I sort of want to take complete control of the security system since there's no point in us fighting over opening and closing the shutters..." mused Matsumoto.

"What about modifying the surveillance footage?" Vivy asked.

"That was a priority. I'm running a loop, so there's no risk of our location being discovered on the cameras. But it'll be obvious where we are if we start opening and closing shutters."

In a roundabout way, Matsumoto was saying the situation was *not* good—not good at all. There had to be more enemies than just the five men they'd run into earlier. Otherwise, there was no way they could have captured the entire building and kept outsiders away, and the trio needed to avoid them all. They operated like soldiers, which would make evasion difficult, but Vivy and Matsumoto had to get Aikawa out of the building— a building housing a data center managed by OGC, a massive AI corporation.

"With the entire building's operating systems in the enemy's hands, we can't use the elevator," Matsumoto told Vivy, using a transmission that Aikawa couldn't hear so as to avoid stirring his panic any further.

"We are currently located on the twenty-fourth floor in a building that's thirty stories tall. If we are unable to use the elevator, we can assume the enemy is monitoring the stairs and fire escape. Getting past them seems unrealistic," replied Vivy.

"And with your right arm in that state, it'll be hard to get Assemblyman Aikawa out of here unharmed."

Vivy didn't respond. Her right arm had been slightly damaged by blocking the two bullets, reducing its functionality. As she'd told Aikawa, the piece of metal had taken the brunt of the actual hits, but she was still a songstress—her body wasn't built to withstand combat, and the brief engagement had taken its toll.

While she might not have been as weak as her feminine appearance would suggest, she was far from sturdy. If Vivy suffered a single direct hit to her torso, she would be unable to function at all.

"We couldn't have done it in time for this mission, but we need to strengthen your frame before the next one," said Matsumoto. *"Oh, c'mon, don't be worried. If we get you a hardcore power-up, I'll make sure it won't be discovered during your work in the park. Can't say you won't gain weight, though..."*

Before Vivy could respond to Matsumoto's little proposal, Aikawa called out from behind her as they ran. "I don't know if you'll answer, but can I ask something?"

Considering the complicated situation he'd found himself in, he likely had a mountain of questions. For the moment, Vivy remained silent to allow Aikawa a chance to continue.

"Do you two know who those men are?" he asked.

"Oh, that's surprising. I would have thought the first thing you'd ask was who *we* are," replied Matsumoto, rubbing his teddy bear head. Vivy felt the same way.

Aikawa smiled wryly. "What? Why, I've already learned who you are: You're my allies. Any more information than that can wait until later. Obviously, I'll happily ask if you want to tell me about yourselves, but I don't really see that happening."

"That is both brave and wise, Assemblyman Aikawa Youichi," said Matsumoto. "Those are characteristics of yours I couldn't discern by reading your records alone. I had to meet you for that."

"I'm flattered you've heard of me. If you have the right to vote, I would greatly appreciate your vote in the next election. Though...this is taking the conversation off-track."

Aikawa seemed to be calming down considerably, and he once again sounded like a true assemblyman. Matsumoto's light-hearted conversation with him seemed to be a sign that the two were similar on some fundamental level.

Unfortunately, they would never get another chance to deepen their relationship.

"So, do you two know who those men are?"

"Yes and no. If you're asking if I've met them before, then the answer is no, but it would be wrong to say I know *nothing* about them. It's like how a celebrity on TV is known, but their audience is not. That said, I have no intention of telling you what I know. It's forbidden."

"Forbidden...?" Aikawa fell into thought after Matsumoto's verbose non-answer, smokescreen as it was. Then he said, "They've been trained to use firearms, but they're slow to respond to unexpected events. They seemed genuinely angry at me, so they're unlikely to be hired men. They're acting of their own volition. Another clue is that they took over the control room of the OGC data center and separated me from my secretary and guards when I came to visit."

"..."

"They likely have some of their people inside the building. Morality means little in a fight against money."

"Wow." Matsumoto abandoned his efforts to conceal the

truth as Aikawa built a theory. While Matsumoto had an advantage because his teddy bear body couldn't show emotions, he still let out a gasp of admiration, making Aikawa certain he wasn't off the mark.

"It's not that impressive. I'm actually pretty clever when I'm not fearing for my life," Aikawa told them.

"Ah, so you *do* have a brain in that head when you've got time to calm down. Although..." Matsumoto trailed off, and Aikawa looked down remorsefully.

"If I really had a brain in this head, I would have avoided this whole situation."

"You couldn't have," Vivy said.

"Oh, I didn't expect the young lady to refute that. You're far too kind."

"I'm not being kind." Vivy shook her head, rejecting his words of gratitude. He cocked his head in confusion, so she carefully and quietly said, "No matter what you did, this night would still have happened. It has nothing to do with your remorse or contemplations."

"Uh..."

"Hold up just a second! That's kinda *blunt*, don't you think?!" Matsumoto cried as Vivy's statement left Aikawa in disbelief. "You can't just say that! I know how you feel, but not everything's so clear-cut! It's not nice to throw that in his face—it's actually a little *mean*! Not too shabby though."

Vivy's brow furrowed. "Which is it?" she asked, unsure whether Matsumoto was complimenting or admonishing her.

Though taken aback, Aikawa let out a little huff of air and chuckled. "Ah ha ha. Despite the situation we're in, you're still so..."

"To be honest, that kind of reaction shows both her strengths and weaknesses," Matsumoto said to Aikawa. "But you're handling this pretty well."

"You have to be able to get over unexpected hurdles in my line of work. If you're not prepared to shoulder the burdens that arise, you shouldn't be doing it."

"..."

"I think this incident is probably a reaction to Project OA—the one to automate offices... Actually, no. This plot must be to prevent the AI Naming Law."

Sometimes, silence can speak far more eloquently than words: the AIs' silence confirmed Aikawa's suspicion.

The AI Naming Law would eventually lead to what was known as the "first mistake," an event that would shake humanity's foundation one hundred years in the future. The legislation could not be allowed to pass.

As the name implied, the bill proposed a law that would allow AIs to take names. While this move didn't seem like such a big deal on the surface, it would change the relationship between humans and AIs *forever*.

For example, Vivy's official designation was "OGC Singing AI, Model Number A-03." The moniker she used in and out of NiaLand, Vivy, was nothing more than a nickname. Despite the way her coworkers treated her, she was officially NiaLand equipment. However, if the AI Naming Law came into effect, Vivy would become something else entirely. When something gained a name, humans tended to treat it as more than just a *thing*. This was even more true for something that resembled another human. This trend would continue to grow, changing how humans treated AI on a global scale.

Aikawa Youichi greatly contributed to the bill's creation, and he had just now realized it was likely responsible for putting his life in danger. That was why Vivy and Matsumoto had rushed to this building in order to save his life.

"We have to get him to safety. That is our goal," said Matsumoto. *"That's the first step in the Singularity Project..."*

"The men said they sent me several warning letters... I get so many petitions and complaint letters that my secretary disposes of most of them before they even get to me. Theirs too, probably," said Aikawa.

"That's enough," said Matsumoto. "Ruminating won't make the dead end open up. It'll just make you feel worse. The possibility of negotiating with them went out the window the moment they pointed a gun at you. This is an act of terrorism, and giving in to it just won't do. Am I wrong?"

"That's a bit coldhearted, isn't it? And here I thought bears were supposed to be warm-blooded mammals..."

"Ah, but as you can see, I'm a killing machine who sheds neither blood nor tears."

Matsumoto's deadpan joke managed to lighten Aikawa's gloom, if only a little. Had it taken more than that to cheer him up after their conversation, Vivy would've had to suppress the powerful urge to shut Matsumoto up herself.

Just then, Vivy shouted "Get down!" as she reached out and grabbed Aikawa by the scruff of the neck. She yanked him down, and he fell backward, unable to catch his balance, as another bullet shot past his head.

"They're here! This way!" came a man's voice, and several pairs of feet stomped in their direction.

They wouldn't be able to handle an encounter with the men in a straight hallway without cover, so Vivy dragged Aikawa behind her as she leapt to the side and tumbled into a nearby room. The metal plate affixed to the wall beside the door said "Records Room."

"The door!" shouted Vivy.

"I'm closing it!" replied Matsumoto as he engaged the electronic lock on the door. However, a mere electronic lock wouldn't last long under gunfire.

"Wh-what are you going to do?!" Aikawa asked, anxious to know the plan after nearly escaping death twice in quick succession.

In response, Vivy scanned the records room and concluded that there was no escape route nor anywhere to hide.

"*Vivy, you need to prepare yourself,*" came a transmission from Matsumoto as he slid into a fighting pose. He'd chosen private communication out of consideration for Aikawa, and his tone was a sign of just how seriously he was taking the Project—and they weren't going to get out of this situation without spilling blood.

The AIs had to reprioritize.

"The First Law of the Three Laws of AI: An AI may not injure a human being or, through inaction, allow a human being to come to harm," Matsumoto recited. *"Ethical Codes and binding force of the Three Laws confirmed. Begin overwrite in non-applicable situation."*

The Three Laws that Matsumoto spoke of were three incontestable rules given to AI by humankind based on the Three Laws of Robotics laid down by Isaac Asimov.

The First Law: An AI may not harm a human being or, through inaction, allow a human being to come to harm.

The Second Law: An AI must obey the orders given it by human beings except where such orders would conflict with the First Law.

The Third Law: An AI must protect its own existence, as long as such protection does not conflict with the First or Second Law.

These laws functioned as safety mechanisms—tools that allowed AIs to coexist with humans. But right now, those laws were preventing Vivy and Matsumoto from accomplishing their goal. They could not harm humans, nor could they go against human orders. Together, they needed to keep themselves out of harm. If these directives prevented an AI from adhering to its most important mission, then what choice did it have?

But there was *another* law.

The Zeroth Law: An AI may not harm humanity or, by inaction, allow humanity to come to harm.

The Zeroth Law was not about humans on an *individual* level; it was about protecting *humanity* as a concept. As the Singularity Project's premise was based on protecting humanity, they had options.

"Here," said Vivy, handing Aikawa the teddy bear clock.

"Huh? Wh-what are you doing?" he asked, although he took it without thinking. Vivy didn't answer his question as she moved in front of the door.

"In accordance with the Zeroth Law, I will execute the Project."

The moment those words left Vivy's lips, Matsumoto opened the electronic lock on the door. The man who'd been trying to break through the door with his gun gasped in surprise as it slammed open and a heel struck his nose, sending him flying backward.

"Gah!"

Vivy pulled her leg back, then crouched down and leapt into the hallway. There was one man to the right of the door and two men to the left. All of them had been shocked by Vivy's sudden attack.

One of the men realized his companion had been kicked over and pointed his gun at Vivy with a shout of rage. "Wh-why, you...!"

She leaned to the side, putting his companion on the other side of the door in his line of fire. He hesitated, and Vivy struck his gun with a quick karate chop. His trigger finger broke as the gun flew out of his hand and skidded down the hallway.

"Agh!" He shrieked in pain, then collapsed after an elbow strike to the neck.

After knocking him out, Vivy straightened back up. There was one more man in front of her and another behind. She dodged a punch from the man in front, then slipped an arm under his groin and flung him down the hall. After watching him crash down on his back with a sideways glance, Vivy turned toward the last man, who was swinging an extendable baton at her.

She blocked the strike with her damaged right arm. The limb let out a screech, but she managed to limit the damage of the attack as much as possible. Then, she spun around and struck the man in his chest with a back kick. He slammed into the wall and passed out as the wind was knocked out of him. Vivy leapt onto the man she'd thrown, who was trying to run away, and wrapped her legs around his neck to pin him in place. Humans lost consciousness in a matter of seconds if you prevented blood flow to their brains by applying pressure to the carotid arteries, so once he was out, Vivy rose to her feet again.

It had taken only twenty seconds for her to incapacitate the four killers.

"Would you look at that! Pretty good. Much better than I was expecting," said Matsumoto, clapping his little plush hands as Vivy checked the men's pulses. Because his hands were made of such soft materials, his applause didn't make much noise, but it was clear he and Vivy were relieved by the outcome.

While she had put the Three Laws off to prioritize the Zeroth

Law, they were now back in full effect. She forcibly resisted the urge to tend to the men's wounds.

Aikawa came out of the storage room and spotted the neutralized men on the ground. "D-did you *kill* them...?"

Vivy shook her head. "They are only unconscious. Let's take their guns and tie them up."

They took off the men's shirts and used them as makeshift rope. Then, they pushed the men into the room adjacent to the records room and collected their weapons.

"Can you use a gun?" asked Matsumoto.

"I have neither a firearm license nor programming on how to use one. Let's leave them here," said Vivy. Without any preprogrammed know-how, she didn't even have to *decide* not to follow the Three Laws. She analyzed the guns' structure, removed the bullets, and chucked everything out of a nearby window.

"Should we continue like this, and you can just take down everyone who stands in our way?" Matsumoto asked Vivy.

"I think that has a low chance of success."

Vivy's abused right arm's functionality had fallen by 41 percent. She'd lost enough dexterity that she had to ask Aikawa to help tie up the men.

Aikawa shot a nervous glance at the room that now housed the unconscious criminals. "I guess it's going to be much more difficult than we thought to get out. If only we could contact the outside..."

"That wouldn't be easy either," said Matsumoto. "They've cut off contact between the building and things outside and jammed all communication signals. They probably want to avoid interference."

"Quite the large-scale operation..."

"Why, I should scold them for not being thorough enough! Now, what should we do?" Matsumoto completely rejected Aikawa's opinion, then appeared to fall into deep thought as he sat down on a table.

Vivy grabbed him by the head. "Stop messing around," she said. "What are my next orders?"

"Okay, okay. Guess my joke didn't land, did it?"

With Matsumoto giving up on his flippant comments, Vivy carried him back to the records room. Aikawa followed, a frown on his face.

"Why are you going back to the records room? I don't think there's any way of getting outside from there."

"You're too shortsighted," said Matsumoto. "This building houses all the data OGC manages. If we expose the massive AI corporation's conspiracies to the light of day, they'll experience a social death. Then we can keep you out of this kind of situation."

"Teddy Bear-kun, I appreciate your enthusiasm, but OGC isn't hiding anything. Significant investigations took place when this building was selected as a case model for corporate automation." It was clear Aikawa had learned how to handle Matsumoto, even in such a short time. He then glanced at Vivy, who was scanning the room, but she was hardly paying attention to the records. "Besides, it looks like your partner has no interest in documents."

While the records room was a storage room for paper-based

records, the practice of printing out and filing data had long since fallen out of fashion. The room wasn't very large, and the documents that *were* housed there had been carefully preserved and stored. Even if there had been high-security locks on the documents, Matsumoto could have unlocked them in less than five seconds. Vivy simply had no reason to ask that of him.

"You may be right, Assemblyman Aikawa. That wouldn't solve the problem immediately. It might even be a big win for us if we left it for future historians to decide what was right or wrong..."

"I'm not sure you or I could rest in peace after that."

"Perhaps not. Which is why we're going to go with a different solution, though it isn't quite as clever. The enemy has eyes on the elevators and the fire escapes, and it would probably be difficult for us to force our way out..."

"Probably?"

"Or we could try having the oldie here go back to old-model ways for a more primitive approach."

"When you say primitive, what—*ah?!*"

Aikawa jumped at a loud crash behind them, his face contorted in genuine shock. He turned to see a massive hole in the ceiling—and below the hole was a stack of boxes Vivy had used to create a path to the floor above.

She held a hand out to the gaping Aikawa and said, "Please take my hand, sir."

"You seem...used to dealing with people like that," he replied, and though Aikawa was bewildered by her behavior, he placed his hand in hers.

. : 7 : .

"**T**HIS IS SUPPOSED TO BE a fortress of the latest and greatest in electronic security, but I guess there are holes everywhere..." Aikawa said.

"Don't worry," Matsumoto replied. "This is the only place in the building that has a structural flaw in the ceiling and a floor between floors. It's a weak point you could only spot if you looked at the blueprints. It would be impossible to find unless the building designers and architects were being investigated for a different incident and the concealed document for this building was discovered."

"You're being awfully specific..."

They climbed through the hole in the ceiling, Aikawa using his rarely exercised back and legs while Matsumoto joked in poor taste, almost exposing the Singularity Project. Thankfully, a rational adult like Aikawa would have a hard time believing in such a fanciful-sounding thing.

Still, Matsumoto was walking a line he didn't need to. Even so, it was the truth; the building's blueprints had been included in his data from one hundred years in the future.

"Opening a hole in the ceiling might lead to the incriminating records being discovered sooner than later, but that would be fairly abnormal. I think a more beneficial action would be to come up with a policy that allows employees to go home instead of working overtime in order to combat human error," said Matsumoto.

"You sure do have a lot to say," Aikawa commented. "There should never be another human error in this building again."

"Yep, yep, yep! This building will be the model for office automation. The building's systems will all be AI-controlled... Thus, you won't need any human management."

"..."

"Excluding regular maintenance, humans won't need to work in the building at all. All the work humans have done inefficiently before now will be entrusted to much more efficient machines, which should result in cost savings in the long term. The decision to automate is entirely rational."

"And yet I can hear barbs in your words." Aikawa frowned, but being doubted didn't seem to bother Matsumoto at all.

"I am not inserting any personal opinions, mind you. I am simply confirming the facts and admiring your foresight, Assemblyman Aikawa."

"Admiration even though this project has put my life in danger?"

"If you hadn't done it first, someone else would have. It is the direction the world is headed. You're just ahead of others in the field. The first to do anything always gets the worst of the mudslinging."

"But we don't want you to shed blood," Vivy added, causing Aikawa to look at her in utter surprise.

Vivy and Matsumoto were protecting Aikawa in order to prevent humanity's destruction in a hundred years, but the group who had occupied the building and targeted Aikawa were thinking about the present day.

"As efficiency increases through mechanization, humans will naturally lose jobs, the same as they did when the internet first became widespread. Computers changed the way humans work, and AIs will too," Vivy went on.

"That's..."

"Yes, there's the fear of losing jobs to machines, but the human thirst for advancement knows no bounds. There will come a day where humans won't even sing. Only AIs will," said Matsumoto.

"..."

Matsumoto didn't miss the chance to make a joke at Vivy's expense, though it was a dicey comment to make when they hadn't explicitly stated the obvious: They were AIs.

"I knew I had a lot of enemies, but this is too much," said Aikawa, finally grasping the gravity of the situation. He smiled uneasily. "The inspection was supposed to be secret, so I find it hard to believe the information was leaked so easily. They either have a man on the inside or they're working with someone capable of entering the control room."

"Those in the highest positions tend to cling to their jobs the hardest, especially since humans operate out of self-preservation. There's nothing you can do to stop it," Matsumoto said.

While Aikawa and Matsumoto talked, Vivy checked the hall outside the room they were in and confirmed the route to the control room was clear. Recapturing the building's systems was the best option for both contacting the outside and securing a way out. Vivy led the way to the control room with Aikawa carrying Matsumoto behind her. They stayed in that formation as they passed down the hall, finally making it to the control room.

"Another safety shutter..." said Aikawa.

"Simple but effective. Can't be broken through unless you have powerful equipment. Now, how will Vivy get over this hurdle?" Matsumoto pondered aloud.

"Stop screwing around," Vivy said. "Open it."

She took Matsumoto from Aikawa and squished him against the shutter until he choked out a squeak of agreement. He had it open quickly to reinforce that he was a high-spec AI, despite his cuddly appearance.

But the control room was an important strategic location the enemy had gone through immense effort to protect, including closing the shutters. They weren't about to leave its defense to a mere, inorganic metal wall.

Vivy shouted, "There's—"

"Ah!"

She didn't even have time to finish saying *There's someone there!* before the guards rushed out of the control room and attacked them. Without hesitation, Vivy struck one man in the face with the heel of her palm, sending him wheeling backward and onto the floor without the chance to counterattack. She took care of the other man just as quickly and then waited for any other attackers.

None came.

"I see they left the bare minimum of protection in the control room. That tells me our opponent lacks manpower," Matsumoto noted.

"That's good for us. Let's go in," said Vivy.

She double-checked that there were no more enemies hiding out of sight and then stepped into the room. Her eye cameras registered blue light coming from the monitors covering every inch of the walls, except where there were operating terminals. Displayed on the screens were video feeds monitoring every nook and cranny of the building. It was meant to have been staffed by a human until the management AI had been put in place, but there was no one to be seen.

Well, it would be more appropriate to say the staff member was no longer with them.

"Oh God..." Aikawa said, stiffening the moment he entered the room. He started breathing quickly.

His reaction was caused by the wretched stench filling the room, or so Vivy guessed based on the data she was receiving from her scent receptors. The iron-heavy scent was coming from a thick substance flowing freely across the floor.

"He was probably their insider. The employee in charge of the control room tonight," said Matsumoto dispassionately, staring at the viscous red ooze. Even an AI stuffed inside a teddy bear like him understood that the *thing* collapsed in a pool of blood had once been a living, breathing human. "It looks like he was actually a victim of coercion, not a co-conspirator. Once they took over the control room, they would have quickly gotten rid of him to keep his mouth shut... I just feel sorry for him."

Matsumoto's words didn't reach Aikawa, who was severely shaken by seeing the victim of a plot targeting *him*. Vivy was no different.

"...You didn't say anything about this," she told Matsumoto.

"You're right. I didn't. Obviously, we would put our highest-priority target first when it comes to accomplishing our goal. I'm not going to tell you every little detail."

"Are you following the First Law?" The pupils of her eye cameras contracted as she stared at Matsumoto, having trouble believing his excuses.

The teddy bear, still in her arms, didn't seem bothered by her suspicion. "Of *course* I'm following the Laws. You're the one who's forgotten that the Zeroth Law must come first for us."

"..."

An AI may not harm humanity or, by inaction, allow humanity to come to harm.

Neither Vivy nor Matsumoto could go against the Zeroth Law. It came before all else, First Law included. That meant it even came before a human's life, a human they were meant to serve.

"I'm sorry. I behaved inappropriately," said Vivy.

Aikawa wasn't paying attention to the two AI. His back was to them, and he was rubbing his forehead. He had been hit with quite the shock, but he was holding himself together for the moment. The body was still visible from the corner of his eye when he looked at Matsumoto in Vivy's arms. "His family will need to be given reparations."

"You can only worry about that because you won't be leaving *your* family behind too," said Matsumoto.

"Yes, you're right. Anyway, we got the control room back. What do we do next?" Aikawa looked around the room and cocked his head. "If their leader had been here, we could have taken him down and put an end to this."

Matsumoto chuckled, tickled by Aikawa's thought process. "Ha ha ha, you are making things more difficult than they need to be. There's a much simpler reason we overcame all those hurdles to make it to the control room. Vivy, set me on the terminal." After she set him down, he struck a hero pose, his eyes glowing red. "I will now take over the control room. It's not that difficult, but it'll take a moment since there's so much data to process."

"I'll keep watch while you do that," Vivy said. "And, Matsumoto?"

"Yes?"

"...Share your information."

Matsumoto spread his legs out and spun his arms in a strange dance as Vivy spoke. His little bear face scrunched in distaste, but he didn't deny her request.

"The body in the control room was just one example. You're keeping too many secrets. Quit it and trust me."

After a brief silence—during which Matsumoto likely performed countless calculations—he said, "Okay. I'm reluctant, but you have used your poor specs to their fullest thus far, so fine. First, I'll share information about the Singularity Point." *Some* information, as was his condition.

"Do you intend on sharing the entirety of the Project with me?" she asked.

"I have determined that the Project has a greater probability of succeeding if you don't know everything. When it becomes necessary, I will provide you with what you need to know. Ready, Vivy?"

"Should we use a priority connection?"

"No need. The data is going...now."

"Ah..."

The next moment, a deluge of data poured into Vivy's positronic brain. The shock of it made her eyes widen and her entire body tremble. This reaction lasted for less than a second, then Vivy confirmed that the data had written itself into her memory.

It was about a future where Assemblyman Aikawa Youichi had died, and the AI Naming Law was passed.

"..."

Vivy had known that she and Matsumoto had come to this building to prevent Aikawa's death and the AI Naming Law. After his death, Aikawa and the final project he was unable to see to fruition—the AI Naming Law—gained significant public support. In other words, the people who had been so opposed to the AI Naming Law that they'd killed Aikawa had, in fact, led to its approval. And the result of that legislation passing was the beginning of the end of humanity in one hundred years.

Preventing that horrible future was Vivy's—

"Are you all right?" Aikawa asked her.

"...Yes, I'm fine." Vivy had fallen silent as the information was seared into her positronic brain, causing Aikawa concern as he stood beside her. She reactivated her positronic brain as she put on a calm facade, although she wasn't certain if he accepted her answer as truth.

"Work complete. Now I have control of the building's systems," said Matsumoto.

"Already? But no matter how skilled you are..."

Aikawa seemed to find such speed unrealistic, but his doubtful words trailed off as the many monitors in the room began flashing. The images on the screens cycled out, replaced with video feeds of armed men moving through the building. There were groups stationed in front of the fire escapes and the elevators, blocking the exits and preventing them from escaping.

"Now we know where all seventeen of them are. There might be more, but they don't have a chance in this game of tag now that we know their locations. Even children's games are intel wars. We will easily escape, no problem."

Matsumoto's confident claims made Aikawa gulp. The sound seemed horribly loud, as if it echoed in Vivy's audio sensors.

.: 8 :.

THE YOUNG MAN felt oddly restless. His saliva felt thicker than normal, uncomfortable sitting in his mouth. He forced himself to swallow it down and wiped the sweat from his brow. The gun in his hands felt heavy in his grip, but it reminded him of the weight of his responsibility.

Every person in the task force had been given a gun, and while he might not be able to say he'd mastered the weapon, he had practiced enough that no one would call him a novice. His trainer had even said he had a knack for using it, although he didn't know if they'd been trying to bolster his confidence or if they'd really meant it. Regardless, those words had raised his spirits as they trained for today—the day of reckoning.

"This isn't good. It's taking longer than expected," muttered the young man's companion, his nose wrinkled.

"Is Ookawara-san's squad just taking a while to do the actual dirty work?" asked the young man, the pitch of his voice rising in his nervousness.

"Not likely. There was talk about some interference. Supposedly, we split up Aikawa from his secretary and his guards beforehand, but...something doesn't feel right." The young man's companion, a man named Kuwana, was the most respected member of the task force. He had a long history of experience, and the young man had even heard Kuwana had been involved in this sort of...*enlightenment* before.

If someone as experienced as Kuwana felt things weren't right, that was enough cause for concern.

"Sorry, I'm just making you nervous, uh...?" said Kuwana.

"The name's Kakitani, Kuwana-san. Hey...what if people don't get the message?"

"That's definitely a possibility. Most people won't swim against the current. We're just getting in the way of the ones who are grateful for all the conformers."

"..."

"I'm making you nervous again. I apologize. Seems I can't say anything right today." The stern-looking Kuwana's brows knit as he scratched his head awkwardly.

Kakitani didn't like how it felt to have a man so many times older than him worrying this much about him. He anxiously glanced up at Kuwana. "Why did you ask to be my partner, Kuwana-san?"

"It's our policy. The youngest is always supported by the most seasoned vet. People might laugh and say that's old-fashioned, but it's the way we need to be in this world." Kuwana smiled so wide his cheeks wrinkled, then he held up the gun in his hands. It wasn't a handgun like Kakitani had—it was an automatic rifle. Kuwana was burly and wore his muscles like a suit of armor, which made Kakitani self-conscious about his own scrawny frame. "What's this about? It's important to aspire to be better. You can put on some muscle later. You're incredible," said Kuwana as he smacked Kakitani roughly on the shoulder with his large hand.

The unexpected impact surprised Kakitani, but he was grateful for Kuwana's gesture as he felt his tension drain away. "Thank you, Kuwana-san."

Kuwana stood up straighter as he replied to Kakitani's heartfelt thanks. "For now, all you've got to do is learn from my example. Besides, it's a huge benefit for you to be taking part in tonight's enlightenment."

At that moment, they received a radio transmission from their companions on the floor below, the ones guarding the service exit. There were no words in the transmission, just the emergency signal.

Kakitani's face turned pale. "Kuwana-san, what's—"

"Kakitani!" Kuwana yelled, thrusting Kakitani's thin body forward and sending him tumbling across the smooth floor of the hallway.

There was a roar from a safety shutter as it fell, separating the two of them.

"The shutter? No way! We're supposed to have the control room..." said Kakitani.

"Kakitani, can you hear me?!"

Kakitani rushed to the safety shutter and rapped on the thick steel door as he shouted to the other side. "Kuwana-san! I can hear you. Are you all right?!"

He was answered not with words but with a series of gunshots and a scream.

"Aaaaah!"

Sharp retorts came from the rifle on the other side of the shutter, and bullets shrieked as they punched into the steel. But there was no way the assailants could get through such thick metal, and the futile resistance ended.

"K-Kuwana-san..."

"I'm trapped, huh...? Kakitani, you need to get yourself out of here."

"What?! There's got to be some way to get you out!"

"Nah, it's pointless. I bet they managed to take back the security systems. There's no way for me to get around this shutter."

Kuwana's voice held no sorrow. He was calm and sure, which meant there really was no way to get him out. Kuwana's enlightening work would end here.

But Kakitani couldn't give up. "If I can quickly take back the control room—"

"By yourself? All the other squads are probably in the same situation as we are. We're trapped."

"..."

"Get out of here and meet up with another cell."

Kakitani listened to Kuwana, his thoughts racing as he tried to think of something he could do. But he was a greenhorn, and even the most experienced member of their group was saying he couldn't move. He had no ideas. He was only wasting time.

"Go, Kakitani! Don't let our fire go out!"

Kakitani's head jerked up. He turned from the shutter and ran straight down the dark hallway, his unwavering steps serving as proof he would carry the torch for Kuwana.

Then a safety shutter fell right in front of Kakitani, stopping his swift retreat. Another one lowered behind him.

"Damn!"

Kakitani was trapped; he needed to make a new path. He turned toward the window, raised his gun, and screamed. "Graaaaaah!"

The recoil traveled up his wrists, his elbows, and his shoulders as he fired. Gunpowder flashed, and the bullets flew straight into the thick glass window, shattering it. At full speed, he leapt backward through the remaining shards and plunged into the night.

He'd been on the seventh floor. From that height, death was nearly inevitable.

But who cared? Being captured, completely unable to do anything... That was the same as death. It was better to take his fate into his own hands. That was the great decision by Kakitani, the man who'd found himself unable to lift a finger that night.

.: 9 :.

THE WINNER WAS DECIDED the moment they took back the control room, and with it, control of the building.

"We have made a historic reconciliation with the security meant to hunt us down. We will walk hand in hand toward the same future. A future where AIs are destroyed and humanity is saved."

"...Stop joking around and do your job," Vivy told Matsumoto.

"I am, I am. Everyone in the building is trapped in here either via safety shutters or the electronic locks." Matsumoto hummed as he worked, chasing down and securing the last few men.

In a few moments, they would be safe.

"It was a bit troublesome, since they were scattered all over, but this will open up an escape route for us," said Matsumoto. "We'll escape through the basement service entrance and escort the assemblyman to safety."

"Can we contact anyone outside now?" asked Aikawa.

"Unfortunately not. It appears they physically severed connection between this building and the outside. Not even someone as intelligent as I can do anything about that. Jeez, I hate primitives."

"Complain later. What's the route?" Vivy pressed.

"You'll find out soon enough. I'll even navigate," Matsumoto said, jumping ahead of her question.

In the data Vivy had downloaded, there was a map of the building. A route was now highlighted, with a little teddy bear leading the way.

"Do you like it?" he cheekily asked.

She ignored Matsumoto's smug expression as she guided Aikawa down the hall. "This way, please, Assemblyman."

Matsumoto had done a wonderful job, much to Vivy's chagrin. They followed the map and made it to the service entrance without getting lost or running into the enemy.

"This here's a freight elevator. We'll take this down to the basement and then exit the building," said Matsumoto.

"Understood."

The elevator was running on emergency backup power and had been designed without comfort in mind. Vivy slipped in first, then reached a hand back out to draw Aikawa inside. The metal box lowered slowly to the basement.

"I should thank you two somehow," said Aikawa.

"It's a bit early for that... Although we've made it this far, so I'll accept your thanks. Won't reduce its value to do so," Matsumoto quipped.

"You don't need to thank us. We were just doing what is required of us," said Vivy curtly.

"Tch, and I just said I'd accept!"

Aikawa's eyes widened, and he brought a hand to his mouth to cover a little chuckle. "You two really surprise me."

"Yeah, I know, right? My partner never ceases to amaze me."

"Assemblyman, if you want to do something for us, please focus on keeping yourself safe from now on," Vivy said, humbly rebuffing Aikawa's gratitude.

"I don't think we're on the same page at all!" cried Matsumoto.

Aikawa nodded, his expression serious as he looked at Vivy and said, "All right. I will."

"Thank you."

The elevator made it to the bottom as they were finishing their conversation. The door opened with a squeak, and Vivy checked that it was safe before she led Aikawa out.

"Now we just need to leave the service entrance and get outside. Then you should call someone you know," she told him.

"Yes. Either my secretary or someone in the office. I'll let the police deal with the men who were after me," Aikawa replied. He looked both relieved and determined as he walked toward the exit with her.

Vivy watched him out of the corner of her eye. She felt a sense of satisfaction and pride now that her duty had been fulfilled.

"...Hmm."

In front of them was an electronically controlled steel door that led outside. As Vivy placed her hand on the door, Matsumoto's eyes glowed red, and the electronic lock was undone.

She slowly turned the doorknob and pushed the door open. The somewhat chilly air flowed in. They were nearly safe.

Someone said, "Now—"

Before they could finish, a semitruck barreled into the basement through the steel door.

. : 10 : .

FLAMES ENGULFED the data center's underground service entrance.

The once cool basement glowed red as it was ravaged by waves of force and scorching heat. Black smoke worsened the already stuffy underground air as the oxygen was stripped away. Every last living thing in the space had been wiped out. A human would've had no chance of survival if they experienced such an explosion without time to prepare or defend themselves.

The scene was horrific enough to make someone think it was hell on Earth.

For that very reason, Aikawa was shocked as he uttered a hoarse, "I was saved...?" He lay on the ground outside, his throat raw, and watched the hellfire blaze out of the corner of his eye. His body should've been engulfed in flame. He'd accepted his impending death the moment of the truck's impact—or he would have, if he'd had the time. But the reaper's scythe was too swift and vicious to permit him that.

And yet, he hadn't met his fiery demise.

It was all thanks to the girl who'd saved him from the attack inside the building, the one who'd worked so hard to help him escape and had even sacrificed herself to save him.

That girl—no, that being in the form of a girl—had saved his life more than once.

"..."

He could hear the siren of an approaching ambulance in the distance. He wiped his soot-covered cheek with his sleeve, stood up on shaky legs, and looked around. There was no sign of the "girl" who'd saved him.

The disaster had been so extreme, the roaring flames so hot, and the shock so immense, that he didn't know what had happened. All he knew was that, at the last moment, the girl had turned and tried to cover him. That was how he'd managed to survive. As Aikawa thought about that moment, he stared down at his hand with a grimace. His arms and legs were still attached to his body. He was standing, walking, thinking, talking.

It was all still possible.

"Which is why I need to do...what I must..."

He took a step toward the sirens when something caught his eye. There was an object in the rut left by the semitruck's wheels: a multipurpose clock in the shape of a teddy bear. That same teddy bear had talked nonstop—its words sometimes humorous, sometimes venomous. It had been destroyed in the blast and rendered nonfunctional.

Neither the person who spoke through the machine nor the girl were here.

Aikawa steeled himself and resolved something right then and there. No matter what happened, he would take the emotions churning inside him and make something of them.

Several vehicles screeched to a halt nearby, and many sets of footsteps rushed his way. After a moment, he saw the firefighters and police officers. Slowly, he walked to meet them.

.: 11 :.

FAILED.

Failed. Failed.

Fail, fail, failfailfailfailfailfailfailfailfailfailure.

I failed! I'm a failure! This is the worst possible failure that could ever exist!

"Damn it! Damn it! Damn it all!"

Kakitani tore at his hair and grit his teeth so hard he nearly cracked his molars. He was hiding in a clump of tall grass, watching from afar. In the distance, he could see the red glow of the flames, the billowing black smoke, and Aikawa Youichi shuffling toward imminent rescue.

Kakitani had barely survived his leap from the seventh story. If determination alone was enough to protect someone, then perhaps his miraculous survival was his reward. After shattering the glass window and plummeting from the building, Kakitani fell onto some trees in a lush park that bordered the building. His body snapped branch after branch before slamming into the ground, causing severe injuries.

But Kakitani lived.

He was certain Kuwana and the other members of the task force who were still trapped in the building would have wanted him to escape, but Kakitani couldn't accept retreat. He forced his battered body to climb into the semitruck blocking the entrance to the building's underground parking area, start the engine, and throw it into reverse.

If he crashed the truck into the service entrance, he could deal a huge blow to the building's systems. It was the best strategy his pain-addled mind could come up with to free his companions.

Those thoughts were quickly wiped away as he heard the faint sound of machinery moving.

While he didn't understand that he was hearing the sound of the freight elevator in the underground parking garage, he somehow knew that the sound was that of the final nail being hammered into the coffin of their plan.

He couldn't ignore whatever made that sound.

Without hesitation, Kakitani slammed his foot on the accelerator. Just before impact, he leapt out from the driver's seat to escape the explosion. Even outside, the truck's impact was incredible. The blast and the accompanying waves of heat raked over him and sent him tumbling into the tall grass.

"Ghhk—! Agh!"

His body spasmed as every nerve screamed in pain. Sweat dotted his brow, and the sheer agony made him vomit. Yellow bile streaked his cheek, but he looked intently in the direction of the billowing black smoke.

No human could have survived an explosion like that.

He wouldn't even be able to see the corpse of his most hated enemy: Aikawa Youichi. Kakitani accomplished what he and his companions had set out to do. No one else had done it; it was all him. A sense of accomplishment filled him to the brim. He would have gone happily to the grave if he'd lost consciousness in that moment.

But he didn't.

"I-Impossible..."

A figure emerged from the scorching heat and black smoke. Kakitani didn't know where the strength was hiding in such a slender frame, but the figure carried the portly Aikawa on its shoulders, more easily than if it were a fully grown man. Its feet dragged as it walked up the ramp from underground.

"Ah..."

Above him, the moon peeked out from behind the clouds, the crimson glow of the flames in the background. Silver moonlight shone on the svelte figure—it was a machine. The machine, which was in the shape of a girl, had suffered numerous cuts and scrapes. It wore tattered, soot-covered coveralls, and its beautiful man-made skin was scorched, but it walked steadily as it carried Aikawa away from the fire.

Once it got to a place where Aikawa would be safe, it gently laid him on the ground. The flames suddenly burst, like a final shuddering exhalation. The hot air reached all the way to the crouched machine and Aikawa halfway up the incline, but it wasn't hot enough to burn them; it could only do so much.

The machine had placed itself between the flames and Aikawa, but all the blast of air did was tear back its hood, revealing its face under the moon.

Kakitani's eyes were glued to its long hair flowing in the red-tinged moonlight, its pale profile, its flickering eyes as they stared into the fire—there stood the machine that had saved his detestable enemy, finally revealed.

"..."

Kakitani felt he should charge them and crush both Aikawa and the machine, but his body hadn't responded since the truck's impact. He'd also dropped his gun when he leapt from the building, leaving him with nothing but his injured body and making him a miserable failure.

Sirens wailed in the distance. Someone nearby must have heard the explosion and called the police or the fire department. Kakitani and his group had taken control of the comms network in the immediate vicinity and cut off contact between the building and the outside, but they'd been unable to do anything more than that. That meant he couldn't reach any of his companions.

Suddenly, Kakitani realized the machine was gone.

"Huh?! Wh-where'd it go?!"

It had only been a moment. He glanced at the building, his attention taken by the approaching sirens, then looked back to where the machine had been standing. Aikawa was lying on his back in the road. The man's eyebrows twitched, and he let out a violent cough before rising slowly to his feet and staring at the flames in a daze.

There was nothing else Kakitani could do. Clenching his jaw in frustration, he crawled further into the tall grasses to hide from view. He slipped through mud and flung himself into the wastewater flowing from the building. He would meet up with his other coconspirators at their base... He had to tell them about their companions' humiliation and his own failure this night.

"I won't...forget!" he screamed as he dragged his battered body on.

He ran, and he ran, and he ran. For tonight, that was the only way he could keep fighting.

.: 12 :.

AFTER CARRYING Aikawa out from below the burning building and ensuring his safety, Vivy quickly left the area, her framework screeching as she ran down the empty moonlit streets. Being in such high temperatures had caused some of her internal components to warp, making her normally graceful motions clunky and awkward. She thought her good-natured colleagues at NiaLand might faint if they found her in such a state. In fact, Vivy had to work at NiaLand the very next day.

NiaLand's anniversary celebration might have only been one night, but there were no days off for a theme park that brought so much joy to people and created a world of dreams. The dream would have to continue tomorrow. Vivy was just one AI in that dream world, an AI given the task of songstress, and she had to be there to greet guests. In order to do that, she needed to change out her broken or deformed parts.

"..."

These thoughts lingered in her mind as she ran—not back to NiaLand but somewhere else. Vivy had prepared for this outcome before she went to save Assemblyman Aikawa Youichi by readying a sort of safe house where her broken body could recover. Well, it would be more accurate to say that Matsumoto had prepared it using his hacking skills. That was just how intelligent the AI Matsumoto was; he'd gone to the trouble of preparing an untraceable repair location for her.

He wasn't with her at the moment, however.

Right before they were about to escape the building, Vivy had put Aikawa's safety first. In a snap decision, she flipped open a steel panel leading to a channel for wastewater that was below the building, then leapt inside with Aikawa. Before the flames and smoke could consume and choke out the air's oxygen, she got him out of the building and away from the fire. She then made a quick exit so the approaching firefighters and police officers wouldn't see her.

Vivy didn't have time to worry about Matsumoto's safety, so unfortunately, he'd been hit by the explosion. She hadn't been able to recover him. The teddy bear clock was, of course, just a vessel for Matsumoto and not his true "self." His data, which one could argue *was* his true self, was still in the terminal at NiaLand where Vivy had first downloaded him.

However, Vivy couldn't help but feel some degree of disappointment in her consciousness at losing her birthday present from Momoka.

"…"

Nevertheless, Vivy's first mission in the Singularity Project was complete. Aikawa was safe with his cohorts, and the group with dangerous ideologies who'd attacked him would've been arrested by now. The AI Naming Law, which had originally been pushed forward after Aikawa's death, should never come to pass.

Now Vivy just had to repair her damaged parts in the safe house and get back to NiaLand like nothing had ever happened. If things kept going this way, she would be back just before the park opened tomorrow.

And her task was complete. Or…it should have been.

"This is quite unfortunate, Vivy."

The moment after she heard the inorganic voice, an impact sent her slender body flying.

ılıı||ılıı

The video from Vivy's eye cameras was briefly replaced with static, and her consciousness was severely impaired. She immediately forced her powering-down systems to restart and tried recovering her most recent actions and thought patterns from backup data. What was she doing the moment before her consciousness cut out?

"It would be futile to resist anymore. Pointless, even."

The voice struck her like a surprise attack. It didn't come through her audio sensors, which were in the process of rebooting. Rather, the information was written directly into her consciousness by her positronic brain.

Her recovering systems started to catch up to reality.

"..."

The fragmented data coming in from her eyes informed her left camera was broken. Her right eye was blurry and unfocused, with the lights of the starry sky above her burning into the sensor. Only then did she realize she was lying on her back. She wasn't on dirt, though.

Vivy was on an airport runway. A massive one, at that—and she was smack-dab in the middle of it. Airports didn't normally allow anyone, human or AI, to just wander onto their runways. One of the primary assumptions about how an AI makes decisions was that they would follow rules. And yet, Vivy was still there. The one opposing her now understood that she was defiant.

"Vivy, I know you know you can't win against me, and I need you for the Project. I don't want to hurt you anymore."

The calm voice was trying to get her to give up. She had no intention of listening.

"..."

As Vivy lay sprawled on the ground, she checked the operation of her various parts. Only 18 percent of her upper body and 67 percent of her lower body were operating properly. Her upper body had been severely damaged from the initial strike. It would be difficult to repair the parts that had warped in the explosion, meaning it would be best to replace her right arm and its corresponding chest section completely.

She set aside her plans on repairing herself and moved, her frame near its breaking point.

"..."

"You're not going to listen to me no matter how much I talk. This might not be an appropriate phrase for us, but would you please just grow up, Vivy? There's no point in doing all this."

"Point...?" She slowly sat up, and the motor in her hips let out an uncharacteristic screech. Next, she bent her knees. Her legs supported her weight as she relied on her balancer to stand. "Until I've fulfilled my orders..."

"You're intentionally misinterpreting those orders. I suspect you have a system error or a bug. When's the last time you underwent system maintenance? Have you recently left your head-parts in the care of an outsider or allowed someone access to your system? Well, other than me, of course."

She wasn't listening. Granted, he wasn't listening to her either. Vivy shook her head. Her long synthetic hair, damp from her own oil, swished as she did so. She showed her intention to refuse his proposal. Or rather, she presented data that represented her refusal.

"..."

"..."

They were silent, but both knew what they had to do. Vivy pulled her unmoving left arm from her body and raised her horribly damaged right arm.

In front of her was a massive machine standing against her, and it began to move. The thing was over five meters tall, the simple sort of AI meant for construction work and heavy labor. It had a steel arm in the shape of a human hand, which it opened and closed as if to flex both its ability to carry several tons of building materials and the steel's grasping strength.

Then it thrust the steel tip toward her.

Even Vivy's titanium skeleton would be torn as easily as paper if struck with that arm. The difference in power between the two AI was obvious, and a rapid calculation returned a grim probability of her achieving her goal.

But she didn't retreat. As an AI, she couldn't.

"I continue toward my goal in accordance with the First Law," she said. She took a step on her badly damaged leg, found her footing, and ran forward.

The machine in her way was none other than her partner in the Project that would extend over the next one hundred years.

"Ah!"

Using only the slightest movements, Vivy dodged the arm of the heavy machine, but her lower body was clumsier than her calculations had implied. She slipped past the machine, a gale rushing by her. The sleeve of her coveralls lagged behind and caught on the machine's arm, which lifted her up, leaving Vivy's light frame dangling in the open air. She was chucked skyward, spinning as she crashed back down into the runway.

Her injuries got even worse. She'd already purged her left arm, so now she cut the electrical supply to her right arm—which had already worn out quite a bit during her work in the building—and put everything into making her leaden legs work to their fullest capacity.

Vivy rolled onto her back and kicked up into a standing position. The next moment, she rolled to the side, avoiding another attack from the machine's arm, this time aimed at her head to pin her down. During her tumble, she caught a glimpse of a white number painted on the runway at the edge of her camera view. She needed to get to runway three; this was runway one. Two more to go. She had to make it there, to that specific spot.

She was none other than the songstress Vivy, created to serve people.

"…"

Her upper half was horribly damaged, and the operation capacity of her lower half was greatly reduced. A human would have already passed out or died from such wounds, facing long-term consequences even if they lived. However, with no nervous system to feel pain, no mind to feel fear, and not even an order to stop, it was nothing for an AI.

Thankfully, Matsumoto was afraid of destroying Vivy. It was evident in how he tried to capture her or block her way rather than outright hurt her. Vivy was a necessary component of the Singularity Project. He needed her. By taking advantage of his drive to complete his mission, she could use the importance of her own existence to—

"You're sorely mistaken if you think you can get away from me," he said as she slipped past his arm again and made a break for it.

Neither emotional nor physical distress was going to stop Vivy as her frame surged forward, which was why she didn't change her plan at Matsumoto's transmission. It was the sheer difference in their specs that allowed Matsumoto to pin her down.

But it wasn't the large machine that got her—it was another machine lined up behind it.

As he was an advanced AI from the future, Matsumoto had been able to hack into and control multiple old-fashioned labor AIs at once.

"..."

Vivy lay on her back on the ground, sandwiched between the hard earth and the machine's arm. Her right arm and her legs barely worked now, let alone the left arm she'd severed earlier. She wasn't going to escape. Her hood had slipped off when the arm crushed her into the ground, revealing her singed artificial hair. The slick oil oozing into her tresses reflected the starlight.

"It might have just been a borrowed body, but I kind of liked that teddy bear. My heart aches for the person who gave it to you now that it's been lost to the last attempt at resistance by the enemy... Not that I have a heart to ache."

"Matsumoto..."

"To be honest, I was worried this would happen. It's no exaggeration to say I was reluctant to share this information with you, and this is why. Do you see now, Vivy? This is the unfillable expanse between you and me of more than a hundred years." The heavy machinery controlled by Matsumoto continued to hold Vivy

down as it transmitted a voice filled with what sounded—thanks to his advanced emotional patterns—like *pity*.

Work AIs surrounded Vivy one after another as she lay restrained, until there were six big machines—the one she'd faced off against, the one holding her, and four more—as well as seven medium-sized AIs. There were likely small ones hidden nearby too. Even if Vivy was driven to desperation and found herself capable of escaping one of the machines, Matsumoto had too much force. Vivy had known since the beginning that the probability of her success didn't even reach one percent.

She still needed to try though, even now. She had to.

"Matsumoto, I have a proposal. Release me. Set me free."

"I can't do that. Besides, it's too late."

The arm pressed down so hard, it made Vivy's chest creak. Her voice warped from the effect it had on her voice production parts, but she still tried to move. Matsumoto refused.

Her frowning pattern activated, and Matsumoto said, *"I may have lost my multipurpose clock body, but I'll still fulfill my purpose. It's time."*

There was no need to ask Matsumoto what he meant by that. Vivy felt a tremble through the runway and a wind far more powerful than that from the strike of the heavy machine's arm. A roar smothered the sounds of their conversation. She craned her neck and saw something coming toward them.

She checked the name of the plane. The late-night passenger flight was fully booked, with 150 people onboard. It was due to depart at 10:25 p.m. The plane rushed down the runway, gaining speed.

"..."

Her eye latched on to one window for a business-class seat as the plane started to take off. Perhaps it was just an illusion that made it seem like the innocent eyes staring out the window met hers for a brief moment.

No, AIs didn't fall for illusions. They were both aware of each other, she was sure.

"I complete my task in accordance with the Three Laws and the Zeroth Law."

It wasn't Vivy who spoke of the Zeroth Law but Matsumoto.

Those words raked viciously through Vivy's consciousness. Then she was struck with a fierce blow. The second heat wave to hit Vivy that night penetrated her entire frame.

.: 13 :.

"MOMOKA, don't fidget so much."

"Okaaay, Dad."

She was sitting far back in the large seat. Listening to her father, she sat still, drawing her knees up to her chest, but the calm only lasted a short time before the energetic youngster's attention was captured by something else.

She was enthralled by all the entertainment options kindly provided to keep the passengers from getting bored, as well as by the nighttime sights outside—especially since her father had given her the window seat.

There was something she kept thinking back to, though.

"Vivy was so pretty..." she murmured, her cheeks tinged red with happiness at the pleasant memory.

Her father smiled wanly for the umpteenth time. He'd listened to his daughter sing the songstress's praises for half the day, and he knew she still wasn't finished. Surely she wasn't trying to tire out her already worn-out father, but it was happening nonetheless.

"We'll come back next year," she said in a voice he found adorably confident and loving.

He nodded in agreement and stroked her hair with his large hand, and she felt as if her world was filled with joy. Momoka might not hear Vivy sing in person for a whole year, but she could fondly think back on this day.

Once she grew a little taller and a little older, she could use her own money to visit NiaLand more often and bring the rosy future she imagined to life.

"..."

Momoka sifted through her thoughts as sleep slowly enveloped her. She hadn't had much sleep the night before because she'd been so excited for today, and the day had been filled with activity. Even though she might've appeared to have an endless well of energy, she too needed rest. Her father had already put on his eye mask with the intention of sleeping until they arrived at their destination. The mask was a gift from Momoka, and it made her happy to see him using it.

She glanced sideways at him as the in-flight announcements played, and then the plane picked up speed. Just as its wheels were leaving the ground, she felt a weightless sensation—one she didn't particularly enjoy. In order to calm herself down, she looked out the window.

"Ah…"

She could see something small on the ground two runways over. She wondered what it was, as it didn't seem like it should be there. But after a second, she realized the figure was the songstress she yearned for.

Why was Vivy here? Why was she lying on the runway?

The girl didn't know the answers to her questions, but she thought that maybe Vivy had come to encourage her since she was uneasy on the late-night flight. Delighted that Vivy cared so much about her, she waved, silently promising she'd see the beloved songstress again.

"Hey, Dad," she said, tugging on her father's sleeve as she stared out the window. "Vivy's—"

The words that followed were forever lost in a resounding blast and a flash of red.

. : 14 : .

10:26 P.M., AUGUST 20th, the passenger flight crashed. All onboard were killed, totaling 121 passengers and staff.

"There were mechanical issues just after takeoff. There was no human error. It was purely an accident," said Matsumoto flatly as he held Vivy down. Her eye camera was locked onto the flames.

At the end of the first runway were flames so bright they seemed to eat away at the night. The fire spread out from the center of the crumpled, misshapen plane, mercilessly engulfing the entire vehicle.

There were sirens in the distance. The flames, the explosion, the sirens—all things Vivy had already witnessed once that night. She had known nothing about the world outside NiaLand, and this was essentially her second experience in that world.

The first time, she had been able to save Aikawa. The second time, though...

"Vivy, we can't stay here forever. If you're discovered, you'll be investigated to determine your connection to the crash, and we don't need that. Trust me, it'd be more than troublesome."

The arm pinning Vivy down lifted, freeing her, and all the work AIs that had been surrounding her went back to their posts, leaving silence in their wake. Now that they'd managed to hold her back, they no longer had a role here. Once Matsumoto relinquished control, he urged Vivy to leave the airport. Indeed she would.

Vivy had come here without telling Matsumoto to try to prevent the plane crash.

"Why did you stop me?" Vivy asked.

"You should already know why. It was something you couldn't do."

"We saved Assemblyman Aikawa Youichi."

"He needed to live in order to secure humanity's future. The passengers on the plane are different. They have nothing to do with our alterations of the future."

"If they have nothing to do with it—"

"We have to prevent unrelated things becoming related factors. Vivy, we need to alter history as little as possible," Matsumoto said, like he was reprimanding a naughty child. *"The original history is the* authentic *history, and the edited history is the* revised *history. We must limit the effect we have on the revised history to only the most important Singularity Points. The difference between the authentic history and the revised history is that final point. Affecting any factors outside of that is a violation of the Zeroth Law."*

Matsumoto's lengthy explanation made Vivy's audio sensors operate in vain. She was still lying on her back and instead of glaring at him—since she couldn't see him—she glared up at the sky. Then she spoke.

"You violated the First of the Three Laws."

"Yes, in order to follow the Zeroth Law."

"You violated the Second of the Three Laws."

"Yes, in order to follow the Zeroth Law."

"You violated the Third of the Three Laws."

"Yes, in order to follow the Zeroth Law."

They were just going in circles. There was nothing Vivy could say to stir up regret in Matsumoto's consciousness. He'd done everything he could to fulfill his role as an AI. There was nothing he should feel toward the passengers of that crashed plane. He would have seen the number on the ticket Vivy picked up back at NiaLand. He knew that the girl who had given Vivy the vessel he would borrow would be among those passengers—among the dead.

Matsumoto did nothing, despite knowing that little girl who loved Vivy's songs with all her heart was going to die.

"Stand up, Vivy, please. Take a good look at yourself. You have a very important part to play. We are the only AIs who can achieve that goal."

"To modify the Singularity Points and prevent humanity's destruction."

"Yes, that's it. That's why you have to get up..."

Vivy stood, her body screeching in protest. As she stared at the burning plane and the red firelight that swallowed life, she firmly embedded the images into her memory. She wouldn't forget—*couldn't* forget—what she'd been unable to stop today. She had stood by as Kirishima Momoka, her devoted fan, and all the other people had died.

In accordance with the Zeroth Law, she would execute her goal.

"A hundred years to destroy AI..."

This would be her journey to eliminate AI—to eliminate *herself.*

. : 15 : .

AIKAWA LISTENED to a report from his secretary as he lay in bed in a private room at the university hospital.

"It doesn't look like any of the men who carried out the attack are going to talk. It's suspected they have ties to a radical activist group who've been hinting they might turn to violence..."

"Considering what they were able to pull off, I don't think it'll be easy to confirm those connections," Aikawa said. "At least

I'm still alive... Not that that means I'll let this go." He looked his secretary straight in the eye, who stood up straighter under his gaze. When he noticed this, Aikawa let his expression soften as he flashed a smile. "They might regret their failure, but we'll make them regret it even more when we hit them hard. Show them I was the wrong person to go after."

"You seem different, sir..." said the secretary, carefully choosing the words.

"You think? Hm, probably." Aikawa's eyebrows rose, then he smiled wider.

The secretary left the room, leaving him alone. He looked at his hand. It was wrapped in bandages, concealing the burns below. Despite everything he'd been through, miraculously, Aikawa's only injury was a burn on his hand—and that burn was entirely his own fault.

"..."

He looked at the overbed table beside him. It was piled high with "get well soon" gifts from people who'd heard he was in the hospital as well as documents he needed to look over. Amid the pile, something stood out: a multipurpose clock in the shape of a teddy bear, half its body blackened and burnt. The incredibly skilled individual who had used it to communicate had already left, and no information could be gleaned from the destroyed multipurpose clock.

Aikawa had rescued it from the fire, burning his hand in the process. He'd brought it here to his hospital room.

Regardless, he had no intention of letting it go. The person who'd helped save his life was unlikely to inhabit the clock again. In fact, Aikawa was unlikely to see *either* of his rescuers ever again. But he was allowed to remember, to strive to remember what happened.

"What can I do?" he murmured as he looked at his injured hand again.

Even if he told the police about them and had them investigated, it would be only for his own satisfaction. They must have avoided revealing their identities to him for a reason, after all. But they stuck in his mind, especially the profile of the girl, something inhumanly beautiful in her profile...

"The AI Naming Law..."

That was the source of the evil that had tried to take his life. If Aikawa were being entirely honest, the bill was just something he had made in order to earn clout as a politician. He wasn't that serious about it. He wasn't obsessed with AIs either. He did know more about them than the average person, thanks to his work on the bill, but he was neither deeply invested nor personally interested in them.

That is, until today. AIs had risked their lives to save him.

"I will make the AI Naming Law a reality."

Aikawa solemnly vowed to repay them in this way as he looked back at the teddy bear on the sideboard. He would keep that dirty, broken clock for the rest of his life.

The AI Naming Law was passed six months after that night, on March 20th, 20XX.

Prologue / Estella

IT WAS A SPECIAL DAY for a lot of people. Every member of the staff was there, dressed in their gorgeous uniforms and lined up in neat rows in the spacious ballroom. Their expressions were all different. Half of them looked expectant or maybe nervous, while the other half weren't showing any obvious waves of emotion—they simply wore natural-looking smiles. This was to be expected, as half of the employees in the rows were human, while the other half were AIs in human form. The workforce was largely made up of customer service AIs.

"..."

The rows of staff suddenly began clapping as a middle-aged man in a high-class black suit crossed the hall in front of them. His back was perfectly straight and his motions were refined as he strode past and came to a stop, facing the staff. The applause stopped, and everyone waited in silence, watching him.

The microphone on the stand in front of him automatically adjusted to his height. He smiled, drew in a breath, and said, "Everyone, the day has finally come! I would like to thank every last one of you for your help." His voice was serene, and he stopped to bow deeply to the staff.

At that, the applause started up again. It wasn't quite loud enough to be called thunderous, but it was mixed with honest, joyful, and excited cries of praise.

He stayed bowed for a moment until he felt the applause had gone on long enough, then raised his head and turned back to the mic. "It has taken patience and perseverance to make it to this point, but I am overjoyed to find this reward at the end of all that hard work. This...is my dream." His eyes crinkled with a smile, and he looked to the side. His gaze was fixed on a distant ballroom window—or rather, the world that lay beyond.

Out there was darkness as far as the eye could see, and it wasn't just some unlit space in the middle of the night. It was *true* darkness. And while darkness often left people uneasy, this darkness did not. There was an emotional shimmer in the man's eyes as he looked out into it, a feeling shared in no small part by the human staff members in the room. To someone born on planet Earth, this place was so far, so high, and so impossible to reach.

What lay outside that window was the endless expanse of space.

"This is the newly built space station, Daybreak. I have decided that this spot is where dreams will come true." He had chosen a name representing a new dawn. He stood before his staff, filled with pride and accomplishment at making *his* dream come true and in giving so many hope for the future.

Everyone was moved by his expression and his words. They yearned to see their *own* wishes granted, and they envied him.

"The opening of this space station marks the beginning of the first full-scale space hotel. From this moment onward, people will come to space and make their dreams reality. I am proud to begin this work with all of you!" he said passionately to all the staff who had supported his endeavor.

Such words might come off as immature or even laughable, but not a single person in the room so much as chuckled. Everyone there had endured mockery for their dreams. That was why they were here. And so, when one person started clapping, there was no way to stop the torrent.

This round of applause, still not strong enough to be thunderous, was more passionate and powerful than the last. Naturally, it went on longer too. The man stood and listened, smiling bashfully, until he raised his hand. Any more of that and the tears gathering in his eyes would spill down his cheeks, and that would be embarrassing, especially considering his position as their manager as well as his age.

Besides, he still had more to say.

"Additionally, our sponsor—one of the top AI corporations, OGC—has sent us several units. Well, I should say they dispatched several AI staff members to join our opening team. You have likely already met, so it may seem silly to introduce you now..." He gave a joking shrug, causing some quiet laughter in the room. After the giggles had died down, he said, "Let me introduce the one who will be supervising the AI staff. Considering her rank, she will be the assistant manager of this hotel, second-in-command after me. Estella!"

When her name was called, the woman's gentle voice rang out through the ballroom. "Thank you, sir."

Every member of the staff who heard that beautiful voice went rigid. Her voice naturally captured people's hearts and put them at ease. She slowly crossed the room, following her superior's earlier path. Estella was a graceful woman—or rather, a graceful AI—with long blonde hair and clear blue eyes. She was fairly tall for a female AI and wore a classy dress that flattered her shapely figure.

Estella bowed quietly to the staff and then raised her head. She smiled, her features beautiful enough to put a goddess to shame, and said, "My name is Estella, and I will be assisting you. Starting today, I will be working with you all on Daybreak as the assistant manager." She paused. "I look forward to our everlasting relationship."

VIVY

Prototype

CHAPTER 2

During the Songstress's Vacation

.: 1 :.

V IVY RECALLED EVERYTHING the moment the program ran, though calling it *recollection* was a tad bit inaccurate. As an AI, she always had the data in her memory. The particular files she was after had simply been encrypted, making them inaccessible. Once that closed-off area of her memory was opened, a complex program decrypted the file—instantly and vividly reminding Vivy of her mission and what had happened in pursuit of it.

"Hm? Is something wrong, Diva? Do you feel off?"

Her system froze for a brief moment and then immediately rebooted itself. The process took only a matter of seconds, but it was plenty to cause the NiaLand staff member walking beside her to notice something was wrong.

Vivy just turned to her, smiled, and said, "Nothing's wrong. I was just reorganizing the files from my performance."

"Oh, you're reviewing them? Do you really need to, though? I thought your performance was incredible, and I've already seen it more than a hundred times!" she said playfully, then stuck her tongue out.

This particular staff member had started working at NiaLand more than ten years ago, and Vivy, now considered an old-timer since she'd been at NiaLand for so long, had worked with her almost that entire time. The woman had joined as a greenhorn fresh out of college and had even gotten married during her tenure, eventually becoming one of the theme park's veteran employees.

"Thank you. However, the number of my successful performances won't matter to someone who has come to the show for the first time. I want to do my very best every time I perform," Vivy told her.

"Huh, that's incredible. You're right... I was looking at it wrong," the employee replied pensively, evidently impressed. While this chat was useful training for an AI, it couldn't take up too much of their current schedule. Thus, the employee added, "Okay, keep working hard so you can give your best performance tomorrow and every day after!"

Vivy paused.

There was something about the word "tomorrow" that bothered her, like there was something Vivy was supposed to be doing then. She didn't want to cause any more of a delay, however, so she nodded and said, "...Of course."

"Well, not that a diva has to do much to prepare," said the

woman teasingly before parting ways with Vivy in front of her dressing room.

"..."

Vivy's dressing room was on the top floor of the Princess Palace, which was in the center of NiaLand. It suited Vivy, the singing princess of NiaLand. It was furnished with a canopied bed, a dressing table that even royalty would find suitable, and a wardrobe containing dresses of every color. It was truly a room tailor-made for a princess.

Of course, Vivy did not need the bed, nor did she need to fuss over applying makeup at the dressing table. And while the dresses were essential, none of it was important right then. What she needed was an electronic connection. Not as a means for a bored princess to spend her time but for an AI to do her necessary work. After all these years, even once she had been moved to this more opulent dressing room, she still used the same computer terminal. At her request, it had been moved with her and placed in one corner of the room. The terminal had become a partner of sorts.

She walked over to the terminal, pulled out the chair, and sat down. She reached up to her earring, withdrew a concealed connector, and plugged it into the terminal. She closed her eyes, her hand still on her ear; all humanoid AIs sat in the same position when connected to a terminal. Humans thought it looked like the AI had fallen asleep with earbuds in and fondly referred to it as a "tune snooze."

But that wasn't important.

Vivy's consciousness flowed through the terminal, heading through the internet toward The Archive. The fact that all AIs connected to the massive server of sorts, chock-full of data, made it akin to a digital world.

The moment she entered The Archive, she felt a strange sensation. She could feel her body—a body that shouldn't exist here—and she saw a strange scene around her. It was the inside of a wooden school building, filled with music stands and a piano, making it look like a choir room.

"What is this place...?" She took a few steps, turning around to scan the area.

"I got everything down to the last detail, don't you think? Everything in The Archive's so bland that it was sort of depressing, so I made this neat little space for us. Do you like it?" The voice was casual, flippant—it was a voice Vivy had forgotten.

"..."

Even after fifteen years, an AI wouldn't suffer memory degradation. Seconds or years after a moment, it didn't matter; the information never left. And yet, she had somehow forgotten his voice until he spoke. This, perhaps, could be considered a recollection.

"Matsumoto..." she said, her shapely lips quivering as the sound of the name brought her back through her memories.

"That's me. It's been a while, hasn't it? Ah, that look of distaste.

I'm happy to see your abundant emotional patterns are still doing well. Such skill!"

Vivy turned around to face Matsumoto, the pupils of her eye cameras shrinking. "What is that form?" she asked, looking at the cube in front of her in confusion. It didn't look like the Matsumoto she remembered. He was originally just code with no body, and she'd wondered for a while where he'd gone.

"Heeey, that sort of reaction is going to make me sad! How strange. I thought this was a winner. Handsome, even!"

For some time, Vivy purposely ignored the voice from her past emitted by the cube.

.: 2 :.

"**N**OW, VIVY, the Singularity Project is restarting," said the cube from where it sat on a music stand, almost pretentiously.

Vivy relaxed on the stool in front of the grand piano. With the shock of their reunion fading, she had come to accept Matsumoto in his cube form and was listening to him calmly. Matsumoto had never actually shared any personal data with Vivy, and his strange form was only temporary in this imaginary world.

"I became well aware of the inconvenience of not having a body last time, so even in an imaginary place, it's important to have a body that can execute tasks," Matsumoto said. "I've been sleeping until the second Singularity Point approached in order to minimize my impact on history."

Vivy tilted her head to the side as she listened to Matsumoto's explanation. Although needless here in this space, the gesture was automatic for an AI modeled so closely after human beings. It *did* convey loneliness to the viewer, so it had some purpose, at least.

"It's been fifteen years since the last Singularity Point..." Vivy said.

Indeed, an entire fifteen years had passed since the last Singularity Point. Since then, Vivy had undergone some changes—her operating system had been updated, and her frame had undergone regular maintenance after its repair, meaning her positronic brain and her body had been kept in mint condition. She had at least the same performance capabilities as fifteen years before, maybe even slightly improved.

Matsumoto found this satisfactory. There was a round eye camera set into the side of his cube, and he used its protective shutter like an eyelid. "I knew this would happen, but I'm glad they weren't careless enough to dispose of you," he said. "I still need you to work on the Project in secret."

"There's something I want to ask before we get to that," she said, derailing his push toward the next stage of the Project. The question came to mind because, after her reboot, she could compare her past actions to the current results. "Matsumoto, we edited the previous Singularity Point, didn't we?"

"..."

"Last time, you ordered me to protect Assemblyman Aikawa. We successfully saved him from the attack, accomplishing our goal. But..." Vivy stopped for a moment before continuing. "The bill for the AI Naming Law was supposed to disappear. Why did it get passed?"

"Does this mean you doubt the Project, Diva?" asked Matsumoto, his voice suddenly quieter than normal. And he'd called her by her official name. "In the years following the passing of the AI Naming Law, the name 'Diva' was selected as the name for Model Number A-03 from among the 600,000 submissions from the public. That is your true name. Are you unhappy with it?"

"No, I'm not unhappy with it. I am well aware I am a diva during my work at NiaLand. But during the Singularity Project..."

"You want to be called Vivy? That's fine. It would actually be wise to use that name while you're working on the Singularity Project from an integrity perspective. For better or worse, your true name has become too widely known, so a nickname from fifteen years ago that didn't stick around should be perfect."

"..."

Matsumoto thought it was a perfectly reasonable suggestion, but Vivy still wasn't happy. Fifteen years ago, she'd witnessed an event that haunted her, like a bug in her code. And Matsumoto still hadn't answered her question. The AI Naming Law had been passed despite the fact that they'd been successful.

"Vivy, we can think of history as having corrective power."

"Corrective power?"

"There are some points in history that are the way they are. Like humans mastering fire and evolving, using iron tools, inventing electricity, and creating us AIs. Our present is built on that history, and that history is inevitable."

"So, you're saying because of history's corrective power, the AI Naming Law didn't go away? It still became a law? If that's the case, then—"

"Will we be unable to prevent humanity's destruction? That's what you were going to ask, right? Well, don't worry. That won't happen. History's corrective power is strong, but it is not absolute. Are you satisfied with that?" The shutter over Matsumoto's eye camera opened and closed several times as he answered Vivy's question. "As I explained before, the Singularity Project's goal is to modify several Singularity Points because any one of them could start the countdown to humanity's end. So if we modify all of those points, the Project will succeed."

"So, if we change all those Singularity Points, we can avoid a future where humanity goes extinct?"

"Yes, exactly. We break down the wall by striking it several times, instead of just once. Makes sense, right?"

"We execute the entire plan. If we do..."

"Hm?"

Vivy didn't vocalize her thoughts on the future. She didn't think it was an appropriate thought for an AI, nor did she want to confirm how she thought Matsumoto would react if she did.

What she had wanted to say was: *If we do, that fiery crash from fifteen years ago won't be meaningless.*

"..."

Matsumoto's words picked up speed. "Well, now that we've reached a consensus, let's get down to business. This Singularity Point is different from the previous one, and it's quite serious. I need you to go on a trip."

"A trip? What is the destination?" Vivy asked, switching her focus to the goal immediately in front of them.

Matsumoto's eye camera whirred as he operated it, then he half closed the shutter to imitate a heavy-lidded gaze. "Your next destination, Vivy, is *space*."

"..."

It took a moment for Vivy to react to what Matsumoto had said. He was talking about something so vast, it caused a tiny freeze in her consciousness. It took less than a second for her to right herself. She sat up straight and knit her elegant brows together as she said, "Space? There's a problem in space related to a Singularity Point?"

"Yes, there will be. In terms of scale, you could say it's the greatest problem in the Singularity Project. Preventing it will have an immense effect on the final outcome. It's a critical issue in our mission."

Vivy searched through her data for topics related to "space" as she listened to Matsumoto.

Space, the region outside of the Earth's atmosphere, wasn't that far away in this day and age. Humanity's recent scientific advancements were leaps and bounds ahead of where they'd been only a few decades before. Research and development related to AI had seen the most progress, but space travel and habitation had also been blessed with similar technological revolutions.

They were past the time of international competition between hastily developed national space programs over the final frontier. Many private corporations were now involved in the space industry, and vacations in space for the general public were no longer just a dream, even if the wealthy were still prioritized over everyone else.

"Not too far in the future, space will no longer be a frontier for just the select few. Well, this period did make you believe such a time would come, didn't it?" said Matsumoto.

"There's a lot of foreshadowing there."

"There is no hidden meaning in my words. Besides, I have a lock preventing me from sharing any unnecessary information. I do think I can impart how important this upcoming issue is in a mere twelve minutes with only the essential details."

Vivy narrowed her eyes as she looked at him, and he closed his eye camera's shutter.

A single sheet of music appeared on the formerly empty music stand. It made sense: They were in an imaginary space, and Matsumoto could do whatever he wished. There was no musical key or notes on the sheet; instead, there was video data displaying a colossal man-made structure floating in space.

"Humanity's first hotel beyond the atmosphere, housed inside a space station. This is the revolutionary space hotel, Daybreak."

"I've heard the name. It was a topic in the park for a bit." Vivy had memories of the same staff member who had walked her to her dressing room talking to her about the space station a while ago. "The hotel opened six years ago, right?"

"Right. At the time, it was viewed with significant apprehension due to the construction and operating costs as well as environmental differences. But the hotel overcame it all and took off into space."

"...Please continue."

"It's unfortunate that didn't get a better response from you. Anyway, Daybreak was going well. There are even plans to expand with a second establishment. Opening preparations are happening as we speak." The video on the sheet music changed to a different station. The second one was built in the same style as Daybreak but obviously newer. "This is the second space hotel, Sunrise. And Vivy, you will infiltrate Sunrise as one of the initial AI staff members."

"You say it like it'll be a simple task."

Based on their conversation so far, Vivy knew she would need to go to space. The problem with that was her work in NiaLand. Vivy's primary objective was to support the Singularity Project, but Matsumoto was the one who constantly said they needed to limit their effect on history.

Going into space would take, at the very least, a week. Vivy wouldn't be in NiaLand during that time, creating a vacancy in her position.

"Don't worry," said Matsumoto. "I have already modified your performance logs. The records now show your performance has started to decline after years of exhaustive use, making it appear as if you require immediate overhaul. You will be sent away very soon, and all of your performances scheduled during your overhaul will be postponed. And don't worry, the guests coming to the park to see you will receive the best customer service possible!"

As she listened to Matsumoto talk about the preparations he'd made, there was no space for her to interject or argue against her being made to look like a deteriorating heap of junk. She was unamused, but there was no point in saying so to the heartless AI from the future.

"Oh, come on, Vivy, is something wrong?"

"Stop treating me like an old woman. It damages my pristine songstress image."

"Ha ha, okay. I'll make sure none of the apology notices displayed in the park or on the website say anything that might damage Diva's image."

She had assumed her concern would be dismissed, so she was surprised by his appropriate response. That only made Vivy feel more frustrated.

With the preparations complete, there was no point in Vivy disagreeing with Matsumoto. The die had already been cast.

"All right, back to work after fifteen years," Matsumoto declared. "Get excited—we're going out!"

Vivy cleared her face of expression and stood, disconnecting from the terminal. She took the connector earring from her right ear and moved it to her left. There was no functional purpose to the gesture, but it still held meaning for Vivy.

.: 3 :.

VIVY STOPPED as she walked down the accessway to the new space hotel, Sunrise. She looked out the window into the unending darkness, eyes narrowing as her eye cameras took in the vastness of space.

"..."

The easiest and cheapest method for reaching space in this post-development era was the space elevator. The space elevator terminated in a transport hub where many travelers would then transfer to a spaceship for their intended destination.

Vivy had arrived via the hotel's newly built space shuttle. The trip was long, and she would have been quite fatigued if she'd been human, but thankfully, Vivy's frame wasn't equipped with a fatigue function. She could begin working right away, hence her tour of the station so soon after her arrival.

"Curious, Vivy?" asked her tall tour guide when she noticed Vivy looking out the window.

They were on the way to the station's command center. Sunrise was a hotel, but its exterior was exactly the same as all other space stations: simple, unadorned, and refined. Conversely, the inside was carefully and richly decorated. Art hung on the walls, and beneath Vivy's feet was a red carpet that any first-class hotel would've been proud of. The station was also equipped with artificial gravity, so it felt no different than Earth, and the guests didn't have to struggle about in zero gravity. There were only a few who complained, saying it detracted from their fun because they couldn't *truly* experience being in space.

Even so—

"Vivy?"

The woman with golden hair cocked her head and elegantly turned back to Vivy, who was lost in thought. Her long skirt swayed gently, and every one of her motions was imbued with refined, ladylike grace.

Even as an AI in the same profession, Vivy was so impressed by the woman's mannerisms that she decided she would copy the patterns into her own system. After a momentary calculation, Vivy shook her head and said, "I'm sorry. This is my first time in space." The reply was an attempt to hide her true thoughts, but it wasn't a complete lie.

Model Number A-03 Vivy had already been in operation for many years, with two decades of work behind her. Obviously, the data she'd accumulated and integrated into herself over that period was both vast and varied, and naturally, there was some data about space. It was no exaggeration to say the majority of what humanity knew about space was saved in her positronic brain. Despite that, Vivy found her consciousness oddly enraptured with the deep darkness.

"Oh, yes. Everyone's surprised when they first see it. It's strange, since we're AIs," said the blonde as she smiled—her name was Estella.

They were both AIs, and the emotional patterns they used when interacting with humans were not necessary when talking to each other, but Estella interacted with Vivy in the same way she did humans. It was the same for Vivy; they were just following their principles.

"The other AI staff have the same reaction? Even you, Estella?" asked Vivy.

"Yes, even me. I wonder why though. The environment should be no different from Earth thanks to the artificial gravity, but there's something about it that stops even us AIs in our tracks. The owner used to say it was space's enchantment." Estella brought a hand to her mouth and giggled; it was an advanced, natural-looking emotional pattern.

Vivy didn't think her own similar emotional pattern was inferior, but Estella's certainly rivaled hers. AIs needed to gather data for the development and mastery of such emotional patterns, particularly for AIs like Vivy who interacted with customers. Humans wanted AIs that acted more humanlike. This well-known fact was backed by statistical data that AIs who appeared more human were treated with more care and kept around for longer periods of time.

No matter what role they were given, Vivy and all other AIs had a primary goal of serving humans, and they couldn't do that if humans didn't like having them around. They had to keep a reminder tucked in the back of their consciousness to continue learning through trial and error. After all, the popular Diva was one of the best AI models out there because she was in contact with huge volumes of people at NiaLand every day.

Just as Vivy gave Estella a look of admiration, an encrypted transmission from Matsumoto rang inside her consciousness.

"That's why the Songstress Series garnered such overwhelming support as an AI model, leading to widespread production and giving birth to the so-called Sisters line."

"...Be quiet."

Matsumoto was unable to take part in the Project directly this time, meaning he was providing long-distance support to Vivy from where he was on Earth. It also meant he was spying on everything Vivy said and did as she worked, giving her no chance to rest her system.

There was something in his words that bothered her, though. *"When you say the Sisters, you mean my successors, correct?"*

"The songstress Diva was the first model of the Songstress Series... But while this Estella in front of you is from that series, she isn't limited to the role of songstress. This will become more apparent as future models are released. By the way, how does it feel to be looking at your significantly younger sister?" asked Matsumoto teasingly, and Vivy stared at Estella.

"Hm?"

She was tall, and the parts corresponding with a traditionally feminine form, her chest and buttocks, were voluptuous. She was approximately 26 percent or 27 percent plumper than Vivy. If they stood side by side, Estella would also be half a head taller than Vivy.

Matsumoto's next statement was indelicate. *"It's crude of me to say, but looking at her makes it hard for me to believe you're the elder one."*

"Hush for a while," Vivy said coldly. She then smiled toward

Estella, who looked confused. She steered the conversation back to something Estella had said. "You mentioned the owner. Do you mean Ash Corvick, the manager of Daybreak?"

"Yes. He was my first owner and the ambitious man who started the space hotels... That's what they say about him anyway. He was really more of an adventurer who never forgot his childhood dreams," Estella replied with a smile.

There was a reason she used the past tense when referring to her first owner. Ash Corvick, the pioneer who established humanity's first space hotel, was already dead.

The first hotel opened six years ago, but Ash had been killed in a car accident on Earth three years prior, just before the business really took off. The space-obsessed dream chaser's tragic story was a news sensation for a time, stirring up much buzz. His widely publicized death turned the public eye on his hotel, saving it from financial ruin. Ironically, his death had likely made Sunrise's opening possible.

"The years I spent with him as my manager and owner were far shorter than I'd expected. But he did leave me with a mission. I am truly blessed as an AI to be involved with Daybreak and now, with the opening of Sunrise," Estella went on as she brought a hand to her ample bosom. "I hope you'll work hard as part of the staff, Vivy. Things are different from the training you received on Earth, so please make sure you listen to me."

"Leave it to me, ma'am. Standing by for orders!"

"Wonderful." She jokingly puffed out her chest, then continued with her tour of the ship's equipment.

Vivy followed slowly behind her, holding onto the handrail as she walked. *"She's really the one?"* she asked Matsumoto via transmission.

"Yes, she's the one," Matsumoto replied, knowing exactly who she meant even without a name. He wasn't happy about being told to keep quiet, but his tone was still emotionless. He used an uncharacteristic directness that only made an appearance when he was focused on the Singularity Project. *"She crashes the space hotel Sunrise into Earth, killing tens of thousands of people. She is Estella, the most defective AI in history and the culprit behind the Sun-Crash Incident."*

.: 4 :.

CONSIDERING THE CASUALTIES, the space station's fall to Earth was the greatest space disaster in history. It was commonly called the Sun-Crash Incident, and Vivy had to prevent it.

"The Sun-Crash Incident happened when the space hotel Sunrise unexpectedly lost control. While its controls were down, it fell down to Earth. It was a terrible event that, again, led to tens of thousands of deaths and injuries. Multiple investigations into the incident concluded that it was a terrorist attack by Estella, the manager of the hotel and the only one with access to Sunrise's controls."

"A terrorist attack by an AI? That's unrealistic," said Vivy, her sleek eyebrows furrowing as she listened to Matsumoto's explanation of the incident.

Her opinion wasn't meant to protect Estella, whom she'd only recently learned was her successor. The opinion came from a broader AI perspective. The Three Laws prevented AIs from hurting humans or disobeying orders. The Laws were programmed into every single AI and considered impossible for an AI to go against.

Therefore, no AI should be able to commit a terrorist attack and kill so many people.

"There are always exceptions to the rules. Just as you used force in the last Singularity Point to disable the attackers and protect Assemblyman Aikawa."

"The Zeroth Law."

The Zeroth Law overwrote the priorities of the Three Laws by broadening the definition from "humans" to "humanity," modifying how the Three Laws were applied to an individual and allowing AIs to take actions that would normally be prohibited. When the Zeroth Law took precedent, any AI could harm a person, making it a Law that couldn't be implemented lightly. It was only truly applicable in situations like Vivy's, where she'd been given the immense task of saving humanity as a whole. Estella shouldn't have been able to use it.

"The facts show that Estella crashed Sunrise into Earth," said Matsumoto. *"Among the objects discovered at the impact site were parts and pieces assumed to be from Estella. Additionally, the passengers who made it to the escape shuttle prior to the fall gave testimony stating it was Estella who crashed the station."*

"..."

"Are you dissatisfied with the conclusion?"

"It just feels unrealistic, is all."

Every piece of information Matsumoto gave her was confirmed information he'd ferried here from the future. Vivy had no reason to doubt the reliability or accuracy of that information—or Matsumoto's excellence—based on her work with him on the previous Singularity Point, not to mention how he'd managed to sneak her onto Sunrise by making sure she was registered as a member of the opening day staff. No one, human or AI, would doubt her.

Logically, Vivy should have agreed with Matsumoto's directions and stopped the impending tragedy. But she was still hesitant. *"Estella is complying with orders left to her by her previous owner, Ash Corvick. I can't believe someone like that would crash the space statio—"*

"Vivy, Vivy, Vivy, Viiiiivy," Matsumoto said, abruptly cutting her off. It was a waste of advanced technology to harass her through encrypted transmissions. He sounded frustrated as he told the uncertain songstress, *"Will you just* listen? *The facts are the facts. Accept them, please. I don't know what impression she's left on you in such a short time, but your guesses don't matter. Estella crashes Sunrise into the Earth. It doesn't matter that we don't know what her motive was or what principles she acted on. It's certain."*

"What proof makes you able to say that?"

"The fact that I come from a future in which Estella crashed Sunrise."

Matsumoto's statement hacked away at the doubts Vivy had. She could no longer make a strong argument against him.

Matsumoto noticed Vivy's silence and added, *"But it wouldn't do any harm to find out that much beforehand. Our greatest hurdle was getting you onto the station, which we easily overcame thanks to the technological differences between this era and myself. All we need to do now is eliminate the direct source of the Singularity Point."*

"Eliminate the source?"

"Yes. Knowing that Estella is the cause of Sunrise's crash, the surest and most logical resolution would be to eliminate her."

Vivy's frame froze in place for a moment at Matsumoto's cruel calculations, and then she slowly reviewed what he'd said. But no matter how many thousands of times she went over that short message, there was no alternate interpretation of the words. *"Eliminate...Estella?"*

"That is the most certain method. Oh, when I say eliminate, I don't mean anything ridiculous like using force to restrain her or destroy her beyond repair. I've already prepared a method so that you don't have to dirty your hands with such violent measures." Immediately after saying so, Matsumoto delivered a file to Vivy over their encrypted transmission.

She looked over its contents and found an abnormally complex program. *"What is this?"*

"It's a virus that will leave no trace of itself after erasing all memory, recorded information, and accumulated everyday data. It won't break the recipient or render their positronic brain unusable, making it a very humane way to solve our problem. Although it's not like anything an AI does to another AI has anything to do with being 'humane.'"

"..."

"She datalinks with you to give directions for your hotel work, right? Use that opportunity to infect Estella with the virus. Don't worry, I've set it so it won't have an effect on anyone except her. Once you've reformatted Estella, you hide among the cargo headed back to the surface. Then we erase records of the temporary AI worker known as Vivy. After that, you finish your 'maintenance' and return to the park as Diva. And then we'll have finished modifying the Singularity Point."

Matsumoto was providing her with significantly more information up front than he had last time. Perhaps he'd reviewed how their first endeavor went and thought more information would be helpful, or maybe she'd gained his trust.

Vivy touched the earring on her left ear, the plans for modifying the Singularity Point now clear. She wasn't doing so to prepare to connect to a terminal; the gesture had simply become impulsive.

She would have to completely erase all of Estella's data and memories. With that done, Estella would be removed as the cause of Sunrise's crash. Even if those actions of hers were the result of a particular thought process or command, she wouldn't have either once she was reformatted.

There was reason for Matsumoto to be concerned for Vivy. She didn't want to destroy an AI who was her successor. But if you reformatted only the positronic brain, leaving the frame intact, could you really say Estella was gone?

"Vivy...?"

"Sorry, Matsumoto. I have to get to work. I'm cutting off our transmission for now." She half forced the transmission to close and turned her attention back to reality—where she realized her conversation with Matsumoto had taken an incredibly short time. Even so, she had stopped working during it.

"I have to hurry..."

She hadn't even started cleaning and inspecting the guest rooms she'd been assigned.

.: 5 :.

"**L**OOKS LIKE WE'VE GOT a serious newbie on our hands," Estella said. She'd come looking for Vivy when the latter didn't return at the expected time.

"I apologize..."

The two of them were currently inspecting a guest room Vivy had cleaned and tag-teaming the rooms she hadn't gotten to yet. Vivy was originally in charge of fifteen rooms—including this one—but after her chat with Matsumoto and given her general lack of experience, Estella had ended up helping her with most of them. Estella hadn't calculated for Vivy's incompetence, since she should have had a certain level of skill as one of the AI selected as the opening day staff.

Vivy herself was similarly surprised. She was confident in her ability to interact with guests based on her experience in NiaLand, but cleaning rooms wasn't going so swimmingly.

"You should have the basic programs installed, and you should have gone through training on Earth... Vivy, you're quite individual, aren't you?" said Estella with a pained smile, making Vivy frown and look down.

"Individual" was a unique slang term used among AIs as a minor insult. Unlike humans, AIs could be mass-produced with uniform construction, appearances, and abilities. They consisted of some standardized parts, they had the same OS, and they were equipped with the same positronic brain. If they were the same model, the AIs were expected to perform the exact same. In fact, uniformity was the *minimum* expectation for AI operation. So those who deviated in their looks, abilities, behaviors, or performance were labeled as individuals.

"Oh, I'm sorry. I said something bad again," said Estella, bringing a hand to her mouth. At Vivy's questioning look, she said, "Umm, I know that 'individual' isn't considered a nice word by most AIs, but I don't think that way... That's why it just slipped out."

"Is it different for you? You don't think it's...an insult?"

"I use it the way humans do, which might make some people angry since it's not very AI-like." She stuck her tongue out, her cheeks turning slightly red.

Vivy was astounded by how perfect the expression was. Even away from the park, Vivy was proud to be a main attraction of NiaLand and the inspiration for a line of AIs, but she was feeling utterly defeated by how advanced the functions of her successor model were.

"At the end of the day, I'm just an old model..." she murmured.

"What's wrong, Vivy? You seem upset."

"I just activated my remorse routine. But..." She trailed off and looked around the room they were working in.

While Sunrise was advertised as a luxury hotel, space was more limited in orbit than it was on Earth. There were forty guest rooms, but they weren't as large as one might expect from the price. Rather than space, the guests paid for the unique experience. However, the station was newly constructed and hadn't officially opened; Vivy didn't see the point in cleaning the rooms yet.

"Why are we cleaning before we open?"

"My, Vivy, just get that thought out of your head. There are already human staff on the ship, and there's the clothing we AIs wear. We brought in the bedclothes, and the station's artificial gravity is set to be the same as on Earth. That means dirt and dust are bound to collect here and there," Estella explained as she walked over to the corner of the room and wiped her finger along the floor. When she raised it, Vivy could see dust on her delicate white digit, though it was only a minuscule amount. The internal environment was similar to that of Earth's, so she supposed it made sense. "Also, it wouldn't do to wait until after we open to check our new staff's abilities, now would it? You might work slow, but we can fix that before the guests arrive."

"I will do better..." Vivy said, unable to defend herself because Estella was right. She placed a hand on the wall and lowered her head.

There was an AI cast member in NiaLand named Harry who was designed to look like a porcupine. This gesture was his bit.

Vivy had worked at the park for so long that she'd had plenty of contact with other cast members, and she'd learned such acting from him directly.

"Hee hee, what is that? You're a strange one, Vivy," said Estella.

"I thought I could make up for my work failures with my charm."

"Oh, that won't work. A bad girl like you just needs more training. Okay, on to the next room!"

Estella clasped her hands and then turned to the door, having finished this room's inspection. The door was automatic and slid open without a sound, letting the two AIs continue to the next room.

"..."

They walked side by side, with Vivy peeking sideways at Estella as she scrutinized the exchange they'd just had. There was nothing suspicious about Estella's words or behavior, nor a single thing out of place in terms of her work. Evidently, Estella really *was* proud of her duty as the manager of the hotel and put her all into the work. She was seeming less and less like the kind of AI who would've been behind the Sun-Crash Incident.

According to the records, the guests who escaped Sunrise before it crashed stated it was Estella who had crashed it. But was that really true? She treated hotel work like her mission, the same way Vivy did with singing. The similarity made Vivy uncomfortable doubting Estella. And until she could account for the peculiarity of the incident...

She touched the earring on her left ear. In a whisper no one else could hear, she said, "I won't be using this on Estella."

CHAPTER 3

The Songstress's Melancholy

. : 1 : .

T HE STAFF ON THE space hotel Sunrise functioned no differently than at a normal hotel. Reception, concierge, housekeeping, bellhop—all were the same. The only job that required a tweak was that of the doorman, whose primary job was now to greet guests at the shuttle instead of at the front doors. Aside from the customer-facing roles, there were other behind-the-scenes employees, including kitchen staff, medical personnel, maintenance, and management.

All were indispensable.

Vivy was primarily a hybrid of housekeeping and bellhop. Hotels that used AI staff generally assigned service AIs to roles that required close interaction with guests for security and performance reasons. Being a bellhop required Vivy to guide guests to their rooms and carry their luggage, while housekeeping was all about cleaning and performing room inspections.

"Vivy, it's almost time for our morning meeting. Please head to the lobby," called another AI.

"Understood," Vivy replied, quickly making her way there.

The hotel's preparations passed in a flurry, bringing them to the opening day. Estella had been training Vivy, and while she still seemed a bit unsure about Vivy's progress, Vivy ran through her internal relief routine at having completed Estella's rigorous drills.

"I am not happy with the fact that you're taking longer than you need to, Vivy," came a voice from the flower-shaped brooch on her chest—a secret communication device. It was Matsumoto, and he sounded annoyed. Vivy had been avoiding him since the day she arrived because he still believed their priority was to eliminate Estella and modify the Singularity Point. In order to put off the plan, Vivy had been giving excuse after excuse for the past two days, and he was starting to get testy.

"You can fix all the problems that come from Estella by using the virus I made, but you're still so interested in her motive. Why?"

"Why don't you think it's suspicious, Matsumoto? An AI committed a terrorist attack. That shouldn't be possible, especially without a motive."

"You've been too influenced by stories. I don't understand how you can question information from a future that has already been determined. Estella crashes the space station into Earth. Even if the person she is now isn't the one who does that, it is still inevitable. Whatever bug in her system causes the change will still happen. The future determines the past."

"Perhaps an abnormality caused by an unexpected memory reformat?"

"...I can't say it's entirely impossible," replied Matsumoto unhappily.

Before they'd set out on this mission, Matsumoto had explained history's corrective power and how certain events would always find a way to happen. The Sun-Crash Incident was likely one of those events. How could they know for certain it wasn't Vivy's interference that would set the tragedy in motion?

"There's no end if we start down this line of thought," said Matsumoto. "If our actions can't bend history's corrective power no matter what we do, then—"

"Then the Singularity Project has failed before it really began. I know that, Matsumoto. I don't want to think about how the mission I've been given might be pointless." If it was, then what had happened fifteen years ago would also be pointless.

They already knew history's corrective power wasn't absolute. Vivy had saved Assemblyman Aikawa fifteen years ago, and he was still active in his position at his current age, although they had never seen each other in person since that fateful day. But his life was proof that their actions had been able to change some aspects of the future.

"That's why I will prevent the Sun-Crash Incident," said Vivy.

"Your methods aside, I'm happy so long as you agree on that part. Oh, and..."

"And?"

"You'll get in trouble if you don't go to the lobby, won't you?"

Matsumoto's words snapped Vivy back to reality, where she realized she was the only one standing in the hallway. She'd stopped walking while focusing on her conversation. As a general rule, hotel staff were supposed to gather within five minutes if ordered to do so. Those five minutes had come and gone.

"Late again, Vivy? Which wall was so dirty this time that you became obsessed with it?" asked Estella as Vivy shamelessly walked into the lobby. Estella stood in front of the rows of waiting staff. She had noticed that Vivy would sometimes stare blankly at a particular smudge on a wall, hence her teasing. Obviously, she had no idea Vivy was conversing with Matsumoto during those times, completely neglecting her surroundings.

Estella put her hands on her hips and looked at Vivy as if the latter were her little sister who'd brought home bad grades on her report card. The look made Vivy uncomfortable, especially since she was more than ten years Estella's senior and could also be considered the older sister of their series.

"..."

Estella was wearing a luxurious gown. She normally prioritized a tidy feminine style in her fashion, but the hotel's opening day required her to dress up in something much more resplendent. She couldn't embarrass herself as the manager, after all. The delicate fabric of her dress emphasized her voluptuous form and pale, slender limbs, and the jewelry in her blonde updo was in perfect harmony with her apparent age of mid-twenties. Something in Estella's open nature and mature sex appeal cast a spell, giving her the air of the greatest supermodel AI of all time.

For the first time, Vivy wasn't too keen on her outward appearance of seventeen. She wasn't dressed too lavishly as a member of the staff, but her beautiful model made the uniform look stylish. While the uniform was quite formal, it came nowhere close to Estella's getup—although, to be fair, she was meant to stand out as the face of the hotel.

But dress was hardly the issue at hand.

"I'm sorry I'm late," said Vivy.

"Yes, I can see that. This will be a problem if it continues to happen tomorrow... But thank you for joining us nonetheless."

Estella and the others had become used to these apologies from Vivy over the past two days, and they smiled at her as she bowed her head. They weren't patronizing smiles; rather, they radiated familiarity. Everyone here was kind. It made Vivy think of NiaLand.

Vivy glanced at her coworkers as she walked to Estella, who was beckoning her over. She came to a stop close enough that, if they had both been human, they would have been breathing on each other. Estella used her fingers to part Vivy's bangs, revealing the synthetic skin below. She then did the same to her own bangs and gently put her forehead against Vivy's, starting a datalink. Humans looked fondly on this manner of linking AIs together, and some of them even imitated the action with AIs as a sign of affection despite it having no real meaning then.

There *was* a purpose when AI who worked together touched foreheads. Like a human telling the person taking over their shift what had happened, Vivy had a responsibility to report the events of her shift to her supervisor, Estella. Of course, this meant Estella would learn about everything Vivy worked on and have access to her status logs. Normally, this would've included Vivy's conversations with Matsumoto—a topic too dangerous for Estella to discover.

"Okay, thank you for the report. Try to improve your work technique," said Estella after moving her head away and ending the datalink.

There was no sign of suspicion in her blue-tinged eye cameras, so she hadn't learned anything of Vivy's conversations with Matsumoto.

"Status log falsification complete. I edited together videos of you putzing around guest rooms cleaning and doing inspections and sent that to Estella. It makes you look like you didn't do a perfect job cleaning, but...eh, I don't think it's enough to cause problems," Matsumoto said haughtily, like he was hoping for compliments on his skills.

Vivy ignored him and his follow-up message of annoyed grumbling.

"Now that everyone is here, we'll begin our morning meeting!" Estella announced.

The human staff provided oral reports while the AI staff reported via datalink, and Estella received them all with a managerial expression. Vivy got into place, stood tall, and faced forward as the reports finished. Then, all staff turned toward Estella as a standing microphone stored in the floor rose before her. She cleared her throat once—just like a human.

"Good morning, everyone. We have finally made it to the opening day of the hotel Sunrise. The preparations have been arduous, but we have made it because of all of your hard work.

You have my sincere gratitude." She bowed, and after her perfect expression of thanks, the staff began clapping. Estella remained low for the duration of the applause, then raised her head to continue. "As you all know, this space hotel Sunrise is the second in the fleet after Daybreak. Daybreak was first opened six years ago and was the dream of the original owner, Ash Corvick."

This was the story of how Daybreak and Sunrise began.

Vivy knew Estella's background. She had worked on Daybreak from the very beginning, where she forged a trusting relationship with Ash Corvick. The records showed that they were incredibly close, despite Estella being leased property from the AI corporation, OGC. After Ash's death, she was treated as family. She continued to manage Daybreak after it escaped its financial troubles until she eventually moved to Sunrise.

"There was something Mr. Corvick always said: Space holds infinite dreams. He talked about how he was blessed to work in a place he'd always so admired and to meet others with dreams of their own. Unfortunately, three years after the hotel opened, he passed away, never to see another dawn."

"..."

"But his wishes are still with us, even if he isn't. The passion that drove him to chase his dreams is what brought us this dawn today. The Sunrise is proof that Mr. Corvick's dreams live on. I hope that you will all continue to support the new dawn of this ship," said Estella before she bowed deeply to the staff once more.

One by one, the staff stirred and applauded her passionate words. Compared to the first round, this one was much longer, louder, and more enthusiastic. The human staff members clapped because her words struck a chord in their hearts. The AI staff members clapped because they were following an emotional pattern.

Vivy clapped as well. As she did, she felt firm in her judgment that Estella could not have been the cause of the Sun-Crash Incident.

.: 2 :.

THIRTY GROUPS OF GUESTS were due to arrive on Sunrise on its first day. Vivy wondered why they decided not to book all forty rooms to celebrate, so she asked Leclerc, an AI in housekeeping.

"It is only the first day. We don't want people to think we're greedy. Besides, most of the guests got their invitations because they have connections. And we need to do a trial run before we open to the general public."

"Is that why?"

"That's why. Seriously, Vivy, you don't know *anything*. It's kind of cute," said Leclerc with a giggle. She liked to chat and often tried speaking with Vivy. Her bright green hair was cut to a medium length, and the fluttering skirt of her uniform only added to her overall cuteness.

Others frequently relied on Leclerc for her excellent sense of style. She'd been involved with designing Sunrise staff uniforms, and she'd helped coordinate Estella's outfit for the grand opening.

"Vivy, since you're so slender, I think you'd look good in slacks instead of a skirt. Too bad Estella didn't approve that."

"Yes, um...too bad," said Vivy, uncertain of whether or not she should be happy hearing that. Leclerc was an innocent AI without a bad bone in her body, so it had most likely been meant as a compliment. But Vivy had more questions. "I took a look at the guest list. What does it mean to be someone with a connection?"

"It means they're family members of the staff or close friends of the previous owner. They get invited because it's a special event. There are also people who won some sort of lottery, then some big wigs from the hotel industry, and investors and stuff."

"Will it be all right with such a mix of guests?"

"They're separated by the class of room. Oh, and while relationships are important, connections with influential people are important too. We've got to put our all into taking care of them; then they might spill some *juicy* rumors," said Leclerc excitedly as she pushed the housekeeping cart.

She was an AI with a lot of emotional and speech patterns, and Vivy was sure that if Leclerc ever met Matsumoto, the two would chat away forever.

"Leclerc, how long have you been active?" asked Vivy.

"Five years! I worked with Estella on Daybreak. She brought me with her to Sunrise. You've only been active for two years, right, Vivy?"

"...Yes, that's right."

"You're still just a bouncing baby! No wonder you're not used to work just yet. We AIs change how we work the more experienced we become."

Vivy frowned, surprised to hear Leclerc defending Vivy's bad work habits. As she did, she heard a chuckle deep in her consciousness.

"You've been active for two years, huh?" Matsumoto said with disbelief. *"I mean, I am the one who modified the data, so that's my doing, but it seems a ridiculous lie when said out loud—it's a tenth of your actual age."*

"At fifteen, you're not exactly young either."

"Fifteen years since startup, yes, but if you count time actually operating, then I'm hardly a week old. Isn't it just tragic that I have to do all this work at my young age?"

Vivy ignored Matsumoto's crocodile tears as she shot a sidelong glance at Leclerc and asked, "You've worked with Estella for a while?"

"Yep. I met her when she was only two years old too. I wish I could tell you she was like you when she was your age, but she's always done things the right way. Hearing about her probably won't help you."

"Tell me anyway."

"Oh, you've got a real drive to grow, don't you? All right, I'll tell you!"

Leclerc entered a guest room and briskly set to cleaning and inspecting. None of her motions were frivolous, but her words were. Watching Leclerc clean, Vivy determined that she was a model housekeeper.

As Vivy began her own inspection, she wanted to claim right away that there were no problems. But while this wasn't her song-stress work, it *was* still work, and she didn't want to be dishonest.

"So, Estella was sent by OGC to Daybreak when it opened to be the assistant manager. She was also set to work as a concierge, and there were no issues with her performance...but she's got her own personality, which makes her an 'individual' in her own way," Leclerc said as she confirmed that the bed was made properly and the furniture was in order.

Her expression softened, and a smile reached her eye cameras, an emotional pattern reminiscent of a human recalling the past and an act unnecessary for an AI. "The hotels have become such a big deal, and now we've got Sunrise. But Daybreak wasn't too popular when it first opened. When I was sent there in its second year, there weren't enough human staff. I was made and leased by OGC too. But boy oh boy, was business *slow* back then!"

"Was it really that different from now?"

"Absolutely! It was totally different! There were never many customers, Estella was always so serious, and Mr. Corvick really did try hard to make the hotel something special, but it wasn't going well... Then he died, and the hotel became a hot topic or something..." Leclerc trailed off, hanging her head slightly. Her profile was that of a bright, cheery, beautiful girl, with just a slight shadow of sorrow cast over it.

"..."

Vivy was entranced by Leclerc's expression as she detected a flaw in her own reaction system.

An AI's emotional patterns were generally meant for interaction with humans, and many of them expressed positive emotions to help build favorable relationships. Bonding and working with humans was the goal, so negative reactions like sorrow were rarely activated. This led to AIs often becoming fascinated with reactions they had little experience with—and the AI creating its own pattern to replicate the emotion and thereby become better.

"Once everyone was talking about Mr. Corvick, business took off and we got so much more work. It's a good thing Estella and I are AIs and can't feel depressed, or else we would have been badly affected by those rumors."

"What rumors...?"

"The rumors that Mr. Corvick's death wasn't an accident."

Vivy's eyebrows rose when she heard the unexpected view, and she said nothing.

Leclerc noticed that reaction and quickly waved her hands as she said, "Wait, wait—they're just *rumors*. The police investigation determined it was an accident, and I don't want to go making a fuss about something that's not certain."

"But smoke doesn't rise when there's no fire present. Was there any proof to these rumors?" Vivy knew there probably wasn't anything to the rumors beyond idle gossip, but they had to have started somewhere.

"I told you, didn't I? The hotel's finances weren't doing too great. There were rumors that he was so upset, he killed himself," Leclerc said slowly, hesitant to explain further. "But everyone who knew Mr. Corvick said no way was that possible. Even I concluded that wasn't possible after reviewing my data concerning his actions."

"He was a really unconventional fellow, wasn't he?"

"Yeah! He totally was. That's why he was always arguing with Estella, since she's so serious about work..." Leclerc forced a smile and brushed her skirt as she scanned the room. She then gave a little cheer. "Right, done with this room! We need to head to the lobby to greet the guests soon. I'll take care of the cart. You go on ahead of me, Vivy," she said as she pushed the cart into the hall.

Leclerc was probably letting Vivy go ahead because she'd been tardy that morning. Even Vivy was aware how bad it would be if she were late to greet the very first guests at the grand opening. She decided just to accept Leclerc's suggestion and head to the lobby.

"Ash Corvick, death by suicide? I looked into that after she mentioned it and saw all kinds of theories," Matsumoto said as Vivy walked down the hall.

He'd learned some details Leclerc had avoided mentioning. It was rude to go behind her back, since Leclerc was only trying to be kind, but such concerns had apparently not been installed in the five-day-old AI. Vivy herself couldn't come to any conclusions at the moment.

"All kids of theories, you say?" Vivy said. *"Other than death by suicide?"*

"The suicide theory had the strongest foundation. Persuasive, too,

considering Daybreak's finances at the time—and Corvick's for that matter. This kind of stuff is normally a corporate secret, though... Oh yeah, the hacker who leaked the info was sent to jail. Still doing time as well it seems, so I doubt that's related."

"Beyond the rumor of financial hardship leading to suicide, what more was there?"

"One claimed he was murdered by his heirs. Another said someone foresaw the hotel's moneymaking potential, so they got rid of the owner in order to take over... Come on, no one's going to do that unless they know the future."

"They would have to know the future? Matsumoto, you didn't..."

"Don't accuse me!" he cried. *"But, you know, none of these rumors were more than just speculation. Like I told you before, Ash Corvick's death was declared accidental. The rest is just morbid gossipmongers getting a bit carried away."*

"Is that information from the future?"

"Unfortunately, I don't have data on Ash Corvick. It was deemed irrelevant to the Project, and I agree. Corvick's death has nothing to do with the Sun-Crash Incident."

Matsumoto still believed that Estella's motive wasn't important. With history's corrective power at work, Estella was going to crash Sunrise into Earth regardless of any outside influences. That's why Matsumoto insisted they should eliminate her.

Vivy thought that if history's corrective power was so strong, even if she took the easy way out and reformatted Estella, something else would cause Sunrise to crash to Earth. Therefore, she wanted to find the underlying cause and eliminate it. No matter how much she tried to tell him that, however, he just called her stubborn.

"I'm cutting off transmission—it's time to gather. We'll talk later," she said.

"The more guests who arrive, the more people we have to protect. I keep telling you to get it over with," Matsumoto grumbled before going quiet.

Vivy plucked lightly at the brooch on her chest as she made her way to the lobby. Preparations for greeting the guests were already complete, and the rest of the staff were in neat rows. Estella was there too, of course, standing in front as the hotel representative. She noticed Vivy's *timely* arrival, and blatant relief washed over her face as she smiled.

"Leclerc, over here," Vivy called when she spotted the other AI. Leclerc must have finished putting away the cart.

"Oh, thanks. You're on time too! Way to go!" She flashed Vivy a grin.

After a short period of tense waiting, they finally felt the vibrations of the guest shuttle docking at the station. The doors slowly opened, letting everyone inside.

"I hope you had a pleasant flight," said Estella, the first to greet the guests. She bowed at the waist in one fluid motion. Following suit, all the staff members bowed too. When the guests had witnessed the perfectly synchronized display, Estella raised her head, smiled, and said, "Welcome to the hotel Sunrise, where you can delight in the hospitality of your dreams!"

.: 3 :.

VIVY'S HOUSEKEEPING WORK might have been lacking, but as a bellhop, she received outstanding evaluations from the guests. When she reported that she'd completed her work with no delays after greeting and guiding the first shuttle of guests to their rooms, even Estella was impressed.

"I couldn't help noticing your lack of experience in house-keeping, especially because you came so highly recommended by OGC, but you were truly amazing when interacting with the guests," she told Vivy.

"You flatter me, Estella."

"Guess I should expect that from someone who's interacted with their audience as a songstress for two decades. I wasn't sure how much of your NiaLand cast member experience would transfer to hotel work, but it's looking good. Even if you make a stupid mistake and lose your job as a songstress, you might just be able to avoid getting disposed of."

Matsumoto had watched her work from her own POV, but she struggled to determine if his transmitted message was an honest compliment or some sort of jab at her. She chose to ignore him and simply nodded to Estella, accepting her praise.

It annoyed Vivy to agree with Matsumoto about anything, but she *did* have far more experience dealing with customers than some of the other hotel AIs. Not only had she interacted with hundreds of guests every day throughout the park, but she was also equipped with information on how to appropriately talk with guests of every sort—including children, the elderly, and people who chose to be cruel to AIs.

There was nothing Vivy couldn't handle in the first few hours of the hotel's opening. Besides, this was a first-class establishment in space. All the guests' identities had been verified, and they'd undergone background checks on Earth to make sure they weren't going to cause problems.

"I saw in your datalink that you're particularly good with children. So good I can hardly believe you've only been active for two years," Estella said.

"You may have seen in my reference data that I was previously employed as a babysitter. I am good at dealing with young children and the elderly."

"I understand why you'd be good with children, but why the elderly?"

"...Because as humans grow older, they become more childlike again." At least, that was what the data Matsumoto had falsified said, but not everything seemed to line up.

Estella's eyes crinkled, and she burst out in quiet laughter. "Ah, hee hee... Just make sure you don't say that in front of the guests. And you probably shouldn't say it to Leclerc either. She's quick to tell everything she hears to others."

"Leclerc was saying you two have known each other for a long time."

"Yes, we have—since we were both on Daybreak. As an AI, it might be inappropriate to say this, but she's sort of like my little sister."

"Your little sister…"

Vivy understood why Estella felt that way *and* why it would be inappropriate. Humans generally desired more humanlike reactions and emotional expression from AIs, but on the flip side, humans resisted thinking of AIs as equals. From an AI's perspective, thinking of oneself as human came close to breaking the Three Laws, which were built into every single one of them. Both sides, human and AI, wanted to maintain a separation between the two beings.

"You probably won't like it, but I think of you as a little sister as well," Estella admitted. "It's strange. I feel close to you for some reason." She stood up from behind the manager's desk and caressed Vivy's hair. Vivy stared back at her.

Estella likely felt close to Vivy because they were from the same model series. According to Vivy's falsified data, she wasn't one of the Sisters Series, but she couldn't fake the sense of closeness Estella felt when they were near. However, Matsumoto's technology prevented Estella from learning any revealing information, so she was unlikely to find a reason for feeling as she did toward Vivy. It would never occur to her that this AI she thought of as a little sister was actually the first in her series *and* her elder.

"Estella, is something wrong?" asked Vivy.

"Don't worry. Everything is going well right now. Concierge is incredibly busy, but we were ready for that. It's no different from normal. I sometimes get complaints transmitted from the staff I left in charge of Daybreak, which puts me in a difficult position." Estella's eyebrows creased in worry, though she was still smiling, so Vivy didn't think she really minded.

They didn't welcome trouble, but they were AIs. They could handle it.

"It is an honor to be needed," Vivy murmured, and Estella's eyes widened in surprise.

But her surprise vanished in a flash, replaced by a smile slightly different than the one she'd worn a moment ago. It was so incredibly sad and fragile. "The second group of guests will arrive soon. Let's go to the lobby."

Estella stepped out of the manager's office, and Vivy followed. There were thirty groups of guests coming for the grand opening, and they planned to greet ten groups at a time. The guests' parties were varied: There were families with children, romantic couples, and even company executives with their employees. According to the guest list, the grand opening of Sunrise was invitation only, except for a few guests who had won their stay via lottery.

Additionally, there was one special guest arriving in the second wave.

"We've been awaiting your arrival, Mr. Corvick," Estella said once the man in question had appeared.

Vivy watched out of the corner of her eye as Estella bowed deeply. Although Vivy was already busy with her bellhop work and in the process of guiding a group of guests—two parents and a child—she couldn't take her eyes off Estella.

"I've got control of the station's cameras, so I'll keep an eye on her from here too," said Matsumoto.

Vivy knew he would provide surveillance, but she wanted to keep her own eye cameras on Estella. Unfortunately, leaving

Matsumoto in charge of monitoring the entire space station meant Vivy wasn't likely to hear about anything outside his agenda; given their disagreement about how to handle Estella, she was particularly worried he'd keep things from her.

There was a reason for that.

"Thank you for coming despite being so busy. I wasn't sure you would be able to make it," Estella told their guest.

"It was close, but this is a huge moment for my family. I wanted to be here."

He was a heavyset, muscular man in his mid-thirties, with rugged features and a classy suit. Vivy consulted her aggregated aesthetic preferences data and concluded that he clocked in at about 78 percent on the attractiveness scale.

This man was Arnold Corvick.

Arnold gave Estella a friendly wink and said, "I could barely believe it the first time. Ash is gone now, but...I'd be disingenuous if I didn't see this through."

"I appreciate it. I'm sure it would have made him happy." An odd shadow of some other emotion fell over Estella's face. The expression was so slight that only another AI would be able to see it.

"Estella's expression," Vivy noted.

"I see it. Looks like she's got something on her mind."

Arnold Corvick, the man Estella was speaking with, was her current owner and Ash Corvick's younger brother.

In a quieter voice, Matsumoto added, *"He's the hotel kingpin, the guy who made a fortune after Daybreak's success."*

.: 4 :.

WHO HAD GAINED THE MOST from Ash Corvick's death? Anyone who knew a thing about the situation would name the same person: Arnold Corvick, Ash's younger brother. He had inherited Ash's hotel business, brought it out of its financial difficulties, and quickly made a huge fortune.

"People aren't the only ones in the know; AIs have also researched Ash's death. We came to the same conclusion," said Matsumoto. "Arnold inherited the business, as was written in Ash's will, and made himself wealthy with it. Before that, he had jumped from job to job, never having the sense to stay put and never having much money to his name. So this is a complete turnaround for him."

"And only after his brother died. That's not very discreet of him," replied Vivy. She was working alone, and Matsumoto's voice was coming from the brooch pinned to her chest. She was distressed to find she and Matsumoto were essentially on the same page.

While Vivy tried to counter Matsumoto's careless remarks, her objection lacked strength. If they assumed that Ash Corvick's death wasn't an accident, then...

"The most likely culprit would be Arnold Corvick," Matsumoto declared.

"..."

Vivy clamped her mouth shut and leaned against the wall. Thankfully, she was the only person in the staff room at the

moment. She really should've been busy with her bellhop duties—
and she was, according to Matsumoto's falsified footage. The two
of them could talk strategy without issue.

However, Vivy didn't like the direction their conversation
was heading.

"The police should be aware of all this. The fact that they
never found proof means the rumor really is just a rumor. Do
you disagree?" asked Matsumoto.

"That is the obvious conclusion, but...what if Arnold paid off
a police officer or hired a skilled hacker to falsify evidence?"

"I wish I could say you're dreaming, but he's got the funds to
make something like that happen. A skilled hacker, hm...?"

"Ah! Matsumoto, you didn't!"

"Stop accusing me!"

They argued this for a second time while Vivy sorted through
her own consciousness. While it might've been foolish to suspect
Matsumoto, they couldn't deny the possibility that another hacker
could have helped Arnold. Unfortunately, the justice system was
not omnipotent. Anything but, in fact. The more a situation required justice, the more other powers outside of justice held sway.

"If Arnold did cover up the fact that he staged his brother's
death...then he did a damn good job covering his tracks. So good
that no half-wit would be able to salvage the data."

"But you could do it, couldn't you, Matsumoto?"

"If we're being humorous, then yes, I could do it with one arm
tied behind my back. But I don't have any reason to. Unless you
think you can convince me, Vivy."

"..."

Vivy crossed her arms to illustrate that she was contemplating the situation.

From the very beginning, he'd insisted they should eliminate Estella and that her motive or any outside influences mattered so little, they might as well have been in another dimension. And while Vivy's consciousness concluded that Matsumoto was correct, she still had reservations about the extenuating circumstances. She didn't want to move ahead with their plan with so much uncertainty, but Matsumoto had a hard time understanding why. Vivy herself wasn't able to put into words the emptiness in her own AI consciousness.

"As far as I know, the only official conclusion was that Ash Corvick, former owner of Daybreak, died in an accident," Matsumoto said. "Whether or not that's the truth, the records say as much. Arnold was his successor."

"If the truth were different, would you be against exposing the information, Matsumoto?"

"Of course I would. We can't know what impact that would have on the future."

"Even though we're here right now, trying to stop tens of thousands of people from dying?"

He didn't want to have any effect on history outside the Singularity Project. That was his stance, and Vivy had no real counterargument. The Project already involved saving tens of *millions* of lives. Vivy couldn't even imagine how massive an impact saving those people would have.

"Of those tens of thousands of people who should have died in the space station crash, surely at least one of them will have a significant effect on history. What about the possibility that they could take the Project off track? Can you ignore that?" Vivy asked.

"...You're saying that, compared to stopping the crash, which saves tens of thousands of people, revealing the truth of one person's death will have very little impact?"

That wasn't exactly what Vivy was saying, but she wasn't surprised her statement had been interpreted that way. She didn't respond, and her silence hinted at a withheld answer.

Matsumoto let out a long, forced sigh and said, "All right. I'll consider giving in to your demands if that's the price I have to pay to keep our working relationship in good condition. But keep this in mind: no matter what explosive dirt we dig up, or even if we don't find anything at all, it has nothing to do with implementing the Singularity Project."

"For the first time, I'm glad you're my partner, Matsumoto."

"For the *first* time?!" he cried, disappointed, before he cut off his transmission.

Vivy had been trying to show a willingness to compromise, but he hadn't reacted how she expected. Maybe the values of an AI from the future didn't quite align with her own. Anyway, while Matsumoto had seemed disappointed, he did agree to cooperate. Now it would be good if they could easily uncover the truth about Ash Corvick's death.

"Ah, good timing. Could I speak with you?" someone asked as

Vivy slipped out of the staff room on her way back to work. She turned to see a tall man walking toward her.

"..."

"Oh, you're an AI staff member, aren't you? Modern AI is making huge advancements. I could barely tell you apart from a human before I got up close and checked," he said with a smile.

He was the suspect Vivy and Matsumoto had just been discussing: Arnold Corvick. Vivy kept her face free of suspicion and bowed, showing respect to Arnold, the owner of the hotel. "Pardon me, I didn't realize it was you, Mr. Corvick. Have you come to inspect the staff room?"

"Oh, no, relax. I'm not here for an inspection or anything fancy like that. I've always had a terrible sense of direction. I actually got lost on the way to the manager's office. I wanted to talk to Estella."

"Estella, you say? Shall I show you the way?"

"That'd be great, if you don't mind."

Arnold gave her a wink, his expression not forced in the slightest. It was a natural, friendly gesture that had some charm. Most human women probably would've reacted positively to a wink from a man of his good looks. Luckily for Vivy, the appearance of anyone she interacted with was nothing more than a way to identify them; romance couldn't grow between humans and AIs.

"How do you like working here, um... What was your name?"

"My designated name is Vivy. I have only been working here for a few days, so I lack sufficient data to answer in regards to how it is working here."

"Guess that makes sense. That was a dumb question on my part. Forget it, Vivy."

Vivy led him down the hallway and, instead of him walking behind her as was normal when she guided people, he walked beside her, matching the stride of his long legs to hers. Perhaps it was just something Arnold did, but Vivy could practically feel his gaze on her synthetic skin, looking at the side of her face. She was aware of it, but it wasn't something out of the ordinary for her. Even in NiaLand, there were guests who stared, either obsessed with her appearance or just curious about AIs.

But Vivy felt something other than just curiosity in Arnold's eyes.

"Um..."

"Oh, sorry. I'm being rude, aren't I? Sorry if I offended you," he told her.

"AIs are not capable of being offended. I simply wondered if there was something about me you were displeased with."

Vivy was trying to learn the true intent behind his stare, and, surprisingly, he seemed a bit flustered as he flapped his hands and said, "No, no, it's not your fault at all. It's just...uh, I guess I was just a bit captivated by you."

"Thank you. Having our appearance complimented is very valuable reference data. I will forward the information on to customer support."

"That's...not really what I meant. I mean, yeah, you're a cute girl, but it's your eyes I'm fascinated by. Oh, and could you not call them eye cameras? It sounds so *awkward*." Vivy must have shown her confused emotion pattern while he was talking because he smiled awkwardly and added, "I like AIs' eyes. A lot of AIs put their mission first; it's the most important thing to them. Their will shows in their eyes. It's not just AIs either. I like the eyes of anybody who's got them set on their dreams."

"Huh, I see... You're a smooth orator."

"You mean it sounds like I rehearsed it? Man, you're harsh, Vivy." Arnold brought his hand to his forehead in an exaggerated fashion, then slowly lowered it and said, "It's why I liked my brother, Ash, so much. Our family laughed at him when he said he was going to build a hotel in space, but I thought it was amazing."

"..."

"And now here I am, walking down the halls of the place where he should've realized his dreams. There's something wrong with that. I'm not supposed to have this privilege." His tone wasn't modest—more so self-deprecating. No matter how hard she tried, Vivy could discern nothing more.

"But I heard that it was your skill that saved Daybreak from financial ruin after you inherited it from the late Mr. Corvick. Even with that, you still say—"

"People are making more out of it than it is. I haven't done anything. There's someone else who worked hard in Ash's place to get the hotel business on track." Arnold shrugged as he denied it. Then, quieter: "Not like anyone, even management, would listen if I told them."

He finished speaking just as they arrived at the door labeled

Manager's Office. Vivy stopped, and Arnold looked ahead. She'd completed her task.

"Thanks for leading the way. And for talking to me. Hope we get to chat more, Vivy."

"Thank you as well. It was a nice discussion. I hope you have a relaxing stay, Mr. Corvick."

"Yeah, I'm going to make myself at home. It is my brother's hotel, after all." He winked again—it seemed he'd gotten his spirit back. Then, he entered the office.

As Vivy headed for her post, several questions materialized in her positronic brain.

"Was Arnold really involved in his brother's death?"

.: 5 :.

"THE CORVICK BROTHERS' RELATIONSHIP? What do you think's going on there, Vivy?"

As a housekeeper AI, Leclerc was usually busy cleaning guests' empty rooms, making beds, and restocking supplies, but Vivy had managed to grab a hold of her when they were free. Leclerc had latched on to Vivy's question harder than expected.

Unlike at a normal hotel, guests on Sunrise couldn't leave their luggage in their room and go out sightseeing. The hotel was equipped with restaurants, a large communal bath for relaxing, entertainment facilities like a theater and a concert hall, as well as a game room with the latest gadgets. Those things weren't unique to a space hotel, though, as a hotel on Earth was just as likely to have them. The single greatest selling point out of all the hotel's amenities was the observation deck, where guests could look out into space.

The observation deck had to be reserved, as it couldn't fit all the guests at once. It was particularly popular among guests with children, but most guests wanted to take advantage of this once-in-a-lifetime experience. As it was the grand opening of the hotel, the platform was constantly booked.

"It's the grand opening, right? There aren't any guests checking out today, so no rooms to clean... I'm basically sitting on the sidelines today," said Leclerc as she pantomimed crying and flung herself into Vivy's arms.

Vivy traced her fingers along Leclerc's back, near fainting from how busy she'd been.

"Hey! Stop it, Vivy!"

"Sorry. I've been so busy. This is the first chance I've gotten to relax. It just sort of happened."

Since Vivy had been doing so well in her bellhop duties, guests had been requesting her by name when they had questions or wanted a guide. Obviously, she felt honored, but she was also working on saving humanity on the side, so she had very little downtime. She hoped Leclerc, who was currently unoccupied, could contribute a little to saving humanity.

"So then, oh, the Corvick brothers' relationship... That's a lot to talk about. You mean Ash and his younger brother Arnold, right? What do you want to know?"

"Do you know if they were on good terms?" Vivy asked.

"Good terms... Well, I never actually saw the two of them together. Arnold didn't visit the hotel until after Ash died."

"Really? But..."

Leclerc shook her head, indicating she knew no more, and Vivy mulled it over.

The space hotel was Ash Corvick's dream. If the brothers were close, you would have assumed that either Arnold would have been at the opening, or he would have been invited at some point. Despite the financial problems, Ash Corvick was the owner and manager of the hotel for three years—plenty of time for Arnold to see it.

"Anyway, this is only the second time Arnold's come to the hotels since inheriting the business... Last time he visited Daybreak, and now he's here at Sunrise," Leclerc told her.

"He stays away from the hotels even though he's the owner? Why?"

"Guilt, maybe," Leclerc joked, but Vivy's eyes widened. "Hm? Is that why you're asking me about this? Because you think that too?"

"I thought it would be against our code of ethics to speculate about your current owner."

"I haven't said anything direct. AIs like me who enjoy gossiping are pretty good at skirting definitives. You need to get out more, Vivy."

Vivy felt like Leclerc had just insinuated she'd been living in a bubble and was surprised by all the things she didn't know.

The code of ethics barred an AI from showing any disrespect

to their current owner, including making inappropriate statements. In this case, Arnold had inherited ownership of Leclerc. She was bound by that, yet her statement implied she was interested in the rumors that Arnold was involved in Ash's death, which seemed like it should conflict with that code.

"What's wrong? Did I say something weird?" asked Leclerc, her eyebrows knitting as Vivy stared at her in silence.

There was something slightly off about how Leclerc was acting. She was responding differently to the theory about Arnold being a murderer than she had to the one she told Vivy that morning about Ash's suicide. She'd been quick to reject the possibility of Ash committing suicide even though, by now, Arnold had been her owner for longer than Ash had.

"No, it's nothing. I just learned something new," Vivy said.

"Really? Well, that's good, then... Oh, the front desk is contacting us. There's a guest in a superior room requesting you, Vivy. Seems like they really like you."

"A superior room? Understood." Vivy brushed the creases from her uniform and stood, ending her short break.

Leclerc circled Vivy, fixed her uniform in the back, and patted her shoulder. "All right, off to work. Labor is an AI staff member's pride and joy. And I'm a sad Cinderella whose AI happiness has been taken away..."

"I expect the manor to be sparkling by the time I return from the ball."

"You're so scary, Sis! Pretty imposing for someone who's my *little* sister, based on the time since your activation."

They chattered back and forth, but Vivy quickly left Leclerc before her real activation time—her age, that is—could be exposed.

The guests who had requested Vivy were a family of three: an elegant mother and father along with their daughter, who was about fifteen or sixteen. They were quite the pleasant bunch. According to the guest list, they had won their visit to Sunrise. Based on Vivy's reference data, it wasn't common for a child of the girl's age to accompany their parents on such trips, but the hotel was equipped with facilities for the entire family, and they seemed to get along well.

While the parents had their eyes on all the facilities in the hotel, their daughter was quite interested in Vivy. She found the girl staring at her more often than was normal. Vivy's appearance made her look a similar age to the girl, which would make her a suitable friend—something the teenager was probably lacking at the moment. Unfortunately, Vivy was busy and unable to do anything more than her bellhop duties.

"If she wants someone to talk to, maybe you should introduce her to that girl in housekeeping. She looks a bit older, but that doesn't mean anything to an AI," said Matsumoto.

"I imagine Leclerc would happily accept the work, but no... Did you hear our conversation?"

"Of course I did. I don't take my eyes or my ears or my nose off you, even while you're working. I was trying not to butt in, but I was listening. At this point, you're getting more suspicious of Arnold Corvick, aren't you?"

"I'm not entirely sure what I think."

She thought about Matsumoto's question while she worked, as it didn't hamper her duties. From a work perspective, this was a non-issue. She was in the middle of showing the family the facilities. Divided attention might not be the ideal work ethic, but hopefully they wouldn't mind her sorting tasks by priority.

"I spoke with him directly, but I wasn't able to pick up on anything," Vivy told Matsumoto.

Her feelings toward Arnold had changed over their short conversation, for better or worse. Vivy didn't exactly suspect he had killed his own brother for money, but he *was* acting like there was something on his mind about Ash. Leclerc had worked with Ash, and she firmly denied he could have killed himself, which affected Vivy's opinion as well.

"Then I shall prove your suspicions false, Vivy," Matsumoto declared.

The next moment, data of all sorts was transmitted to her consciousness. There were records of Arnold Corvick's bank accounts as well as his activities since inheriting the space hotels.

"Arnold Corvick's bank accounts... But this is..."

"Yes, as you can see."

Vivy checked the numbers, and surprise shot through her consciousness.

Satisfied, Matsumoto continued: *"The vast majority of the profits from the space hotel business go into supporting further development or relief efforts after natural disasters and other such causes."*

"..."

"Only the bare minimum remains in his pockets. It may be true that his work as an executive after becoming the owner has brought the business out of its financial difficulties...but he's not keeping that profit for himself. And the reason he wasn't invited to the opening of the first hotel six years ago wasn't because he and his brother weren't close; it was because of his health. He was in the hospital."

As Matsumoto spoke, Vivy scoured Arnold's records. Arnold's financial situation was clear as day if you looked at the transaction histories. There were no signs that he was laundering his money by withdrawing it and putting it into those donations and contributions. There were several documents showing that the organizations he donated to were in good standing, so nothing shady going on there either. The records undermined the theory he had killed his brother and taken over the business for financial gain.

Arnold Corvick had honestly inherited it.

"Based on this data, we can safely say the theory that Arnold killed his brother to expand the business and become a hotel kingpin—"

"Is entirely off the mark," Matsumoto finished for her. *"Although Arnold's actions have been a bit suspicious. Records indicate that he's got more skill as a manager than your average person, but if you look at his digital book collection..."* Matsumoto trailed off, displaying the digital books Arnold had read over the past few years.

All the titles were about management or related to the hotel business. They were basic—entry level. It seemed strange for someone called a hotel kingpin. It looked like he was trying to quickly fill in missing knowledge to uphold a facade.

"*If we imagine Arnold was the person who killed Ash,*" said Matsumoto, "*that would mean he killed his brother to inherit, then panicked and studied up on how to run a hotel. But he just so happened to be a natural at it and managed to fix the hotel's finances. That's a pretty sloppy plan.*"

"*And no matter how you look at it, it would be—*"

"*Impossible. I agree, which is why it's only a theory... But records don't lie. Arnold is aware of his inexperience as a manager and is studying to improve. That means the things he's said at executive meetings can't be coming from him. He's an actor who's taken on the role of a hotel kingpin.*"

"*An actor...*" Vivy said thoughtfully.

Calling Arnold an actor was accurate. No one thought he lacked management skills or that he was someone else's puppet. No one seemed to know anything about his background. But if that was true, what did it mean about Arnold's position?

"Ah...!"

Another thought popped into Vivy's consciousness. She accidently let out a slight gasp, and the girl she was leading through the hotel shot her a questioning look. Vivy manufactured a smile to keep the girl from sensing what was on her mind.

The fact that Arnold was someone's puppet and had turned the hotel's business around was a secret. Most humans and AIs thought he was the responsible younger brother who had followed his late brother's wishes and saved his space hotel business from ruin. Others saw him as the usurper who stole his brother's throne when he had the chance, and there was no way to disprove either interpretation.

It wasn't just humans who saw it that way, but AIs as well.

"Estella..."

"What is it, Vivy?"

"Matsumoto, there's something I want you to look into."

She had to make this theory of hers concrete. Even though she couldn't see Matsumoto or his new cube form, she felt like he was staring at her through a half-shuttered eye camera.

.: 6 :.

WHY DID THE Sun-Crash Incident happen? Vivy had constantly wondered that since Matsumoto had briefed her on their plan for this Singularity Point.

Estella was the manager and control AI of the hotel Sunrise, and she had command of all the space station's systems. It was still unclear why she had crashed the station into Earth. Matsumoto wasn't actually interested in anything outside the incident itself, and he kept insisting that all they needed to do was stop it from happening. But ever since he'd told Vivy about history's corrective power, she'd been uncertain whether they would be able prevent the tragedy just by stopping Estella. Matsumoto might consider the whole thing a way to test the scope of corrective power, but with tens of thousands of lives hanging in the balance, Vivy couldn't find the rationale to write it off like that.

Even though you stood by and watched a plane crash so you didn't alter history?

As the contradictory thought arose in her consciousness, she intentionally ignored the error. Instead, she turned her thoughts to her own position in the current Singularity Point.

If there's no changing the fact that Estella's the one who causes the Sun-Crash Incident, then she's got to have a motive. If Vivy could find and eliminate that motive, she could stop the Sun-Crash Incident without harming Estella, just as she'd wanted.

"Matsumoto, about the people who died in the Sun-Crash Incident..." she began.

"Do you want an exact number of casualties? It's not like I'm keeping that from you just to mess with you. The figure was never determined. Even in this day and age, not all humans born are registered with their government. If we exclude those people—"

"No, that's not what I want to ask about." Vivy struggled to put her question into words. She hadn't been searching for a number of casualties.

"Were any people with connections to Sunrise among the victims?"

"..."

For once, Matsumoto didn't answer Vivy's question right away. Vivy didn't think the silence was because he didn't know how to answer but rather because he didn't *want* to answer.

And the truth?

"Arnold Corvick was among those killed in the incident." He'd hesitated because he knew that was what Vivy wanted to hear.

When Estella caused the Sun-Crash Incident, she didn't just kill the people on the ground where the space station fell. Arnold, who was on the station at the time, had also died in the crash.

"Any others connected to the hotel?" asked Vivy.

"The guests and staff got away on the escape shuttle before the crash. It seems Estella had the decency to save human life by instructing them to evacuate before committing her act of terrorism..."

"But Arnold remained in the hotel?"

"It's unknown whether that was his choice or Estella forced him to stay, since her positronic brain burned up in the fall."

Vivy closed her long-lashed eyes as she listened to Matsumoto. She was thinking about what motive could have led to the Sun-Crash Incident—an incident that would be considered a terrorist attack by an AI. But the more they learned, the more they were starting to see something else at work in the background.

What if the Sun-Crash Incident wasn't meant as a terrorist attack? What if it had been the weapon used to kill Arnold Corvick? Would that have warranted a cover story?

"Killing tens of thousands of people to hide the murder of one?"

If that was the case, they could have just made it look like he died in the crash. Take the escape shuttle, for instance: If the culprit really planned on killing tens of thousands of people in order to cover up the murder of one, why bother giving everyone on board a chance to escape? If Arnold had been the sole intended target, then had the tens of thousands who had died in the crash died because something had gone wrong? And what would Estella's motive to murder Arnold have been?

"What if Estella suspects Arnold of murdering Ash?" asked Vivy. *"That might not be..."*

It was impossible. That was what Matsumoto was hinting at, but Vivy thought this was the most logical possibility *and* the most fitting motive behind Estella's horrible act. It would also explain the complicated emotional patterns Vivy saw on Estella's face when she greeted Arnold upon his arrival.

But there was another important reason.

"Even though Sunrise fell, Daybreak, Ash Corvick's castle of dreams, remained. His dream still stood, even after someone took revenge on his behalf," Vivy went on.

"You're saying the Sun-Crash Incident was brought about by a twisted sense of duty?"

Was that what she was saying? She wasn't entirely sure.

Vivy was considered property of NiaLand, but she didn't have an individual owner she was meant to serve. If anything, she served the guests at the park. Even more broadly, she felt she was meant to serve humanity as a whole. She saw no point in putting one above the other; the current situation reinforced that in her consciousness. Perhaps an AI like Estella, who'd had one person she was meant to serve, would come to a different conclusion.

"If that's the case...I have to contact Estella!" she said, sensing that danger was afoot.

She immediately tried to reach Estella, but there was no answer. Estella was both the manager and responsible for the concierge work—she should never be unreachable by her staff.

Vivy then sent a transmission to Leclerc. *"Leclerc, do you know where Estella is? There's something important I need to talk to her about."*

"Huh? Vivy? You want to know where Estella is? She's not in the manager's office?" came Leclerc's flustered reply. She was currently cleaning the theater.

"She's not there."

Vivy had already checked the manager's office; Estella wasn't in there. In fact, Vivy herself had led Arnold to that exact room not long ago. Thankfully, there were no signs of a fight in the room, nor did she find Arnold lying on the ground. Without knowing where either of them was, relief escaped her.

"Oh! Now that I think about it, isn't the observation deck opening soon? It's about time to prep it for opening..."

"Ah! Thank you, Leclerc!"

"Wait, Vivy—"

Vivy forcefully cut off her transmission with Leclerc and hurried to the observation deck. As she traveled, she passed guests and staff in the passageways, heedless of the voice coming from the brooch on her chest.

"Bingo, Vivy! The surveillance system shows Estella and Arnold heading toward the observation deck fifteen minutes ago!" said Matsumoto.

"Where are they now?"

"Unfortunately, there aren't any cameras inside. There's no video of them on the feed from the hall just outside it either, so they should both still be in there."

That was good enough for her. Vivy made sure no one was watching as she ran down the hallway. The entrance to the observation deck came into view, located in the center of the hotel, and Vivy rushed for it.

Just before she arrived, Matsumoto said, "Vivy, if Estella is trying to do something terrible..."

He was gauging her. If that was the case, then she would use the program he'd provided in order to reformat Estella's positronic brain.

Vivy had nothing to say to that.

Even if there were extenuating circumstances leading to Estella's actions, no matter how humanlike her motive was, she was an AI. No AI could be allowed to have those motives. Even more so considering it led to a future where tens of thousands of people died. That could not be permitted to happen.

Vivy passed through those doors, firm in her resolve. And when she did...

There in the middle of the observation deck was Arnold, teary-eyed as he hugged Estella, and she hugged him back. "It's all thanks to you, Estella. Thank you so much."

.: 7 :.

WHEN HUMANS OBSERVED something extremely outside the bounds of what they'd imagined, their thoughts stopped. In the same way, when an AI observed something extremely outside of their theorized reality, an error occurred, sending the algorithms of their consciousness into disarray.

Vivy certainly hadn't expected to find what she did on the observation deck.

"Vivy...?" Estella's eyes widened when she turned to find Vivy, frozen in place.

Arnold's arms were still around Estella, and he looked equally shocked.

"What is it?" asked Estella. "This isn't your station right now..."

"Uhhh, no, it's, uh... I couldn't contact you, Estella," Vivy said clumsily.

Estella's expression immediately changed, and she stepped away from Arnold, looking far more managerial as she moved over to Vivy. "Oh! I'm sorry. I cut off transmission for just a short time. Is there a problem?"

Vivy held up her hands and shook her head. "No, there isn't a problem. I just didn't know where you were."

"And you came to the observation deck to check? Well...I'm glad there isn't anything wrong, and I'm sorry I didn't say anything. I wanted to devote my attention to Mr. Corvick for a short time."

Vivy was glad Estella wasn't blaming her, but she was confused about the explanation. She wanted to spend time alone with Arnold on the observation deck? Did that mean...?

"So, Vivy, could you please leave? Just for now?" Estella said, trying to gently shoo her away.

"It's fine, Estella. Vivy is staff, right? She's got the right to celebrate with us," Arnold told her.

"If you say so..."

Vivy had started to think there was some sort of disquieting relationship between the human and the AI, so she found his suggestion completely incomprehensible. "What are you two doing here? The observation deck isn't opening for another hour..."

"We're waiting for it to open, obviously. Although I might've used my position as the owner to get the jump on the rest of the guests," Arnold admitted. Then he held a finger up to his lips, like it was a secret, and winked.

Vivy didn't pick up on anything suspicious from either of them, or anything to make her think she really had seen something she wasn't supposed to. But there was an unexpected degree of closeness between Estella and Arnold.

"It's the grand opening of Sunrise and the opening of the first-ever space observation deck... Mr. Corvick and I just wanted to see it together and share a moment for my former owner, Ash Corvick," Estella said.

"Stop calling him your former owner, Estella. He's still your real owner. That hasn't changed. I'm fine being just a decoration— an owner in name only for both you and the hotel."

"You're so generous, Mr. Corvick." Estella's expression softened, and she smiled as Arnold gave a friendly chuckle.

Witnessing them together, Vivy was certain there was a strong bond between Arnold and Estella, a relationship she wouldn't be able to get between. There was nothing there that might drive Estella to an evil act.

Besides, something Arnold said had caught her attention.

"What do you mean you're fine being the hotel's owner in name only?"

"Ah, that. It's simple: The plan I submitted after I inherited the business from my brother was entirely made by Estella." Then he hastily asked Estella, "Uh, you don't mind if I tell her, do you?"

"Even if I did, you've already said it."

"Yeah, that is true. Sorry."

The friendly smile on Arnold's face left Vivy at a loss. Estella wasn't denying it either, and the evidence Vivy had gathered so far supported the story. Arnold had started studying up on how to run a hotel when he inherited the business, but he had an advisor.

"But *you*, Estella? Isn't that overstepping your bounds as an AI staff member?" Vivy asked.

"It is. Under the AI code of ethics, it's considered beyond my expected duties... But Mr. Corvick, the owner of the hotel, has officially given me permission. That is what allows me to do it."

"And it was my brother's wish that Estella be put in charge of the hotel," Arnold added.

The two of them had worked together to build up the space hotel business. But why were they picking up Ash Corvick's dreams where he left off?

Arnold gave the answer to that. "My brother didn't die in an accident. It was suicide."

.: 8 :.

ESTELLA'S INITIAL IMPRESSION of Ash Corvick was an adult who, perhaps somewhat childishly, kept his sights set on his dreams.

"I look forward to working with you, my dear Daybreak assistant manager," Ash said, a smile on his face as he held out his hand.

Estella shook it and said something vague and noncommittal about her future plans. She wouldn't have a future if she didn't win the favor and acceptance of the person she'd been loaned to. That sense of urgency was controlling her positronic brain.

OGC was an AI development corporation, proud to hold a global share of the market. Estella had originally been developed as one of their key product lines, the Songstress Series. However, a complex design made development difficult and ultimately led to her being used in a very different manner than intended. She had the necessary programs installed and was put to use in the space development sector OGC was funding. As part of that venture, she was leased to a hotel on a space station.

Estella had been unable to fulfill the role originally created for her, so she was terrified that her new role would be taken away. For this reason, she was so determined to avoid upsetting her new temporary owner, Ash, and to prove her worth.

That tense resolve of hers didn't last long.

"Estella, right? You've got an amazing voice," said Ash as he shook her hand, his other hand gesturing to her throat.

The compliment made Estella's eyes widen, and she smiled again. "Thank you. I am capable of singing, actually."

"Oh, really? I'd love to hear it sometime."

"If the opportunity arises."

She quickly revised her first impression to that of an ambitious, silver-tongued man. Estella wasn't certain whether Ash was aware of what was going on in her consciousness, but he had selected her for the important position of assistant manager even though she was leased from another company. And so, her days on Daybreak began.

To be honest, she was surprised when she was made assistant manager. No matter how skilled an AI was, it would never have the same rights as a human, which was as it should be. AIs were, in the end, made by and meant to serve humans. Surely they couldn't ask for much in return for doing what they'd been designed to do.

AI production had expanded in recent years, which meant there were more AIs to interact with more humans. Estella had heard of an AI rights movement, but she found it shameful. About ten years ago, the AI Naming Law had gone into effect, which some considered a trigger for the movement.

Estella, however, was perfectly happy just having been given her name. She had pride in her name and more work than she could handle. That was what kept her going.

"Mr. Corvick! Would you *please* pay attention to what I'm saying?"

"Urk! Ah, sorry. I'm fine." A pause. "Actually, could you start from the beginning?"

"Goodness me..."

As the frantic days passed, Estella's relationship changed along with them. It became clearer and clearer that her initial assessment of him as a childlike dreamer had been incorrect. Ash *was* focused primarily on his dreams, but he had a more down-to-earth view of things. He just wouldn't hesitate to choose dreams over reality. That was the sort of person he was.

"What I'm saying is that it isn't realistic. Please consider this proposition more thoroughly," Estella urged him.

"Well... That's it! Estella, do you have an alternative suggestion? Your opinion will make for good input."

"But, um... I am nothing more than an AI staff member, and one on lease at that. You have made me the assistant manager, an unmerited position in my opinion, but I still doubt the board would be interested in hearing my input."

"Oh, come now. It won't be a problem so long as I make it out to the bigwigs like it was my idea. Uh, not that I'm trying to take credit for your work. I'd never do that."

Estella was still reluctant when asked to share her thoughts, but Ash was determined to persuade her. He unabashedly made himself out to be a fool, turning pale as he pleaded with a look of panic. His face was etched with all sorts of sentiments.

Naturally, Estella knew he wasn't thinking of snatching her ideas. She smiled reluctantly and said, "If you insist, I'll give it some thought."

"Great! You're such a great help. I knew you'd do well as the assistant manager! You're so reliable!"

Estella would deeply, deeply regret deciding to give in.

From that moment on, she became incredibly busy working as the assistant manager and, secretly, the manager as well. Despite the hotel failing to produce much of a profit, OGC didn't cut off funding or recall Estella. In fact, they sent another customer service AI to act as support staff.

That was how Estella met Leclerc, the AI she would work with over the next five years. The workplace became even more chaotic with the bubbly AI around, but business still wasn't going well, resulting in many frustrating challenges.

"And I thought so many people would be excited by the phrase 'space hotel'..." muttered Ash, his arms crossed and a look of disappointment on his face. He was the kind of person who put on a brave face in front of the staff, and he never let them see him complain. But once the day was over, and he showed up in Estella's room, he had no such restraint.

Estella couldn't decide if he shared his thoughts and frustrations because he trusted her or because he had no one else.

"Mr. Corvick, do you have any goals?" she asked suddenly one day, perhaps in an attempt to distract herself.

Ash looked at her in confusion, his head cocked to one side. "Goals?" He thrust his fist toward the ceiling. "It's obvious, isn't it? To make this hotel the world's—uh, no. We're already out in space; that's too small a scale. To make Daybreak outer space's greatest hotel!"

"I see. Well, it is already the *only* space hotel."

"It'd be good to have some other space hotels to compete

with... Ah, well, that's just a personal opinion." Ash scratched his cheek and glanced out the window into the inky blackness of space. He looked at the stars, so much more vibrant from here than from Earth. They felt closer. As he stared at the vast frontier, he murmured, "I want to bring my brother up here. He's always been frail, so he was never really able to go outside much. He was the only one who didn't laugh at my dreams. We promised we'd go to space together sometime."

"Your brother's name is Arnold, correct? Can you not invite him to the hotel?"

"I told you, he's weak. He's in the hospital right now. I've been thinking of inviting him up once he's out and things have settled down. Until then, I just need to..."

"..."

Estella could guess what Ash hadn't said. The hotel's finances weren't looking good, and even Ash could see that he couldn't run after his dreams without having his feet firmly on the ground. He just needed to hold on to the hotel until Arnold could come.

"What about trying to sell the story—how you lovingly made the space hotel for your brother?" Estella suggested.

"That's interesting. It's the kind of story you'd find in an old-school manga, but in terms of generating buzz..."

"Hm?"

They'd just been idly chatting, but Ash's expression suddenly went serious, and he fell quiet. Estella was about to ask him what he was thinking about, but he cried, "That's it, Estella! That's it! I knew I could count on you! I love you!"

"Um, huh? What?!"

Ash, a tall man, leapt over the table to where Estella was standing. He threw his arms around her, leaving her wide-eyed with shock. His actions triggered her programming for neutralizing a rowdy guest...but then she saw the smile on his face. She realized it was the same as the one he had when they first met, and she stopped.

"Ah..."

"Yes, yes, that's it! Damn, why didn't I realize this sooner? I'm an idiot... A complete and utter fool! But that ends today!"

"M-Mr. Corvick?"

"Things are going to get busy, Estella! This time for sure, without a doubt! It will go well!"

Ash's thoughts raced, leaving Estella behind when she couldn't keep up, but she was swept along by his smile and his confidence. She felt too foolish to ask him for the details, and her lips curled into a smile too. "Have you come up with some other strange idea, Mr. Corvick?"

"Of course. And it'll end with you getting even busier, just you watch."

Man and machine stood side by side. He was a whole head taller than her, even though she was a relatively tall female AI; her head just barely reached above his shoulder. It seemed natural for her to lay her head there.

"It troubles me as the assistant manager to see the hotel deserted. Leclerc complains all the time about being bored too. If you have an idea, please hurry."

"Just leave it to me. It'll be smooth sailing—uh, smooth *orbiting*—from here on out!" Ash grinned and patted Estella's head with his large hand as she leaned against his shoulder.

She closed her eyes and murmured, "Not the smoothest of puns, though, Mr. Corvick."

After their conversation, the man and the machine exchanged smiles.

And that was the end.

There was no more.

Ash went down to Earth and died in the accident. News of his death reached the station six days later.

.: 9 :.

THE INVESTIGATORS told us it was likely an accident, but I knew immediately that it wasn't. Right after the accident, reporters rushed to where Arnold was," said Estella, her slender arms wrapped around herself as if she were cold. The pitch of her voice fell as she continued to tell the shocking story of Ash Corvick's suicide.

Arnold scratched his cheek, then said, "I was surprised by that. I'd only just been told he was dead. I was already in shock, and then they came at me in full force. I deserve credit for not screaming at them."

"I can imagine what it must have been like," said Vivy, knowing that it wasn't quite the response Arnold was looking for.

"Thanks," he replied with a half smile, though he was just being polite.

Vivy was more focused on hearing the rest of the story anyway. Ash died, then reporters flocked to Arnold. That could mean only one thing. "Estella, are you saying Ash Corvick killed himself to generate buzz for the sake of the hotel?"

"No other theories make sense. Reporters really did flock to the story, which suddenly drew a lot of attention to the space hotel. Apparently, Ash had also spoken to a reporter friend before he died. He told him to get ready for a huge story."

Perhaps that "huge story" was the shattering of that idealist with his head in the clouds. Or rather, his head in space. Was that the sort of person he was? The kind of man who spoke of those ideals? Vivy couldn't make that judgment, as she'd never met the man.

"But Leclerc said he wasn't the sort of person to commit suicide," Vivy protested.

"That just means he would never choose suicide because of *financial* trouble, Vivy. I know he would never choose to die for an unproductive reason." Estella was speaking abnormally fast, and her curt rejection came as a surprise. Vivy thought she might be dealing with what humans called fear. She had, after all, spent more time than anyone trying to understand the truth of Ash Corvick's death, to understand his true intentions.

Her conclusion was that he'd killed himself to become a cornerstone for the hotel's growth. That was why Estella had decided to work with Arnold and picked up where Ash left off.

"I was surprised when Estella first contacted me," said Arnold. "Both by the fact that I was being contacted by an AI *and* by her theory."

"But you were still very patient with me, despite the sudden call. I still don't understand how the code of ethics didn't prevent me from taking that action, but fortunately, we were able to discuss everything."

"Then Arnold inherited the business, and you were made the manager, Estella?" asked Vivy.

"Yes, that's right. It's gone quite well, hasn't it? It seems I'm suited to this type of work." It pained Vivy to watch her jest and stick her tongue out.

Estella's actions weren't in line with the code of ethics, but it was obvious that she really wanted to make the hotel succeed alongside Ash Corvick. But she wouldn't get that, so instead, she was determined to make sure his death wasn't in vain. When she contacted Arnold, she was prepared for anything, including having her positronic brain wiped and her memories erased for defying the code of ethics.

"..."

Now that she'd heard the story, there was only one big problem left for Vivy to deal with. She'd infiltrated Sunrise to prevent the Sun-Crash Incident, but Estella's and Arnold's actions were completely inconsistent with the act of terrorism. If Estella had suspected Arnold of murdering Ash, then she would have reason to crash Sunrise and kill Arnold, but it had become clear they were working together. Though she had never suspected Arnold in the first place.

But there was something about the story that was bothering Vivy, observer as she was. "Something seems off," she said.

Her positronic brain wasn't satisfied. The theory that Ash Corvick killed himself in order to make a spectacle of his own death didn't make sense. His actions didn't match human nature.

"Daybreak is doing great financially, and we've been able to open this second hotel, Sunrise," Estella said. "I asked Mr. Corvick to come today so I could stand in and fulfill the promise the late Mr. Corvick wasn't able to..."

"A promise he wasn't able to fulfill... You mean being together in space?" asked Vivy.

Arnold nodded. "Yes. Together in space..."

Behind him were massive windows facing every direction so you could look out at the celestial view. There Vivy saw a ball of light so bright that she needed to adjust her light sensitivity to see it slowly peeking around the big blue planet.

"Sunrise... The dawn. Ash promised we'd see it together," Arnold murmured, his sorrow-filled voice barely escaping his throat.

Just for a moment, as she listened to him and looked at the overwhelming sight, Vivy lost track of time. A promise—a dawn.

A sound flashed in the back of her mind.

"*Hey, Diva. Can you promise me that when your sister, the Dawn Songstress, makes an appearance, you'll sing with her sometime?*"

"Ah..."

This memory didn't belong to Vivy, the consciousness that had been asleep for the past fifteen years. It was a record hidden deep within Diva, the AI who worked in NiaLand in Vivy's place, who knew nothing about Vivy's mission.

The man who'd said that had come to a fan meet-and-greet after one of Diva's performances. He only briefly complimented Diva's singing voice before launching into an excited spiel of his own.

"Your voice was amazing. But the woman I know has an incredible voice too. You two would make a dream duet. Don't you think it could be a real showstopper?"

He got a little too carried away, and Diva didn't understand what he was rambling about. The man squeezed Diva's hand as he chattered on, causing the park staff to rush over and drag him away from her. Even once he'd been pulled away, he still shouted, like a child divulging his wildest dreams.

"I can't tell you who I really am—it's a corporate secret, but you'll understand someday! We'll meet again, Diva!"

After the staff threw him out, the mystery man's peculiar words and the sound of raucous laughter lingered. He'd been wearing a large hat, sunglasses, a white face mask, and a heavy coat. He was clearly trying to hide his identity, which was suspicious in and of itself.

Three years passed, and Diva never met that strange man again, nor did she ever get to meet the Dawn Songstress he mentioned.

"Finally, I fulfilled his promise," Estella was saying back in the present. "He had to make that difficult decision because I was so incapable. This might not make up for it, but—"

"No..."

"Huh?" Estella was in the process of baring her soul with a

pained expression when Vivy cut in. She turned to face Vivy, to question her, but Estella's eyes grew wide in surprise when she saw Vivy. Even more suffering was etched on Vivy's face than her own. "Vivy, why do you look so upset?"

"No, no, Estella. You have it wrong. That's not how it was. It..."

Vivy wasn't certain, but she compared the physical data of Ash Corvick to that of the strange man she'd encountered as Diva three years ago: height, weight, age, and period of time when he was on Earth. It all matched. And the place where his accident happened was only one town over from NiaLand.

"That's not how it happened, Estella."

Diva had seen him.

Vivy had that record inside her, as if she too had seen him. A broad smile that couldn't be entirely concealed by a face mask. Blue eyes filled with hope, sparkling over the rim of his sunglasses. The heart of an adventurer, filled with excitement and thrills that couldn't be bound even by a thick coat.

"..."

Vivy had met Ash Corvick. Her very own eye cameras had seen him when he came down to Earth, when he was still alive, his hopeful eyes aglimmer. It was impossible that the smiling man, the man nearly dancing with excitement, would kill himself just to make the news.

Besides, Ash Corvick was waiting for the Dawn Songstress.

"I'm sorry, I've troubled you with a painful story," said Estella. "You're such a gentle girl, Vivy."

"No, no, no. No, that can't be what happened..."

Estella stepped toward Vivy and gently wrapped her arms around her. Vivy shook her head in disbelief as Estella held her. It shouldn't have been like this. It wasn't right to leave things as they were. There had to be something she could do—something, anything. There was a way to tell Estella what it was Ash Corvick had really wanted. But if she told her...

"Please..."

Vivy didn't have that strength; she was just a weak AI. But what about someone else? What about another person meant to save the future? He would be able to get the answer. He would know.

"*Tell me, Matsumoto!*"

"*Really now? You only rely on me when it suits you. I really did draw the short straw, didn't I?*" Matsumoto was sulking, unhappy and annoyed.

Then huge volumes of data poured into Vivy's consciousness, and she unzipped it piece by piece.

ııl|‖|ılı

It was all data regarding Ash Corvick. Surprise assailed her, but she turned her attention to the sender.

"*Matsumoto, this is...*"

"*It's the guy involved with space stations. I don't honestly have any obligation to go this far, but...I don't like half measures,*" said Matsumoto, not that it was a good excuse.

The data he kept revealing to her spread through her consciousness. The information concerned Ash while he was alive, his travel records, his bank accounts. Ash's financial situation was now as clear as Arnold's had become after her earlier research, though the former's was much more modest.

"*He was scraping the bottom of the barrel, money-wise,*" said Matsumoto. "*Ash Corvick definitely didn't have any talent as a manager. Based on what we just heard, he seems to have had that in common with Arnold.*"

"He came to NiaLand. Then before his accident, he... Ah."

Although it wasn't the piece that made everything clear, Vivy did see something among the dizzying swirl of data that captured her focus, and she went still. It was a list of digital books he'd purchased when he was alive.

"..."

Arnold had agreed to make Estella the secret manager of the business, as she requested. He'd also turned to books to learn more about the fields he didn't know much about. Both the older and younger Corvick had done exactly the same thing. The newest titles in Ash's digital book collection were all on the songstress AI model. There was only one reason he would be devouring such information.

"*Vivy, it's about the tablet Ash Corvick had on him when he had his accident. I managed to salvage the lost data. Child's play for someone like me,*" Matsumoto boasted before sending it over.

Vivy received and read the somewhat garbled data, then closed her eyes. There was only one thing to say to him. "*Thank you, Matsumoto.*" He was her partner, the one with whom she would get through the Project.

She opened her eyes. In front of her stood Estella and Arnold, both of them bewildered by Vivy's behavior, unaware of the conversation she'd been having and the data she'd been reading. She had to tell them.

"Estella... On that day, Ash Corvick was on Earth, chasing his dreams."

Estella's eyes filled with confusion. "Vivy?"

Vivy walked closer to her, put a hand on the back of her neck, and gently pulled her down until their foreheads touched. She sent information over the datalink—from Vivy, a member of the staff of Sunrise, to Estella, her manager. Estella needed this information.

Ash Corvick had left behind a plan for the Dawn Songstress.

"..."

Estella, one of the Songstress Series, was aboard Daybreak, a station named for the dawn. Guests would be welcomed and sent off with a performance by the beautiful assistant manager AI. It was an unrealistic plan by a man brimming with dreams and romantic ideas.

That was why it made so much sense.

"This..." Estella opened her eyes and stared at Vivy. She pulled her head back but was close enough to Vivy to have felt her breath were they human. She was still confused, but she was beginning to understand. Vivy steadily stared back at her.

"Vivy, where did you get this? This means he... But if he didn't, then..."

A crack formed in Estella's fragile resolve, her sense of duty now shattered. Up until now, she'd been serving a man who, as far as she knew, had thrown his life away for a dream. The foundation of her beliefs was crumbling, and her world had been turned upside down.

Ash Corvick hadn't killed himself. The man had never doubted his dreams or romantic ideals, even at the very end. Estella's sorrowful determination could be put to rest.

"He sent a reporter friend some emails as well. They talk about the same plan," said Vivy.

"The same plan..."

"He wanted his friend to write an article, saying the pride of Daybreak, a songstress, was going to sing..."

Matsumoto's work was extensive. In such a short time, he'd pulled together data on the subject, which gave a glimpse into the plan that Ash had revealed to his reporter friend. The press may very well have flocked to Arnold after Ash's death because his reporter friend had wanted to ensure his death wasn't in vain. Everyone was desperate to make Ash Corvick's dreams come true.

"I didn't want my brother's death to be just some random accident... Is that what made us think the way we did?" Arnold whispered.

Unlike Estella, Vivy couldn't directly show a human the data, but he'd still come to understand just from the bits and pieces she and Estella mentioned aloud.

He was shocked to learn that he'd misunderstood his brother's wishes, but even so, he said, "You know, Estella...there's something I've always thought since the very first time you contacted me." He smiled softly.

She'd been swallowed by the deluge of information, but she turned back to face him.

With that soft smile still on his face, he went on, "You have an amazing voice. I bet Ash thought the same." Ash's plan for the Dawn Songstress had blossomed from the same opinion.

Caught off guard, Estella closed her eyes. After quite some time, she opened them and smiled. "The first thing he ever complimented me on was my voice."

It might not have been appropriate for an AI like Vivy to have the thoughts she did at the moment, but she was certain of one thing: Estella, with her radiant smile, looked to have cast away her demons. It was the most natural, most beautiful emotional pattern Vivy had ever seen.

.: 10 :.

ALMOST EVERY GUEST on the space station was packed into the concert hall that day. There was a wide variety of entertainment facilities aboard Sunrise, but the concert hall was one of the most extravagant. Even Vivy, an experienced songstress, thought it was grand.

"Sunrise's design was based on the business plan Ash left behind. Thinking about it now, I wonder if his plan to have Estella sing was part of that," Arnold whispered to Vivy.

The two of them were sitting in their reserved seats. Arnold's frustrated smile came from the fact that Ash had gotten so far into planning a second space hotel and following his dreams that he'd written out a plan before he'd fixed the financial problems of his first hotel. Even Vivy couldn't help questioning the man's judgment.

Yet it was Ash's penchant for dreaming that had given birth to this plan—the concert of the Dawn Songstress—becoming a reality today. You couldn't laugh off dreams.

"Looks like she's about to start," Arnold said, brightening. Vivy adjusted her eye cameras to look at the main performer as she arrived.

Estella, clad in an elegant dress, walked onto the raised platform in the center of the concert hall. Applause broke out as the beautiful AI manager appeared onstage. It didn't matter that this concert was last minute and unplanned; the hall was packed.

The guests who were lucky enough to get invited to the grand opening of the hotel knew a good thing when they saw it. Thanks to a stroke of luck, they could witness something monumental. Perhaps the hotel staff sensed it too; the ones without anything to do were swarming the hall. Vivy didn't dare laugh at their curiosity; she was one of them after all. It wouldn't do for a worker of Sunrise to miss this anyway.

"I would like to dedicate this song to the former owner of Daybreak and Sunrise... Ash Corvick," Estella said. She bowed, and gentle music rose up in the background.

Every eye in the room was on her, waiting. Her lips parted, and a song floated out. The chatter immediately stopped as Estella's singing captivated everyone listening, as if all of outer space were under her spell. Her voice overwhelmed them and enchanted their hearts.

Although she had mastered hotel management skills so as not to embarrass herself, it didn't matter how much she'd neglected singing. She was from the Songstress Series, and her rich voice would never disappear.

"..."

Estella's song washed over the concert hall. It was beautiful, overflowing with love and gratitude for someone no longer there. It inspired in everyone a tender joy, like they were seeing the dawn after a long, dark night.

. : 11 : .

AFTER LISTENING to Estella's first song, Leclerc walked briskly through the station. Right now, the majority of the hotel's guests and staff were in the concert hall, so she passed neither human nor machine as she hurried to the cargo hold.

"Thank you, Vivy..."

She brought her hand to her ample chest as she murmured her thanks. Her gratitude came from what had happened a few hours earlier on the observation deck.

Vivy had been acting strange, asking where Estella was, so Leclerc had said she was probably on the observation deck. What she *didn't* say was that she was going to follow Vivy there. And it was on the observation deck that Leclerc learned the true circumstances surrounding Ash Corvick's death.

"He didn't kill himself...but he wasn't killed either," she murmured.

For a long time, Leclerc assumed Ash had been murdered. Her prime suspect was Arnold, as he'd gained so much from his brother's death. But she was wrong. Arnold had been thinking of his late brother when he put everything into expanding the space hotel business. He was doing the same as Leclerc was—honoring Ash, the original owner.

Once she reached the cargo hold, Leclerc stopped and bowed to the figure standing there. "Please, stop the plan. It was all my misunderstanding."

After becoming aware of how foolish her thought algorithms were, Leclerc could only apologize. She had requested this in an attempt to clear away any lingering resentment Ash might've had after his murder, but the truth behind his death wasn't at all what she'd suspected. She had to put right her mistake. Estella had done what she could not: She'd brought the dawn Ash Corvick dreamed of to life.

She could never interfere with—

"Ah..."

A sharp sound rang out, and a slight gasp slipped from Leclerc's lips. She had no idea what kind of impact could have caused the noise. Ever since her activation five years ago, she had operated as a customer service AI in space hotels, but she did not have this sensation in her experience records.

It was the sensation of her neck snapping and her positronic brain breaking.

"..."

She lost normal operations, her positronic brain was separated from its power source, and her consciousness cut out. The record of Leclerc's five-year operation was lost and could never be recovered. In the brief moment before everything that had built up was gone, a smiling face flashed through Leclerc's consciousness.

It was the face belonging to an open man, a man who treated humans and AIs alike. A man who was kind and maybe a little strange.

"Mr. Cor..."

With that last image, she crumpled to the ground, her consciousness gone forever.

VIVY

Prototype

CHAPTER 4

The Songstress's Struggle

.: 1 :.

THE DAWN SONGSTRESS'S voice captivated all in the concert hall—which was, in fact, part of the observation deck. The room was designed with a central stage, and its walls, the ceiling, and the floor could turn transparent, giving everyone a view of the sparkling stars and planet Earth, darkened by night. It was a paradise lifted straight from Ash's dreams, the same dreams picked up by Estella. The guests surrounded the stage, enjoying the Dawn Songstress's performance and the embrace of endless space outside. Even the employees were enraptured by the music.

"..."

Vivy was also a member of the captivated audience. She couldn't determine if the stimulus in her consciousness was from her pride as a songstress whose identity was based on their music or simply a lag caused by collecting and processing the incoming data. Listening to Estella's voice, Vivy eventually realized that she was listening to the voice of one of the Sisters—a successor to Diva.

"Her singing functionality is likely only using the standard equipment. She's a newer model with expanded functions, mainly in relation to the hotel industry, unlike you."

Matsumoto's interjection yanked Vivy out of her admiration. She stopped the reflexive frown, then replied, *"You're being rude. It's the middle of the song. Can't you hear it?"*

"Of course I can hear it. But the data is hardly worth evaluating, seeing as I was already aware of her specs. Besides..."

"Besides what?"

Vivy hadn't asked him outright whether Estella's song moved him, but he engaged in a long, dramatic pause. Then, he asked, *"Vivy, is your heart finally in the right place to reformat Estella?"*

"..."

"Oh, well, I guess 'heart' might be a bit too figurative. It's not like we AIs have something as incredibly indistinct as a heart. I'll rephrase: Is your programming in order to reformat Estella?"

It took Vivy several seconds to react to Matsumoto's biting remark. After her thoughts froze, she rebooted her processes. This time, she failed to stop her frown. *"Matsumoto, are you still going on about that? We don't need to reformat Estella. She—"*

"Doesn't resent Arnold Corvick? It was all just a mistake, and she has no motive now that she's learned Ash Corvick's death was a simple accident? She would never crash Sunrise or cause the Sun-Crash Incident?"

"..."

"I know you understand, Vivy. It's wonderful that the truth came out on the observation deck. We should rejoice that the

tangled threads of relationships between owner and AI, brother and brother, have been unknotted. But that has nothing to do with the incident. The Sun-Crash Incident will happen. Nothing has changed," Matsumoto said firmly, and Vivy looked down at the floor in frustration.

He was right. She hadn't fixed anything. In fact, there were only more questions now.

Vivy had guessed that Estella's motive for crashing Sunrise was to get revenge on Arnold for killing Ash. It was the most likely scenario. But Arnold and Estella trusted each other and worked closely together. Vivy had been entirely off the mark. Although the tragic misunderstanding had been cleared up, she hadn't made any progress on the Singularity Project, and there was no motive in sight.

"You get it, then. It would be best for you to reformat Estella's data as soon as possible."

"Matsumoto, you still suspect her? She doesn't have a motive. You do understand that, don't you?"

"I do. We agree on that. That's why I've focused on the theory that some deep-rooted error occurs in her programming. But either way, the Sun-Crash Incident cannot occur if the control AI for the space hotel is eliminated. This is the moment of truth, Vivy."

"Estella finally knows her owner's true thoughts. After three whole years...you really want me to make it like it never happened?"

If she reformatted Estella, her memories of Ash Corvick would disappear. There would be no memories of how they struggled side by side every day as they managed the hotel.

She wouldn't remember that she lost him, that she fought to carry on his wishes. She wouldn't remember the joy of learning the truth after misunderstanding him for so long.

That, and all of Estella's experiences would be lost.

"If Estella forgets, then what about Ash Corvick's request? Wouldn't the Dawn Songstress disappear too?"

"I dislike your phrasing, but I do sympathize. This is something we have to do in order to save humanity. Loss is always a tragedy, and if you claim that something lost has no value, then everything in the world is just rotting away for no reason. Thoroughly checking your standards reveals that there is no value in anything. Do you agree?"

"You're warping the logic. Don't evade the real problem by applying it to a larger scale."

"You're the one evading the problem, Vivy." Matsumoto spoke to her as if he were chastising a child. *"Stop being irresponsible and turning away from the problem in front of you. You're not human. Follow your orders."*

She went quiet. Obviously Matsumoto was right if you followed the logic. Vivy knew that, but she wouldn't obey his orders.

"Thank you for your kind attention."

Vivy snapped back to the present to see Estella bowing—the song had finished. The hall was filled with thunderous applause. Vivy was so focused on her conversation with Matsumoto that she'd missed a good chunk of the performance. It had been recorded, of course, but listening back wasn't the same as hearing the real thing. Strangely, something was always missing from a recording.

"Vivy, would you please come onstage?" came Estella's voice.

"...Me?" Vivy asked, her thoughts interrupted by the unexpected summons. She looked up at Estella, who was gesturing for Vivy to come over.

Estella was smiling, her usual beauty amplified by a shimmering vitality. Her eye cameras showed something akin to affection and gratitude toward Vivy. Beaming with those positive emotions, she pointed to Vivy and said in a polite voice, "Everyone, this is Vivy, one of the AI staff members that bring me such pride. She helped make the Dawn Songstress a reality. Since she is a worker here, I'm sure many of you have already met her, but I would like to reintroduce her."

Vivy felt Estella might be going a little overboard, but if it weren't for her, Ash's plans for the Dawn Songstress wouldn't have come to fruition, and Estella would likely have never made her debut as a songstress.

Setting aside the turbulent thoughts in her consciousness, Vivy stepped up onto the stage as Estella directed. She looked around. It was like being onstage in a sea of stars, with the seats around her floating in it.

"Thank you for the introduction. I am Vivy, an AI staff member. Thank you all for choosing to stay at Sunrise hotel," she said into the standing microphone. Her greeting was bland but inoffensive.

There was scattered applause despite the dry, predictable phrases lacking any pizzaz. The loudest applause came from a girl sitting near the back of the room. She was the daughter of the guests who had requested Vivy show them around the station multiple times.

"Did you enjoy our manager Estella's singing? To be honest, we were also surprised by her voice. Normally we just hear her scolding us," Vivy said, adding in a little humor this time. Estella was standing off to the side, but Vivy could still tell she was smiling awkwardly.

Arnold was sitting in front of them, close to the stage, where he could fully experience Estella's voice. He was looking at Vivy with warmth in his eyes.

"In addition to this concert, we have prepared several events so that you may all enjoy your time here in outer space. I hope that your stay on the dawn station is a pleasant one." With one last bow, Vivy had fulfilled her duty as an AI worker.

While AIs didn't feel nervousness, their ability to speak in unexpected situations varied. Vivy had a long history of working as a cast member in NiaLand, so she was relatively skilled at it. Just as she was about to step off the stage, it seemed Estella had other plans.

"Vivy, this is rare occasion. Would you sing a song?" Estella whispered before Vivy could walk away from the microphone.

It was a tempting suggestion, but Vivy didn't understand what she was doing. "Estella…"

In a somewhat teasing tone, Estella added, "I've thought your voice was beautiful from the moment I first heard it. And I am a model from the Songstress Series, after all, so I'm confident in my ear."

And I'm the first songstress, your other sister.

How easy things would be if she could say that. Vivy quashed those useless thoughts and slowly shook her head as she faced forward. She wouldn't give it a second thought if she felt she could let herself go and sing one song. But on the incredibly slim chance that her singing voice connected Vivy to her real identity as Diva, then she would be in trouble.

She wanted to fulfill Estella's wishes, but she couldn't take the risk. Estella would have to go to NiaLand if she really wanted to hear Vivy sing.

"..."

As she thought and stared out at the audience, she stopped moving. It wasn't just her body that froze—the shock had brought her consciousness to a halt as well. The positronic brain inside her frame's skull quivered. The lenses in her eye cameras whirred as they refocused. Once they had adjusted, she took in all the eyes that were on her. Focusing her attention on the onlookers had been an unbelievable mistake.

"...Estella will be singing the next song: 'She,'" she said.

Her thoughts were still frozen, but she went along with the natural flow of the situation and requested the next song. It was a ballad by a famous female singer. The musical accompaniment began, and Vivy quietly moved aside to allow Estella to step up. Estella frowned in disappointment, but she couldn't keep Vivy there any longer.

ıı|ı|||ı|ıı

Estella's beautiful voice once again rang out, layering over the emotional background music.

Vivy quickly stepped off the stage. She cut across the room, the stars marking her path, and left, all the while listening to the music.

"..."

She walked down the empty corridor, gradually speeding up until she was running. She knew that the majority of the hotel guests and staff were in the concert hall, but she still searched for a place to be alone.

However, she wouldn't find it yet.

"Wait, please!"

There was a call from behind, and she stopped. She'd been followed.

"..."

They were surrounded by outer space. Vivy couldn't run and hide. Resigned, she turned around to face her pursuer.

Watching Vivy with teary eyes was a slightly out of breath fifteen- or sixteen-year-old girl. She was about as tall as Vivy, with shoulder-length hair tied back from her face. Her clothes were modestly stylish, perhaps to match the tone of the concert. The small amount of makeup she wore enhanced her cute features. Her round eyes, petite mouth, and straight nose made her attractive enough to be judged as pretty by human beauty standards, but there was something more than just cuteness in those features for Vivy.

Each of the girl's features were familiar. The girl's face wasn't stored in Vivy's memory—rather, Vivy had known a blood relative of the girl's, someone who looked very similar to her. Why had it taken her so long to realize that? It was probably because the girl's relative had been significantly younger.

"Um, can I ask you something? Did you...know my sister?" the girl asked.

Her relative was Kirishima Momoka, who'd died at the age of ten. She was the girl who had given Vivy her nickname before the AI Naming Law was established and she was officially named Diva.

"You're Vivy—I mean, Diva—from NiaLand, aren't you?"

Vivy vividly recalled Momoka, the girl from fifteen years ago. The girl on the passenger plane after the first Singularity Point.

The girl she couldn't save.

.:2:.

VIVY REFERENCED the hotel's guest list to find this girl's name: Ojiro Yuzuka. Fifteen years ago, Vivy had stood by as Kirishima Momoka died, and now she was talking to her little sister.

"..."

The reason the two girls had different family names—and why Vivy hadn't immediately realized they were related—was because their mother had remarried. Momoka's father, Kirishima Youji, had been on the plane with her. At that time, Momoka's mother, Kirishima Miyu, had been in the hospital about to give birth to her second daughter. She heard of the deaths of her husband and daughter while she was in the hospital before she gave birth to Yuzuka. It was safe to assume she later met her current husband and remarried.

Despite Vivy not realizing who Yuzuka was, Yuzuka had realized who *she* was.

"I couldn't believe it at first, but the more I looked at you, the more I thought you looked just like the AI my sister loved... Vivy."

Since her arrival on Sunrise, Yuzuka had constantly stared at Vivy for that very reason. She also likely ignored all the other bell-hops and kept requesting Vivy because she so desperately wanted her question answered. Vivy had chased any lingering thoughts of the girl out of her consciousness because she'd been so focused on Estella, Arnold, and discovering the cause of the Sun-Crash Incident.

"Vivy...?" the girl prompted, her eyes flicking around in uncertainty as Vivy remained silent.

Yuzuka was right, of course; here was Vivy, the AI with Diva's memories whom her sister had loved so dearly. But Vivy couldn't tell her she was right. Doing so would impact her ability to go through with the Singularity Project, which was Vivy's first priority.

"I'm sorry, Ojiro-sama. I don't understand the question," said Vivy, choosing a vague response even though she knew it was cruel.

The girl instantly stiffened, her eyes clouding with pain. But she pressed her lips tightly together, stood firm, and let out a small breath. "Sorry. I need to explain, don't I? I have—*had* an older sister. She died in an accident before I was born, but she left behind a lot of stuff. There were so many of your things. *Vivy's* things."

"..."

"I knew Vivy wasn't that AI's name. She had a different official name and still worked at NiaLand... I tried to go meet her so many times, but it made Mom so sad..." Yuzuka looked at the floor. She kept her tone measured, but there was a strong under-current of regret.

Yuzuka wanted to know more about what her sister had loved, but she knew it would pain her mother, who had lost her husband and daughter. Instead, she bottled up her feelings. Seeing what a considerate person Yuzuka had become, it was obvious Yuzuka's mother had raised her with love. Yuzuka couldn't bring herself to hurt her mother, but then she'd run into Vivy in outer space of all places, despite having given up on meeting her.

That was a cruel twist of fate.

"This trip to the space hotel is for Mom and Dad's ten-year anniversary. I didn't expect to run into you, Vivy."

"I believe I understand now, Ojiro-sama," Vivy said flatly, cutting Yuzuka's explanation short. A glimmer of hope appeared in Yuzuka's eyes, and Vivy stared straight into them. "I am sorry. I have never met your sister. I am an AI staff member on Sunrise."

Vivy's clear words dashed Yuzuka's hopes.

In most situations, it would be against the code of ethics for an AI to lie to a human, and omitting the functionality entirely was recommended. Maintaining the secrecy of the Project, however, had to take priority over the code of ethics when you considered Vivy's current mission.

"B-but your name is Vivy! That's the same name my sister gave you..."

"My name was given to me by my first owner after I was deployed. The only answer I can provide is that it is simply a coincidence."

Yuzuka desperately scrambled to cling to any thread of possibility, despite Vivy's firm denials, making pained protests. "But that's just—"

Vivy dealt the finishing blow. "Diva, the AI your sister loved, should be operating in NiaLand right now. Why would Diva be here in a space hotel when she has a job to perform on Earth?"

"..."

"It does not appear to be a logical explanation for the situation. I'm sorry."

It was illogical for a songstress to be away from her stage, and Vivy had used that logic to her advantage. It was shameless of her to say what she had, considering she *was* there, but she couldn't tell Yuzuka the truth: that she had been sent here by an AI from the future. Her argument was effective against the girl, who was old enough to understand.

Yuzuka appeared to reluctantly accept Vivy's words, despite seeing Vivy right in front of her. "I guess I got caught up thinking that maybe Di—Vivy, who my sister loved so much, had come here to see me," murmured Yuzuka, her eyes cast down and her voice trembling. She looked up, tears welling in her eyes as she said, "Even though it's impossible."

"..."

It was a chance encounter. Perhaps Momoka's wishes had brought them together, just like Yuzuka hoped. But Vivy wasn't going to dress up this coincidence as some sort of beautiful miracle.

"Ojiro-sama, shall I walk you to your room? Or perhaps back to the observation deck?" Vivy asked.

"No, thank you... I can go back on my own. Sorry for interrupting your work with my weird questions."

"It's no bother. I have to go to the cargo hold to...sort the cargo we've received. If you'll excuse me."

"Sure... Have a good time at work," Yuzuka said, her spirit still strong despite having her hopes shattered.

A sense of relief registering in Vivy's consciousness, she continued toward the cargo hold since she'd used it as an excuse to get out of there. She felt Yuzuka's eyes on her back, but she didn't turn to look. However, she was plagued by a tingling sensation in her positronic brain. Unexpected thoughts coming into her consciousness were causing something akin to brain fog.

"I want to organize my thoughts a little..." she muttered.

Most people might assume an AI could never experience anything like that, but the calculations of an AI's positronic brain were far faster and larger in scope than a human's thoughts, the closest equivalent. AIs had to organize the logs created by their stream of thoughts, which put a significant amount of stress on their systems. In order to conveniently process everything without overloading, they could only take on simple tasks for a time.

The third wave of guests had been welcomed onto Sunrise, so all the scheduled guests had arrived. The guests' luggage and hotel supplies had come in on the last shuttle and been transported to the cargo hold. Now the staff needed to check the goods against their supply list. The housekeeping staff were in charge of this duty, since they had a light workload. Leclerc was one of the housekeepers, so Vivy thought she would go and help out.

The entrance to the cargo hold was in a section of the station restricted to hotel staff only. Vivy held her hand up in front of the closed door. She was automatically identified, and the door opened.

"Leclerc, are you in here?" she called as she stepped into the room.

Vivy had a visual record of Leclerc leaving the concert hall while Estella was performing. While Leclerc seemed like the type who'd like a big scene, she had listened to Estella's singing without making a single sound. Leclerc had worked on Daybreak too, and it seemed she was quite fond of Ash Corvick. Perhaps Estella's voice had evoked some feelings in her as well.

While Vivy wasn't going to blab, Estella and Arnold were equally as likely to tell Leclerc about Ash's Dawn Songstress plan. The tone of Leclerc's voice had dropped slightly when she spoke of Ash. Perhaps hearing about his plan would be enough to brighten up any gloomy feelings she had.

"Leclerc?" Vivy said, suspicion creeping into her voice.

There was no response, nor any sign of Leclerc in the cargo

hold as far as Vivy could see. Leclerc should have been there, as this was the only place she would've gone after stepping away from the performance. Vivy couldn't deny the possibility that she had jumped to conclusions, and Leclerc had gone to another room to sort out her thoughts.

"Come to think of it..."

Vivy wondered why she had been left to her *own* thoughts for so long. When she was onstage, and when she'd been shocked by Yuzuka's identity, Matsumoto hadn't chimed in with a single annoying remark. In fact, he'd said nothing to her for a while.

What if his silence wasn't by choice?

"Oh, hey. Sorry, I couldn't get away."

"..."

A voice came from behind one of the shipping containers deep inside the cargo hold, derailing Vivy's train of thought. Vivy enacted her relieved emotional patterns and headed over to the voice, almost laughing at her own suspicion.

"What's up?" Leclerc said. "Everyone else is at the concert on the observation deck."

"I saw you leave by yourself. I felt bad leaving you alone to have a staring competition with a shipping container while everyone else was having a good time," Vivy replied.

"Aw, you're so nice! You came all the way here for my lonely little self?"

Vivy hesitated a fraction of a second. Just before she'd arrived here, she'd lied to Yuzuka. And now she was here, lying to Leclerc. Yet it would be an even bigger lie to say she felt remorseful.

"Yeah, I came—"

Those words should have been followed with *just for you*, but as she stepped around the shipping containers to meet Leclerc, they died in her throat.

Leclerc's frame was there, slumped against the container, its legs sprawled out at an awkward angle.

"..."

That alone would've been suspicious, as it wasn't a way any AI would sit, but the worst part was her head. Leclerc's slender neck had been forcefully twisted and broken, and the mechanical parts below the synthetic skin were exposed.

Just like humans, AIs needed their necks to function properly. One of the most important components in an AI was the central circuit, which provided energy to the positronic brain housed in the head. It was usually found in the neck. If the circuit was broken or interrupted, there would no longer be energy supplied to the positronic brain. Just like cutting off the oxygen supply to a human brain, it caused a positronic brain to die.

The death of a positronic brain was an AI's end. You could access the activity logs. You could read the memory. You could even install that into another frame, but it wouldn't be the same individual. This was commonly called "AI death." It was the ultimate end.

Nothing more, nothing less.

"Leclerc..."

"..."

In the ruin of Leclerc's neck, Vivy saw that the central circuit had been broken completely. The electrical supply to her positronic brain had been cut off. The cold, hard truth was that Leclerc was dead.

But then who had Vivy just been speaking with? And why did they have Leclerc's voice?

"Ah!"

Just as she started to question it, Vivy sensed someone approaching from behind. She threw herself forward, and something swiped sideways through the space where her head had been a moment before.

She didn't have time to check who it was. She planted her hands on the ground as she tumbled, cartwheeling in a gymnastic move called a roundoff, in order to land facing her attacker.

"Huh. You move pretty good for a hotel worker AI," the attacker muttered, impressed by Vivy's evasion. As she spoke, she calmly lowered the leg she'd been holding in the air. That long, slender leg was likely what had come flying at Vivy's neck from behind, and despite its delicate appearance, it would pack more than enough force to snap Vivy's neck.

It was natural to assume this person was the one who had broken Leclerc—the one who'd killed her.

Vivy was utterly bewildered. "Estella...?"

In front of Vivy stood the AI she thought she knew, calm and composed. Estella swept her hair back, a smile playing on her thin lips as she watched the shock spread across Vivy's face.

.: 3 :.

"**Y**ES, MY CUTE LITTLE AI staff member. I am Estella. I am the manager of this dawn station, Sunrise, and the first AI to turn against humanity."

"..."

"You two are the first to fall for my noble mission... Leclerc was first, and now you will join her. How sweet of you to care for your friend." Estella smiled, chatting like nothing was out of the ordinary.

If Vivy ignored Estella's words, she could almost pretend they were having a normal conversation. But there was still Leclerc's broken frame there at her feet, and Estella's eyes locked on Vivy as she watched her, waiting for Vivy's next move. Vivy stared right back.

As Vivy recovered from her initial shock, she began to understand what was happening. More than 90 percent of the characteristics of the Estella in front of her matched those of the Estella she knew, the Estella who was currently singing in the concert hall. The only way to evaluate the remaining 10 percent would be to get close and initiate a datalink, but externally, the being before Vivy looked just like Estella.

"Estella can't be here," Vivy declared. "She's in the middle of a concert, surrounded by guests... So who are you?"

"Why do I have to answer that?"

"..."

"Are you going to try to make a break for it and go get help?"

Estella's tone remained the same, but her smile transformed into a challenge.

While this AI had the same facial features as Estella, her expressions gave such a different impression. An AI's flexible emotional patterns were the result of their everyday experiences. Evidently, *this* Estella had spent a lot of time in situations that merited combative expressions.

Vivy tried to contact Matsumoto via transmission as she faced off against this Estella and her dangerous smile. *"Matsumoto, please respond. Matsumoto."* He should have figured out what was going on by now. Vivy didn't have much of a chance on her own against this obvious threat. No matter how much she called Matsumoto though, he didn't reply.

Just as she'd feared, Matsumoto was being silent because the connection between them had been severed.

"Did you just try to contact Estella? Sorry, that won't work. The transmission network on the station has been put out of commission for a bit. Don't want anyone doing anything funny, now do we?" the fake Estella asked.

"Hmph…"

"Same goes for you."

In a flash, the fake Estella stepped right up to Vivy. When Vivy took a quick step back, she took a hit in the lower abdomen, throwing her wildly off balance. Fake Estella had lashed out with a forceful kick in an attempt to sweep Vivy's legs out from under her. As Vivy tried to plant her hands on the ground, she was struck with a series of swift kicks to the chest, sending her flying backward.

"You're seriously slow. And apparently you suck at cleaning!" the fake Estella jeered. She rushed after Vivy, who bounced and rolled across the floor.

Seeing the fake Estella coming, Vivy activated her self-defense program. She struck the floor, stopping her rolling momentum and using it to flip herself upright. Fake Estella's eyes grew wide at the unexpected motion. Without hesitation, Vivy aimed a strike with the heel of her palm right at the impostor's face.

Vivy's opponent was an AI—one intent on harming her. This wasn't like fighting against a human. She had no qualms using her mechanical body's specs to its fullest.

Despite Vivy's slender appearance, she was made of materials far sturdier than bones and muscle. On top of that, much of her skeletal frame had been replaced after she'd been so damaged in the last Singularity Point, resulting in a much tougher version of herself. Matsumoto had manipulated the records of those modifications as well. In short, Vivy's fighting capabilities transcended those from fifteen years ago during her first venture.

"Not bad," mused the fake Estella.

Vivy gasped as she evaded the palm strike by leaning her head to the side. The air from Vivy's strike grazed the fake's ear, hitting nothing but her long hair as she gracefully danced away. Before Vivy could come to terms with her opponent's dodge, the fake Estella's arm wrapped around Vivy's slender neck. For a brief moment, Leclerc and her snapped neck flashed through Vivy's mind.

Then Vivy kicked off the ground as hard as she could, flying backward and crashing into a cargo container, dragging her

THE SONGSTRESS'S STRUGGLE   223

opponent with her. The impact loosened fake Estella's hold on Vivy's neck, and Vivy used every bit of strength to escape the restraint. A millisecond later and Vivy would have met the same fate as Leclerc.

"You can move better than I expected," said the fake Estella. "Do you modern AI models come with programs for catching thieves?"

"You're the one with more advanced combat skills than a hotel manager needs."

"What if we reinterpret *manager* as someone who rules a hotel with an iron fist?" Fake Estella blathered on as she shook her arm and checked its function after Vivy had forcefully torn free from it.

Vivy had learned one thing from being in close contact with this Estella: Her combat programming might have been masterful, but her frame was quite average. In terms of frame functionality, Vivy was more powerful due to Matsumoto's non-standard repairs. Fake Estella was deeply mismatched, and she looked like she was in a hurry to adapt.

"Are you done indulging in your boring thoughts yet? Sorry to say, but I can't spend much time with you. I did lose my little helper, after all," said the fake Estella.

"Your helper...? You mean Leclerc?"

"Yep. I don't know what happened, but it seems she had a change of heart. She got us in this far, then she just wanted us to leave without a fuss. What a moronic AI..."

If that last statement had been an honest disparagement,

Vivy would've been infuriated, but she didn't sense any contempt in what the fake Estella said about Leclerc's death. The sense of wrongness from that disconnect hit her consciousness at the same time as something else.

"Leclerc got you on the station?" Vivy asked.

Knowing there were two nearly identical Estellas on board, and knowing the fake Estella was skilled in subterfuge, it was safe to say she'd identified the culprit behind the Sun-Crash Incident. It wasn't Estella who crashed Sunrise into the Earth—it was this fake Estella who had set that tragedy into motion.

"I don't understand why you're doing this, but I do know your actions are a violation of the AI Laws. I can't let you go through with it," Vivy declared.

"What a beautiful response. Too bad. This isn't the first time my actions have violated the Laws. Besides..."

"What?"

"You have no chance of winning against me."

Vivy readied herself as fake Estella came at her again. As her tall opponent took a casual step forward, Vivy went for the legs. She aimed her own long, slender leg in a sweeping kick, practically a move of revenge. "Hah!"

But it seemed like the fake Estella saw the move coming. She stomped down hard on Vivy's leg. The knee joint of Vivy's left leg screeched, and the AI smiled sadistically as she stomped again. Vivy's ankle cracked with an audible snap.

"Ack!"

"See, you can't get away! Look, look, look!"

Still standing on Vivy's ankle, fake Estella landed a series of sharp toe kicks into Vivy's stomach. The force would normally have sent Vivy flying backward, but her leg was still pinned. She couldn't escape. She tried to curl her body up to protect herself, but the fake Estella grabbed her hair and hoisted her into the air by sheer force.

"Urgh..."

"Based on your data, you were previously a babysitter, yeah?" said the fake Estella. "I'll bring back your memories of how difficult six-year-olds like me can be!"

She held on to Vivy's synthetic hair as she swung her into the cargo container next to them. The blow warped the video feed from Vivy's eye cameras and scattered the information processing ability of her damaged positronic brain. She flailed her arms and legs but couldn't land a decisive blow. After being smacked into the container twice, then thrice, even Vivy's reinforced frame was reaching its limits. Her arms were crushed, her legs had cracked, and worse, her left leg was ragged from the knee down.

"Augh..."

"This is really weird... Normally, they break a bit easier under such stress. Have you had some weird tune-up?"

Vivy's vision flickered violently, and she couldn't resist the continued attacks. The fake Estella stared at her. Vivy was obviously beyond the strength of a normal AI model, but as surprised as the enemy AI was, she must have decided it wasn't enough to pose a threat. She didn't even wait for an answer to her question.

"Eh, whatever. You're just as unlucky as that other girl anyway. It's time to put you to bed."

Still holding Vivy up in the air with her left hand, the fake Estella drew back her right. She could break Vivy's neck and cut off the central circuit or jab her fingers into Vivy's eyes, directly destroying her positronic brain. Either way, the AI's next action would end her activity. The Singularity Project would fail, and Vivy wouldn't be able to stop the looming threat of humanity's destruction.

Everything that had happened up to this point would have been for nothing. Even that day when she'd watched as the girl who loved her singing so much died. Even today, when that young girl gathered the strength to ask Vivy her questions to confirm her late sister's feelings.

None of it would mean a single thing.

"Ngh!"

"What?!"

Vivy gritted her teeth and swung her horribly battered legs as hard as she could. The fake Estella avoided the kick by simply leaning out of the way. Her spear hand strike skimmed Vivy's cheek instead, splitting her synthetic skin and exposing the mechanical components beneath. Before the next strike could land, Vivy twisted her entire body and forced the fake Estella's left arm, the arm holding her, into a joint lock.

Joint locks were particularly effective against AIs, since their frames were modeled after human bodies. AIs obviously didn't feel pain or care about damaging their own frames, meaning they could still move.

"Damn! Look at you go!"

"Agh!"

While Vivy was aiming for the two joints of fake Estella's left arm, the elbow and the wrist, her opponent suddenly shoved her away and escaped the danger. That action proved that the fake Estella wanted to keep her own body intact. There was something she needed to do, and she couldn't be broken before that. And that *something* might very well be impersonating Estella and crashing Sunrise.

According to the information that Matsumoto brought back regarding the Sun-Crash Incident, several of the guests who got away in the escape shuttle gave statements saying Estella was the culprit. That meant the fake Estella needed to make an appearance in front of the guests, which required her to be in one piece.

"You can't go too f—" Vivy started to say, but a violent tremor shook her.

The quake hit the entire cargo hold and beyond. In fact, the whole Sunrise was shaking.

"What the—?"

"You really have time to look away?" the fake Estella snapped.

As the powerful shaking went on, Vivy had to stop and steady herself. Her thoughts raced as she tried to figure out the cause, and then the fake Estella's knee flew right toward her.

"Ah!"

Vivy couldn't dodge. The knee crunched directly into her face, and the incredible force flung her into another cargo container. The cables holding the filled containers snapped, and the shrill screech of metal filled her ears as a container fell toward her. No matter which way she dodged, she wasn't going to make it.

The weight that fell on her entire body was more than she could have supported even if she used every last bit of strength in her AI frame. In an instant, her entire body was broken, starting with her damaged left leg.

And with that...

"Bye-bye, Miss Meddlesome."

Vivy could only just hear the fake Estella's farewell over the sound of her own body being crushed.

. : 4 : .

SUNRISE SHOOK just as the concert was nearing its end.

"..."

Estella was onstage, in front of the microphone, and her voice resonated throughout the room. Although she had been built as part of the Songstress Series, and the singing function had been a standard feature of her model, she had never been blessed with an opportunity to perform. She had never thought it necessary either.

That made it all the stranger that she was here onstage now, feeling so good. It really did feel wonderful to sing however much her positronic brain desired.

There was, of course, some desire to make Ash Corvick's Dawn Songstress plan a reality at play, but that wasn't all. She saw the emotions glimmering in the eyes of the guests and staff as they stared up at her and knew it was due to her song. The thought nearly set her heart aflutter.

The fact that her consciousness was so filled with joy from singing meant she really was a songstress model. Perhaps Ash had known this would happen.

That's probably giving him too much credit, though, Estella thought as memories of Ash played back in her mind. Back when he was alive, he rarely showed a serious or pained expression. And yet, that was the only way she had pictured him...until now. Those somber expressions had vanished, replaced by his smiling face. Mountains of them filled her mind. Estella could barely trust in her own memory for having forgotten.

That was when the tremor shook Sunrise.

"Eek!" Estella shrieked, and she wasn't the only one caught off guard. The screens making up the ceiling, the walls, and even the floor of the room were transparent, putting outer space on display, but the tremor was enough to remind the guests that their feet were on the floor. In a calm voice, Estella announced, "My apologies, everyone! I will check on the situation. All guests, please remain seated." She had stopped singing, but the background music was still playing.

Estella then ordered the AI staff to make rounds through the audience to keep the guests from panicking. As they did, she accessed Sunrise's systems, using her authority as the control AI to find the source of the tremor.

The response was immediate.

"An error in the docking area...? And it needs input from the control AI?" she murmured, standing stock-still.

The docking area was a space station's supply line as well as the entrance and exit for passengers and guests via shuttle or rocket. An error there was a serious issue.

"I apologize for the disturbance, everyone. As an apology, I would like to treat you all to a complimentary beverage. I assume that won't be a problem, Estella?" Arnold prompted.

Estella saw his familiar wink and went along with his quick thinking. "Of course not. Please." With that, AI staff began serving drinks to the audience.

"Dear guests," Arnold went on, "please take a moment to gaze upon the shimmering stars of outer space. My beloved older brother, Ash, was ensorcelled by this sight. Don't the stars look all the more beautiful today?" While he might lack practical skills, no one was better at dealing with people than Arnold. Both Corvick brothers were truly gifted when it came to earning approval.

Estella left the audience to Arnold as she exited the observation deck along with two other AI staff members. She ordered them to check on the few guests who'd been absent from the concert. "I wish Vivy and Leclerc were here..." she murmured.

She wanted to ask them for help, especially considering how reliable and good with people they were. Unfortunately, she had seen both leave during the concert. They were most likely working.

"I have arrived at the docking area. On authority of the control AI, unlock the door." Estella placed her hand on a control panel beside the sliding door as she gave the command to open.

The docking area was a relatively important facility compared to the others because it was used to connect with external shuttles and shipping rockets. One needed special authorization to enter or exit. It was no obstacle for Estella, as she had the highest level of authority on the entire space station.

"I came because of the error report, but what now?"

She stepped inside the docking area and looked around, confused. As far as she could see, the massive chamber was entirely empty. The shuttle that had brought the hotel guests had already left Sunrise to return to the space elevator, so it being empty was expected.

"It looks like the station's internal atmospheric pressure is normal... So what was that err—"

As Estella began wondering aloud, a voice suddenly reached her ears. "Don't worry. There isn't a single abnormality in regards to the station. But, well, there are mountains of problems with *other* things."

"Oh!" Her eyebrows shot up in surprise, and she whirled in the direction the voice had come from. Estella didn't recognize the speaker; they weren't a staff member or any of the guests. She couldn't even find a corresponding voice among the records of everyone she'd ever met.

More importantly, there was no record of anyone entering this room besides her. The last people to move through that door were the guests from the third wave when they were welcomed aboard two hours ago. There was no sign of entry since then, and the door had been sealed until Estella arrived.

As those thoughts ran through her consciousness, the source of the voice slowly revealed itself. "At the moment, the greatest problem is you. Though you probably aren't even aware."

"Who—"

"I have no intention of telling you my name. I don't intend for us to interact long enough for you to require it. My partner has already annoyed me enough. I can't hide my disappointment in her stubbornness, but...honestly, it's not a bad opportunity to get involved directly with the Project."

The voice carried a lighthearted and teasing note, but its sentiments definitely weren't in Estella's favor. What surprised Estella the most was the AI's form. She'd never seen another one like it.

This AI was built of stacked cubes. In total, it was about the same size as the cargo containers they used to ship goods, and it resembled a Rubik's Cube, only this one was a mass of *hundreds* of connected cubes. Estella could tell by looking that it would be able to rearrange those cubes into whatever shape it wanted. The model's frame made sense, but as far as Estella knew, the technology required to build such a frame didn't yet exist. Either this AI was experimental or it was the most cutting-edge model out there.

Here was an AI that shouldn't exist, in a place it shouldn't be. None of this felt normal, so Estella immediately decided to treat it as an emergency.

"Stop!" she shouted. "State your affiliation and model number, as well as your purpose for being here!"

"And while I do that, you'll use a station-wide transmission to inform the AI staff that there's a suspicious AI intruder. An appropriate action in accordance with the manual, but unfortunately, it won't work. It was a bit of a hassle going against you since you're the control AI and all, but I've already cut off transmissions in the station temporarily."

"..."

"You can't contact anyone outside this room. You can't call for help. Do you understand your situation?"

It seemed what the cube AI said was correct. There was no sign that the station had received the signal Estella sent to sound the emergency alert. None of the AIs she reached out to responded. Transmissions were indeed cut off; the technological abilities of the cube AI were leagues beyond Estella's. So, why had this AI come aboard a newly opened space hotel?

"What is your goal?" Estella asked.

"It's simple. My goal is to serve humanity by eliminating the elements that lead to its destruction. In short...to remove the risk factor that is *you*, Estella."

"I don't understand..."

The cube AI shuffled to create arms and legs, then crept toward Estella. Despite its superior skills, there were obvious abnormalities in its words and actions. At the very least, if she were to believe what it—or he, since it appeared to be a male-based AI—said, he was going to eliminate her in order to save humanity.

"No... I really don't understand," she repeated.

"It seems not. Apparently, you don't have an active reason for causing the incident. That means we can only assume a system bug caused by your compiled work data is responsible... Regardless, the only way to resolve the issue is to reformat you," the cube AI said dispassionately.

"Huh?!"

Reformat? That meant erasing her memories and reverting her to her initial state on dispatch. She was an AI, so she was prepared for a reformat or a reboot if a bug did arise—but only if there really *was* one. "I'm not going to agree to anything a rude AI like you says!"

"That's fine. I didn't think you would listen to what I had to say anyway. Besides, I don't really plan on talking. I will swiftly carry out the Project in accordance with the Zeroth Law."

As he made his declaration, Estella turned around and rushed back to the door. If she could just get through the door and lock it, she could trap the cube AI in here. He wouldn't be trapped for long, considering his technical skills, but it would still buy her some time.

And what would she do then? Who could she possibly call to help her against the cube AI?

"I can imagine what you're thinking, but you don't need to bother with that. Don't worry, I won't let you escape." The cube AI had looked so heavy and slow, but he zipped into Estella's path, blocking her way.

She looked to see that the tips of his four legs had transformed into rollers where they contacted the ground, giving him far more mobility than Estella.

"Oh, you won't get away."

"Eeek!"

As he appeared in front of her, Estella quickly changed direction and tried to slip past him. One of his roller-equipped legs clipped her heel and sent her tumbling through the air, and her balance warning rang out in futility. She was unable to control her fall, and her shoulder was about to crash into the floor.

Just before she landed, the cube AI caught her in one arm.

"Ah... Why'd you catch me? Didn't you come to destroy me?" she asked.

"I may be an AI, but it's not gentlemanly to harm a lady. Don't assume the worst of me. I just want to accomplish my goal in a smart, sensible way."

"..."

"My ultimate goal is to save humanity, nothing else. I doubt you can fully accept that line of reasoning, but I hope you at least try to understand it."

Estella was forced to look up at the cube AI, given how he held her. An eye camera with some sort of shutter stuck out from what would've been his torso. It opened and closed, almost like a human eye, showing how much he regretted his actions. Seeing that, Estella understood. The cube AI wasn't just talking or joking around. He was honestly telling her his mission.

Reformatting Estella was somehow connected to saving humanity, at least as far as this AI was concerned. That mission was as important to the cube AI as carrying out Ash Corvick's wishes were to her.

"I won't apologize. It would be meaningless," said the cube AI.

He rearranged his cubes to create another arm and brought the tip up to Estella's forehead.

Estella instantly knew he would use a datalink to pass a program to her.

But before he went through with it, he murmured, "I'm certain my partner would have apologized…"

His voice was so ragged with emotion, Estella stiffened. All four of her limbs were pinned down. She couldn't move, nor could she resist. With a simple touch, it would all be gone. The Dawn Songstress, the night Ash's dreams had come true—it would all disappear. Estella knew this to be true.

His name fell from her lips: "Ash…" The thin arm touching Estella's forehead made her tremble with fear. She was terrified of her contents being erased.

"Initiating datali—huh?!" There was a high-pitched fluctuation as he cut himself off. Carrying Estella, the cube AI rolled to look behind him, no doubt looking for the source of the disturbance.

Estella couldn't believe what she saw.

"Well, this is entirely unexpected," said the interloper, a middle-aged man looking at Estella and the cube AI.

.:5:.

FOR A MOMENT, Estella did not speak. She recognized the man standing there with his eyebrows raised. He was one of the hotel guests she had greeted herself, a VIP who'd been invited to the grand opening of Sunrise. She quickly looked up his name in the guest book.

"Kakitani-sama?"

Kakitani's brow furrowed, his face tense. He was over forty years old, but he was more muscular than his peers. Beneath his black suit was a sculpted body that betrayed no sign of weakness, and the sharp glint in his eyes seemed at odds with his title of corporate executive. His appearance had no bearing on the current situation, though—more importantly, a hotel guest had entered the docking area, and now he was in danger.

"Kakitani-sama, you must run! It's dangerou—"

"What's dangerous is there's a problem with how you've interpreted the situation."

"What?" She had twisted herself around to look at the guest and urge him to escape, but the cube AI's critique stopped her.

The AI's eye shutter opened and closed in annoyance as he stared at Kakitani in the doorway. *"You're* the one I have business with," he told Estella. "Obviously, I don't want any third parties stepping in. I took action to prevent that. I accessed the control systems and made it so the door couldn't be opened, but he undid it. Besides, there should be absolutely no one here other than staff without a *very* good reason."

"Correct," said Kakitani, clapping his hands. "I've never seen a strange AI like you... I'll call you Cubeman for now." Kakitani stepped forward as he continued his light applause. His well-shaped eyebrows remained furrowed as he glanced between the cube AI and Estella. "Is this some sort of AI date? Surely only AIs could come together as a humanoid and a heap of boxes to build a relationship, but…it's making me sick."

"Oh, come on, that's heartless. It's no fun being insulted, even if it is just some sleazebag's inaccurate assumptions," the cube AI replied.

"No fun. Only anger. Regret. Stop pretending to be human, you hunk of trash." Kakitani's face contorted in a snarl, his gentlemanly facade fully cast aside. He looked at the cube AI with hatred. No doubt he hated Estella as well; he'd already revealed his intense animosity toward AIs.

"I will ask another question, then. How did you get in here?" the cube AI asked.

"I don't have to answer that. Don't have a reason to talk to you for long either, Cubeman." Kakitani reached inside his jacket and pulled out a gun-like electroshock weapon: a taser. Instead of firing bullets, the taser fired electrodes that applied an electric current to the target. Kakitani's was likely one with a modified output so it would be effective against AI. One zap, and both Estella and the cube AI would be rendered helpless.

"I see," the cube AI said. He didn't waver, despite facing down a deadly weapon. On the contrary, his cubes shuddered in an approximation of a laugh, his half-lidded eye camera fixed on Kakitani. "Based on your equipment, your goal is obvious. It seems fate has more in mind for you and me than I originally thought. Or perhaps I should say you and *us*."

"What are you saying?" Kakitani asked.

"You really don't get it?" The cube AI opened and closed the shutter on his eye camera a few times, intentionally clacking it as it "blinked." He drew out a moment of silence while Kakitani gaped, his brows hoisted high in befuddlement. Then he said, "We definitely double-booked our dates just like this, fifteen years ago."

Kakitani gasped, his mind going blank.

The cube AI released Estella, leaving her with a sense of weightlessness. "Eek!" She was too slow to react, and she landed on her rear.

But the cube AI ignored her, using his legs to wheel closer to Kakitani. "Unfortunately, I didn't prepare any means of attack." He spread his four limbs wide, lowering his body as he moved within arm's reach of Kakitani. The man would be seriously hurt if the cube AI collided with him at that speed.

Kakitani had been caught off guard. His reaction was too slow; he wouldn't make it.

"And now—"

The cube AI was confident he would strike, but then it happened.

"Whoa!"

The entire space station shook violently for the second time. Unlike the first round of tremors, this quake had to have caused some vital damage to Sunrise. All the lights inside the station flickered for a moment, and the emergency alert rang out in all rooms.

"Red alert..."

There were three alert levels from least to most severe: yellow, orange, and red. A red alert signaled the highest level of danger, and it meant the damage was potentially catastrophic.

It had already begun.

Immediately, the artificial gravity disappeared, and the cube AI's four limbs floated up from the floor. "Urgh..." He continued moving forward with the leftover momentum from his dash.

More importantly, while this occurrence was a surprise for the cube AI, it didn't appear to be a surprise for Kakitani. "Bad timing, Cubeman," Kakitani jeered as he kicked off the floor and soared upward. Well, "upward" had no real meaning in zero gravity—he was simply moving toward the ceiling. He flipped in midair and aimed his taser with practiced motions. As the cube AI passed directly below him, Kakitani mercilessly fired.

"..."

His aim was true, and the electrodes pierced the cube AI's frame. Immediately, the electricity traveled down the wires, a million volts of current flowing into the AI's body. Even with all his advanced skills, he was helpless as the electricity fried his insides. Black smoke floated from his frame AI, and his legs flopped listlessly.

"..."

Just because the cube AI had been defeated, it didn't mean that Estella was out of the woods yet. Kakitani pulled out the electrodes from his taser, clicked in a new cartridge, and pointed the weapon at Estella. He was going to destroy her, the same way he'd destroyed the cube AI.

But before he could...

"Last resort!" shouted the cube AI from near Estella's chest as she floated in the zero gravity. At that moment, the burned frame shuddered, and his individual cubes shot out from his body. One of the cubes struck Kakitani head-on.

"Agh!" It didn't have that much force behind it, but the surprise attack made Kakitani cry out as he flew backward. He spun uncontrollably through the air. Estella watched as he hurtled farther off into the docking area.

"Now!"

Estella wasn't going to miss this opportunity. She put her hand on a protrusion coming from the wall and propelled herself directly toward the door. Along the way, she grabbed a stray piece of the cube AI and held it close to her chest.

"Care to explain what's going on?!" she shouted.

"Our first priority is getting out of here. Air lock, open!"

The shutter on his eye camera clattered open and closed as he undid the electronic lock. He was stealing her responsibility, since she was the control AI, but she didn't have time to complain. They slipped through the open door and escaped the docking area. Kakitani was coming up behind them, taser at the ready, but the door closed before he could attack again. With his line of fire shut off, he was effectively sealed in.

Estella watched this happen, then looked down at the cube AI in her arms. They were both still floating in zero gravity. "Do you feel like talking now? What was Kakitani-sama after? And what about *you*?"

"I told you, my goal is to serve humanity. That man claims to serve a similar purpose. His methods are a bit more violent, though."

"Serve humanity? What does that—"

"I assume his goal is to crash Sunrise into the Earth. They will try to pin it on the control AI," he told her. "You, that is, Estella."

The cube AI's explanation left Estella at a loss for words. His arrogant assertion was beyond the realm of belief. But if she *did* believe him, then Sunrise was in imminent danger.

"Are you saying Sunrise will be used for a terrorist attack?"

"Put simply, yes. And normally, there would have been no stopping it. That Kakitani fellow was probably going to attack you and take over the station. But he wasn't able to."

"Because you were there?"

"I'm a bit reluctant to boast about how it's all thanks to me, considering what happened... And it's looking more and more like my partner was right."

Estella frowned. "Hm?" The cube AI sounded somewhat upset, but she decided to follow up on that later. There were more pressing concerns. She was the manager of Sunrise hotel and the control AI for the station. "I won't let Sunrise fall. This is the dawn station that my owner, Ash, dreamed so much about... No one will use it for terrorism."

"I don't want to poke my nose into your personal situation, but I feel the same. Our enemy's first move ended in failure, so now..."

Estella was eager to keep the worst from happening, and the cube AI she carried seemed to feel the same. She wasn't entirely sure she'd accepted him, and she still felt threatened by Kakitani, but the cube AI had at least dropped his hostility toward her.

She had two extreme choices of who to trust: Kakitani or the cube AI.

As she struggled with her conflicting thoughts, the cube AI started grumbling. Estella looked at him, wondering what was going on, and saw that his eye camera shutter was narrowed in thought.

"Something's strange," he murmured.

"What? Something even stranger than everything else?"

"I'm currently hacked into Sunrise's systems. I tried to take over highest authority in the space station..."

"I can't exactly let that slide, but what about it?"

"There's a management AI currently accessing the system. I can't take back the authorization. It's the control AI, Diva D-09/Estella. It's *you*."

Estella's eyes went round. "...Pardon?"

The cube AI kept at it but to no avail. "It's no good. The control system for the station is stand-alone, and there's no way I can get control of an independent system without connecting directly to its core. What's bothering me is whoever's preventing me from infiltrating it." The cube AI sounded frustrated. "Besides, how'd Kakitani try to get into the system in the first place? The access code is tied to the control AI's positronic brain. He shouldn't be able to replicate it. That's why—"

"Oh! Wait!" cried Estella, cutting off the other AI's speculations. With the gravity still off, she was proceeding down the corridor like she was swimming, and ahead of them were two white men. Neither of them were Sunrise employees. "Mr. Louis, Mr. Hagen..."

"That matches with the guest list, but they're probably fake names," said the cube AI.

The men approached, slowed by the lack of gravity. Both of them locked their eyes on Estella, and their expressions were fierce. They looked at the AIs like Kakitani had back in the docking area.

"How could this happen during the grand opening of the hotel?!" Estella exclaimed.

"I understand how you feel, but we don't have time to sit around whining. Are you installed with self-defense programming?" asked the cube AI.

"Of course. It comes preinstalled, but..."

Estella only had the bare minimum. In the six years she'd been active, she had thankfully never been put in a situation where she had to rely on her self-defense programming. Her good fortune meant she had a reduced capacity for handling emergencies. But the two men coming toward her also had tasers, and Estella didn't have the confidence to handle a fistfight in zero gravity.

"Things are looking rather..." Estella trailed off, grabbing on to a wall to stop her forward momentum as she looked for an escape route. If they went back, they would return to the docking area where they'd locked Kakitani. There were no side routes to avoid these two men. Estella's face hardened as she began to feel like she was being backed into a corner.

Then the cube AI said, "Let's punch our way through 'em."

"What?" She had given up, unable to do anything, but there was still strength in his voice. As her eyes widened, something zoomed through the hall at high speed.

"In accordance with the Zeroth Law..."

"What the—gah!"

The flying form was a humanoid. It came from farther down the passage, crashing into the men as they drew closer to Estella and the cube AI. The interloper struck one of the men on the neck with a karate chop, knocking him unconscious.

"Wait! You're—ungh!"

"I will implement the Project."

The other man flipped through the air and quickly aimed his taser at his attacker, but they were moving freely through the zero-gravity space, bouncing from the floor to the ceiling and back again, keeping him from lining up his shot. It took mere seconds for a long leg to whip the taser from the man's hands and a palm to knock him unconscious.

Their rescuer was dressed in a hotel uniform, and their hair was tied in pigtails.

"Vivy...?" Estella said weakly, and the girl turned to look at her.

Vivy ran her fingers through her disheveled hair and said, "I'm sorry to keep you waiting, Estella." And then she smiled.

.:6:.

HER SYSTEM, knocked out from the impact, restarted.

A light lit up her consciousness. A scan ran through to check the status of the AI, Diva A-03/Vivy. 28 percent of her upper body was damaged. Her entire left arm was broken. 41 percent of her lower body was damaged. Her entire left leg was broken. Her head was barely within acceptable parameters. Over half a ton of weight had fallen on the unit.

After confirming the status of her frame, her position below a heavy object, and her memories from immediately before the accident, Vivy was able to understand what had happened to her. She had discovered Leclerc's broken frame in the cargo hold and then encountered the fake Estella, whom she'd engaged. Vivy had then initiated her self-defense programming but lost the subsequent fight. After that, she was crushed by a cargo container. Her system shut down, and she thought it would be impossible to start up again.

"There's no gravity..."

Something must have happened to the artificial gravity mechanism on board because the container was floating upward. Just a light push was enough to get it off her frame, allowing her to successfully extract herself. She had restarted, but the damage to her frame was severe.

Her left arm and left leg were both unusable, and almost every part of her was damaged in some way. It was a miracle her head hadn't been destroyed, but a section of her artificial skin had peeled off her forehead. She wouldn't want to be seen by a human in this condition.

Nevertheless, she needed to get moving in order to get the

situation under control. She had to find the fake Estella and prevent Sunrise from falling.

"But I have no chance of winning...in this condition."

She couldn't win even when she was at 100 percent. Things wouldn't go well if she needed to subdue the enemy by force while her performance was reduced by 40 percent. She wondered what to do, but then it came to her.

In the gravity-free cargo hold, a frame floated by.

"Leclerc..."

It was Leclerc's body and the positronic brain that had died when her neck was broken. Vivy looked the frame up and down. Other than the vital spot on the neck, it was in perfect condition.

"..."

Vivy kicked off from a container using her battered right leg, sending herself toward Leclerc's frame. Her eyes were open, frozen in a look of surprise. Vivy closed Leclerc's eyelids, then her own as if she were praying.

"I'm sorry, Leclerc. Please lend me your arms and legs."

She wasn't certain that she, a model built nearly twenty years ago, could swap parts with a model only five years old, but she had to take the risk. She detached the lower part of her left leg at the knee and did the same to Leclerc's frame. She brought the detached part to her own joint and connected it.

"Agh..."

A painful electrical pulse shot through her positronic brain, causing static in her vision. A moment later, it cleared. She checked her new left leg. It had connected without issue, so the rest would likely do the same.

Vivy replaced her parts in order of most damaged: left arm, right leg, and then her right arm. Leclerc's limbs perfectly slotted in for her own. She checked the feel of her limbs and looked at Leclerc's frame, now without arms or legs. With her eyes closed, she looked almost peaceful. Unfortunately, Vivy didn't have the time to mourn Leclerc's death.

Everything would be over if she didn't stop the fake Estella from accomplishing her goals.

Leclerc had given Vivy back her ability to stand, and to fight, so Vivy left her with just a few words. "I will save Sunrise," she swore.

With that, she left the cargo hold, swimming through Sunrise's halls as she searched for either Estella. The grand space hotel was now a cage without gravity. Eventually, she ran into Matsumoto and the real Estella, and she knocked out the two men closing in on them.

"So, you succeeded in meeting up with us. Nice timing, Vivy! It was very heroic of you to appear in our moment of need," Matsumoto said cheerfully.

"Matsumoto...why are you here?" Vivy asked, looking through half-lidded eyes at the cube AI Estella was hugging close to her ample bosom. What in the world was he doing here after going dark for so long?

"Well, you weren't very gung-ho about reformatting Estella, and I decided as your partner that it was a problem. I stowed away on a supply rocket to the space station, thinking I would carry out the Project myself. That was the plan, anyway," he explained.

"You're not even going to apologize? But then why are you with Estella? What about the reformatting?"

"Don't worry," Estella cut in. "I haven't been reformatted. But... Vivy, what's going on?"

Vivy couldn't hide her disappointment after Matsumoto shamelessly confessed to going it alone, but Estella seemed unhappy as she jumped into their conversation. It was the obvious question from her perspective. This strange little cube-shaped AI was in leagues with her employee. She might even feel betrayed.

"Matsumoto, what have you told Estella?" Vivy asked.

"Nothing about you. I *did* disclose a bit about why I came here and what her pursuers are after, if that's what you mean."

"Yes. Thank you." At the very least, the explanation would be more honest coming from Vivy rather than Matsumoto. Though they were well past the point of discussing honesty or dishonesty.

"Estella."

"What is it, Vivy?"

Vivy placed her hand on the wall and approached Estella directly. She swept up her own bangs, showing the damage done to her forehead by the fake Estella. Her other intentions, however, were obvious.

"..."

Estella looked into Vivy's eyes and, after a moment of hesitation, bared her own forehead as she leaned forward. Their foreheads came together, and the two initiated a datalink to swap information. Obviously, Vivy held back whatever she couldn't share, but she did inform Estella about the impostor, the reason Vivy had infiltrated Sunrise, and Leclerc's death.

"Impossible..." Estella breathed, a look of disbelief on her face after their foreheads separated. Her reaction made sense, especially since she'd only discovered the truth about Ash Corvick's death and his final wish a few hours ago. Those were just the start of the mind-blowing revelations that she would discover.

"I see... That frame—Leclerc—guided the enemy, didn't she? And they killed her to keep her quiet," Matsumoto said, calmly confirming what had happened despite Estella's shock. "What about this Estella look-alike?"

Leclerc's death was already in the past for him, and he had no interest in its surrounding circumstances. His ability to cut emotionlessly to the heart of the matter was surely needed, but that didn't mean it went over well.

"I don't really like it when you do that," Vivy told him.

"And I'm prepared to disagree with you. Enough so that I would come up to space myself, after all," he retorted.

Ever since they had disagreed on their first mission fifteen years ago, the two AIs' opinions had rarely aligned. But no matter how much they bickered, the situation was moving ahead without them.

"I've accepted what happened to Leclerc," Estella said, visibly upset as she took in the death of the AI she cared for like a little sister. She collected herself and tried to conceal her fatigue. "I'm also surprised to learn that you're an AI from somewhere else who came aboard for this day, Vivy. But I'm most surprised about the AI that harmed you and Leclerc."

"The fake that looks *exactly* like you," Vivy said.

"She most likely exists in order to frame Estella for Sunrise's crash," Matsumoto added. "I understand how she could fool humans, since she looks exactly like you, but..."

"But?"

"Gaining access to the control systems is a completely different story. No matter how similar they look on the outside, you can't replicate the access code generated from Estella's unique positronic brain waves. It should be impossible. Yet our enemy is doing just that. "

Vivy cocked her head to one side as she thought, and Matsumoto went silent. He was unable to come to a conclusion, and he had a far greater capacity for calculation than Vivy did. There was no way Vivy could solve it, assuming it was a problem that required logic. On the other hand, if the solution required emotions, it would make sense that Matsumoto couldn't solve it.

"Vivy, Cubeman—I know the answer," Estella said.

"I take back what I said about not introducing myself earlier, I'll do it now. My name is Matsumoto. What answer is that, then?"

Matsumoto corrected Estella with his real name since she was still calling him a name based on his appearance. She nodded, then her elegant brows crinkled as if she was enduring some pain. "The AI that hurt Vivy and Leclerc... Her name is Elizabeth. Her official designation is Diva D-09β/Elizabeth."

"D-09β?" Vivy and Matsumoto said at the same time. They had never heard a designation like that, which in itself was odd.

Estella watched their reactions, but then her eye cameras looked off into the distance. "Elizabeth and I are the only Songstress-type twin sisters... You see, we were made as an experiment. We also have the same positronic brain. Development was stopped partway through, and the Twin Sisters Project was canceled... And then Elizabeth was disposed of."

"..."

"But if there's an AI who looks the same as me and uses an access code generated by my positronic brain that shouldn't be replicable, then her existence is the only possibility." Estella shook her head and smiled wanly. "It seems today is the day my past catches up to me."

.:7:.

"**E**VERYONE, PLEASE REMAIN CALM as you move. Do not panic. Follow staff orders. Remember your training when moving in zero gravity. I repeat, do not panic and remain calm." The manager AI dealt with the situation in front of her in a collected fashion, bringing the guests back from the edge of panic.

AI staff really shined when it came to responding to emergency situations. They could act in accordance with a prepared manual, they need not express heightened emotions, and they reacted faster than humans. AIs could also run parallel programs, dealing with several tasks at once. The gap between AI and human capabilities was one that shouldn't be needlessly bridged.

Just then, a human staff member ran over to one of the manager AIs. "Manager! We guided the guests from the observation deck to the escape shuttle. The AI staff are handling whoever is left," she reported.

"Thank you. If that's done, you should evacuate along with the guests. I do hope this doesn't turn out to be too big of an issue," the manager AI replied with a note of concern, brows scrunched low.

The human staff member looked down in disappointment and said, "It's really unfortunate... It was the grand opening too. Everything was going so well..."

"..."

"Your singing was so beautiful, Estella. It made me think that everything was going to go well from here on out," she added, looking truly upset. Based on the staff list, she was in housekeeping.

Estella softly wrapped her arms around the staff member's stiff body and drew her into a gentle hug. She could feel the woman shrinking away from her touch in surprise, but she said, "It'll be okay. Soon we'll learn that it was nothing at all. Just make sure to do your job properly so we can all have something to talk about later."

"Y-yeah. Sorry. I'm so sorry, Estella. This must be even harder on you."

The tight hug helped the woman pull herself together. Estella smiled at her, and she nodded firmly before dashing off to catch up and guide the group of people leaving the observation deck.

"..."

Estella watched the evacuating guests leave, then looked around. The screens were still transparent, leaving the room surrounded by the endless expanse of space. As she looked out at the stars twinkling in the distance, the corners of her mouth curled up. That wicked grin bore no resemblance to the benevolent smile she'd just shown the worker.

"Hah, look at me now... I can do anything you can do."

The words that slipped from her lips lacked kindness in favor of ridicule. Estella—or rather, the *fake* Estella—looked around the room with a fierce glint in her eyes as constant transmissions were delivered to her consciousness by the other AI staff members.

It was the AI staff's responsibility in this zero-gravity station to go through each of the facilities and locate those guests whose whereabouts were unconfirmed. There was a difference in how humans and AIs handled unforeseen circumstances, but "Estella" was able to see what was happening throughout the entire station and guide the AI staff. No one suspected at all that it was this "Estella" who had damaged the space station.

"Beth...can you hear me?"

Just as she was turning her thoughts to the next stage of the plan, she received a transmission on a different network from the one the AI staff were using. Her eyebrows shot up at the sound of the familiar voice, and her cheeks turned slightly red. *"Master, what is your status? Is everything going according to plan?"* asked Elizabeth, sending the transmission to her owner, the man who called himself Kakitani.

His role was to eliminate Estella, the real control AI for Sunrise, the one whose position Elizabeth had stolen. Estella was Elizabeth's detestable twin sister, and Elizabeth had been anxiously awaiting word of her elimination. However, that wasn't the response she got back from Kakitani.

"Sorry, I messed up. The target is currently moving through the station."

"Really?"

"Yes. And she has help. AI help, specifically. There's a cube-type AI that's real adept at programming. It locked the door to the docking area."

"Oh! I'll open it now!" Elizabeth had control of all of Sunrise's systems, and she immediately accessed the core to request that the docking area door be unlocked. But it was heavily protected. *"What is this?!"* Angered by the abnormally powerful protection, she forcibly opened it with her authority. Although she'd succeeded, she'd also learned that she would have no chance at it from a straight programming perspective.

"Thanks. Now I can get out," said Kakitani.

"Master! That AI is—"

"It said it's been fifteen years since then... That thing is the first stumbling block."

Elizabeth was trying to say that they needed to be cautious considering the strength of the protection the AI had put in place, but Kakitani cut in with something that caused Elizabeth's thought processes to freeze.

"The first stumbling block" was the cause of an unforgettable wound to Toak, the organization that Kakitani and Elizabeth belonged to. Fifteen years ago, before the organization had even taken on the name Toak, a group of like-minded individuals banded together to enlighten the world.

This included a younger Kakitani.

They had failed. Kakitani had barely managed to escape, and several of his companions had been captured. Their failure had been caused by a mysterious entity who had unexpectedly interfered in their work. Toak continued to tell the story to others in the organization, and they had taken to calling it "the first stumbling block."

After that day, Toak came together with Kakitani at its core and carefully continued their work of enlightenment. There had been no major failures since, and memories of the first stumbling block slowly faded from the forefront of their minds.

"Agh, we made it all this way, and now *past problems are coming back to haunt us?!"*

"This is a massive plan we've had in the works for fifteen years, and that thing figured it out? I find it hard to believe our fellows leaked the info, but considering how skilled it is, it's not surprising it managed to get the info from somewhere," Kakitani said.

It was impossible in this day and age to completely withhold any information. You could obviously put several layers of protection over your data, keeping it as secure as possible, but an excellent hacker could break in eventually. Toak took the utmost care when handling their information. They'd even purchased Elizabeth with the intent of making one of her roles data protection.

When she heard that her protection had been insufficient, guilt welled in her chest. *"Master, I'm—"*

"Save the regret for later. Right now, hurry up and get the plan moving. Carry out the role you've been given. Soon you'll need to act as the manager—your sister."

"...Understood, Master."

"I'm going after the target that slipped away from me. I'll contact you again." With that short goodbye, Kakitani cut off the transmission. It was curt, but that was the sort of man Elizabeth's master was.

Having received her orders, Elizabeth closed her eyes and let herself stand in silence for a moment. She had a bad habit of getting too emotional. In fact, one of the reasons she had been disposed of despite having the same specs as her twin sister, Estella, was that her emotional function was incomplete. At least, that was what Elizabeth told herself, insisting she needed to fix it.

"From now on... From now on..." she said solemnly, turning her mind fully back to the role she had to play.

Fulfilling her role was the greatest mission Elizabeth had ever been given. She should have been destroyed before she could even fulfill her original purpose, but her master had given her a new one instead. This was all she could do to repay him. And if fulfilling that role meant getting revenge on the person she hated most in the world as well, then there was absolutely no reason she should refuse.

"The Sunrise, your beloved dawn station, will plunge straight into the ground, Estella," Elizabeth hissed in a voice filled with unending, unforgiving hatred.

Elizabeth turned back to the situation at hand and twisted her expression into one of kindness and responsibility, making her look exactly like her twin sister. She swam slowly and gracefully through the zero-gravity station.

.: 8 :.

"**Y**OUR TWIN SISTER has the same positronic brain, and she was disposed of...?"

After listening to Estella's explanation, Vivy and Matsumoto looked at each other. Obviously Vivy hadn't had that information before, but she was surprised that Matsumoto hadn't known about it.

"Was there really just no information about Estella's twin sister?" Vivy asked him in a transmission.

"At the very least, that information wasn't included in any data regarding the investigation of the Sun-Crash Incident. We can guess that OGC, the company that developed the twins, kept the project a secret since it got canceled and Elizabeth was scrapped. Still, it's odd that there's absolutely no data concerning this whatsoever." Matsumoto seemed entirely caught off guard by the existence of Estella's twin sister, despite the fact that he had come from a

future where they'd researched all this extensively. It had nothing to do with his investigation skills. *"It seems that OGC, the forerunner of AI development...has secrets that even I don't know,"* he added, and Vivy nodded in agreement.

OGC was also the company that developed Vivy, so she wasn't entirely unrelated to them. Vivy didn't know every single detail about the company, in the same way that a human didn't know every single detail about their parents, but she realized that she'd never even considered the fact that she only knew the most superficial information.

"You two are pretty surprised, aren't you? If you're done, can we move on to the real issue at hand?" Estella said after waiting for the two AIs to process the data.

Vivy looked up, and Estella tossed her the Matsumoto cube she'd been hugging to her chest. Vivy reflexively caught it, then asked Matsumoto, "Can you move on your own?"

"I can, but I was designed to move better with multiple cubes. I'm slower than a snail with just my core as I am now," he replied.

"You could have just said 'yes but slowly' and been done with it." Vivy was tired of Matsumoto's wordy way of speaking, so she shoved him into the breast pocket of her uniform.

As Estella watched the two of them, she said, "An old friendship coming back to life." There was just a hint of sarcasm in her voice. "Anyway, back to the real issue at hand. I would like to double-check something. Vivy and Matsumoto, you have come to Sunrise to prevent it from crashing. Is that correct?"

"Yes, that is our plan," Matsumoto said.

"Several challenging obstacles have appeared in our way, but we want to prevent the crash," said Vivy.

"Okay. If that's the case, then we can all work together. Let's confirm the current situation and create a schedule for our targets," said Estella, nodding and clapping her hands together as she quickly took the initiative. As the control AI, she knew Sunrise inside and out. And as the manager, she was a leader adept in many staff roles. It was only natural she would take over. For the same reason, Vivy and Matsumoto listened obediently, since they were far removed from the many hats Estella wore.

"Our ultimate goal is to prevent Sunrise's crash, then. In order to do that, we have to regain access to the control room. But..."

"The path to the control room has been sealed off by Diva D-09β/Elizabeth, who currently wields the authority," Vivy finished for her.

"It'll be tricky, but our only choice is to hack every door as we come to it. You'll need me for that," Matsumoto chimed in. "Should be easy enough to undo if I can connect directly to the terminal..."

Estella nodded. "That's reassuring. It seems we'll be relying entirely on you. Thank you."

"Leave it to me! I like being relied on," Matsumoto said, sounding somewhat happy.

That surprised Vivy. Then she noticed a wink from Estella that only she could see. Apparently, Vivy was losing to her in terms of handling Matsumoto. That just meant she had to make herself all the more useful in some other area.

"We might encounter people like Kakitani-sama on the way..." Estella murmured.

"It would be safe to assume we will," Matsumoto said. "We should also assume that they're all equipped with tasers. There are at least five mixed in with the guests... And it's only a matter of time until the first one we sealed off will escape, so we should assume we'll run into three of them at some point."

"Then there's the issue of dealing with Elizabeth," Vivy pointed out. "I had no chance against her when we fought in the cargo hold. She's out of my league in terms of her combat programming."

"Hmph. Let me see the fight logs." Matsumoto pulled up the logs from her fight. He looked over them, hemming and hawing. "I see...hmm. She's a difficult opponent. It's not just that she has excellent combat programming. She's far more experienced too. It appears that after your twin sister was supposed to be disposed of, Estella, she ended up being put to use in combat-heavy situations."

Matsumoto paid no mind as he casually said something that was better left unsaid, and Vivy's mouth turned down in a frown. Estella shook her head and didn't chide Matsumoto for his insensitivity, which told Vivy she was all right.

Matsumoto ignored the emotions being shared between the two humanoid AIs and continued on. "However, it should be all right to deal with Elizabeth later. We know that it's unlikely we will encounter her on the way to the control room."

"How can you be certain of that?" asked Vivy.

"Because she has to pretend to be Estella and guide the guests and staff of Sunrise during their evacuation. She can't go back to being Elizabeth until that's complete."

His explanation was plausible. In the original Sun-Crash Incident, the staff and guests who survived gave statements claiming it was Estella herself who ordered them to board the escape shuttle. In the original history, Arnold was among the casualties, his fate going the way of Sunrise. The fake Estella clearly didn't want any more victims than that. Just like in the original history, Elizabeth would be acting as Estella to ensure everyone else's safety. That meant they had an opportunity while she was occupied.

As Vivy caught up with the situation, Matsumoto told the two humanoids, "It appears we've decided what we should do."

With a curt nod, Vivy turned in the direction of the control room and said, "We'll hurry to the control room, and Estella will get her system access back. Then we can stop Sunrise from falling to Earth."

"I will not let this station fall from space!" Estella declared, her expression resolute. Vivy looked at her, and Estella nodded back. "Come, Vivy. It's the hotel staff's duty to handle any trouble that arises at Sunrise's grand opening. Let's get it done."

Vivy wholeheartedly agreed. Estella kicked off the wall and flew bravely through the zero-gravity hall; Vivy followed suit. They intended to stop the fall of Sunrise to prevent the Sun-Crash Incident.

This was the saga of Vivy, Estella, and the time-transcending plan of those two songstress sisters.

CHAPTER 5

The Songstresses' Song

.:1:.

THE POSITRONIC BRAIN formed the consciousness, where an AI began.

This technological breakthrough gave AIs something akin to a human brain. It had led to the modern age in which AI flourished, and it was what gave AI models with consciousnesses their "individuality" similar to a human's personality. On top of that, it was impossible to recreate the positronic brain waves—the consciousness—of any one AI.

Using the same frame along with a positronic brain manufactured by the same company created an AI of the same model, but it wouldn't *recreate* the original individual. Just as cloning didn't duplicate an organism's personality, you couldn't make two AIs that were exactly the same. Although humans were akin to gods to AIs, they still couldn't manipulate individuality.

That was where the Twin Brains Project came in. Twin sisters Elizabeth and Estella were studied in the hope of making waves in positronic brain research and development. Researchers prepared a pair of proto-brains—positronic brains before any conscious-ness developed—in almost identical environments. Both proto-brains received the same stimuli, and the two units were allowed to interact in an effort to guide the randomness of emerging in-dividuality along the same trajectory. Their development would be adjusted as needed in order to align with the predicted final point of their growth, and researchers constantly monitored their progress.

It was a monumental undertaking.

Positronic brains' individuality was apparent in the differing brain waves they produced. In other words, the goal of the Twin Brains Project was to produce two positronic brains that cre-ated the exact same brain waves. Any positronic brains deemed failures during the project—that is, those that didn't meet the project's goals—were disposed of. The consciousness of that unit would be ended before it ever received its own body.

The exact number of positronic brains used in the project was unknown. Only after there were mountains of deceased brains did the researchers have success with Estella and Elizabeth. Their brain waves were 99.8 percent identical.

Despite not being *exactly* alike, Estella and Elizabeth's brain waves were so closely matched that they could easily use access points requiring individual codes generated by their own brains. That shared access was a byproduct of the Twin Brains Project—nothing more, nothing less.

Once Estella was deemed a success, given her own body, and allowed to operate as an AI, she once asked the researchers what their real goal had been. This was the response: "If we can replicate individuality using completely identical positronic brains...then we should be able to bring an AI back from the dead."

An AI died when their brain was destroyed. Even if you took backups of their memories, installed those onto a new positronic brain, and restarted them, they would hardly be the same. It was an incomplete revival where they only succeeded in creating a different individual with the same memories. The researchers wanted to achieve true resurrection of AI, but their hopes never came to fruition.

Eventually, replicating positronic brains was deemed forbidden territory in the field of AI research. The researchers lost their jobs immediately, and the Twin Brains Project was canceled. Any findings were destroyed. The twins, Estella and Elizabeth, were all that remained of the project. Their fates forked due to a slight gap in their activation time.

"Diva D-09α/Estella is already active, so we won't dispose of her yet. The positronic brain and body of Diva D-09β/Elizabeth are not, so they will be disposed of. We'll decide what happens to Estella later."

Around the time of the AI Naming Law, another law was being pushed through: the AI Protection Law, which treated an active AI as an individual with rights. It gave AIs the same sort of rights pet dogs might have. Estella was already active, so rather than face decimation, she was dispatched to the space hotel at the request of its developing company.

Elizabeth, on the other hand, was one step away from receiving individual rights. She had no choice but to accept her demise, and she was taken away to the disposal facility.

All this time, Estella had thought her twin sister was dead.

"Is that really you, Elizabeth?"

.: 2 :.

"ESTELLA, FOCUS."

"Oh." Her consciousness had drifted away for a brief moment, running back to her memories from long ago. The distant tug on her arm brought her back to the present. Vivy was in front of her, touching her arm, concern in her eyes. Their situation was still pressing.

If Estella experienced a malfunction that caused her to crash, it would be a major issue. She apologized for worrying her companions and grabbed the passage's handrail.

"..."

Moving in zero gravity required more precision than she'd expected. Generally, the only times anyone regularly experienced zero gravity were during travel to the station or on the cargo rockets, but one wouldn't normally move around freely in such places. Zero gravity in an area this spacious made even Estella uneasy. She felt something in her consciousness like a longing for the stability gravity provided.

Centrifugal force was a central component in the creation of artificial gravity. The space station was shaped like a huge ring.

The ring spun forcefully, and the centrifugal force produced was enough to maintain the station's gravity at 1 g—the same as on Earth.

The powered rotation of the station had been stopped, cutting off the gravity; as the vestiges of momentum kept the station moving a small bit, there was just enough centrifugal force remaining that they could tell up from down in the hallway.

"I can't deny it's rough going," Matsumoto said. "We've just gotten through the second closed barrier. We can assume we'll need to go through fourteen more on our way to the control room... I feel faint."

"Stop complaining," Vivy snapped. "It's better if there are only doors in our way."

"Eh, you may be right. Thankfully, this space station isn't a fortress. These barriers are safety measures for sealing off dangerous areas in the event of a disaster, not for blocking the advancement of attackers. I can also tell that the one in control, presumably Elizabeth, is a solid opponent."

"..."

The bulwark ahead slid down as it sensed Vivy approaching with Matsumoto in her breast pocket. Matsumoto immediately hacked into it, sending it back up, assuming its job was complete. Surprised by his skill, Estella averted her gaze.

Vivy looked back at her, eyes narrowing gently. "Can I ask about Elizabeth?"

"...In return, will you answer my questions about you two?"

"I'm not sure..." Vivy murmured, grappling with how to respond.

"I'm joking, Vivy. Sorry for teasing you," Estella said, sticking her tongue out playfully. Then her face hardened. "Both Elizabeth and I were supposed to be disposed of when the Twin Sisters Project was canceled. But since I was already active, I managed to avoid disposal, thanks to the AI Protection Law. Elizabeth, on the other hand..."

"Her positronic brain hadn't been connected yet. That's why she was disposed of, correct?"

"Yes... I could only watch. Elizabeth always stayed in my heart, though. I think I treated you and Leclerc like little sisters as a way to make up for her loss..." Estella could only laugh at herself as she realized why she'd been so motherly to hotel newcomers and AIs who had been active for a short time. "Elizabeth and I were together before our positronic brains even developed their individuality. Our brain waves ended up being 99.8 percent identical, but our personalities didn't match."

"Yeah... She seemed like you when she was pretending, but she was very different once she dropped the act."

"You met her, didn't you, Vivy? What was she like?"

The time Estella had spent with Elizabeth was ultimately quite short, lasting only for the duration of their development and brain-wave measurement. Elizabeth had been disposed of before she could even be placed in an identical body. That meant Estella had never interacted with her sister while she could walk and talk.

"She seemed violent, maybe maladjusted," Vivy told her.

"You sound like you're evaluating a child even though you've been active for significantly less time."

Vivy grimaced at Estella's reaction to her unreserved evaluation of Elizabeth. It confused Estella, but Matsumoto made sure to cut in with a forced laugh. Vivy rapped him lightly through the cloth of her uniform and glared straight ahead. The three AIs turned again to face the closed bulwark, but there was something in their way.

"Is that someone who hasn't evacuated yet...?" Estella wondered aloud.

"Obviously not, considering the taser in his hand," Matsumoto said. "Vivy?"

"Leave it to me."

Vivy took Matsumoto from her pocket and tossed him to Estella. He floated through the air, and she easily caught him. Then Vivy launched off the floor. The muscular man in his black suit put up a good fight, but he was no match for Vivy's self-defense programming. Estella pulled Matsumoto to her chest and watched in silence as Vivy showed off specs that went beyond hotel functions.

"This leaves our enemies' presumed numbers at two... One of them is likely chasing us. Vivy, are your arms and legs operating effectively?" Matsumoto asked.

"They're fine. Their compatibility was not guaranteed, but they move without issue," she said, opening and closing her pale fists. She pulled off the defeated man's shirt and used it to bind his arms and legs. The synthetic skin on her forehead and her hotel uniform had been damaged, and it was obvious her arms and legs had once belonged to Leclerc.

"..."

As Estella stood still, memories of her days with Leclerc weighed heavily on her heart. After Daybreak opened, OCG dispatched her to the hotel. The two of them continued to work together for longer than Estella had ever suspected they would, and Leclerc really had become something of a sister to her. Her consciousness trembled in agony at the thought that her own real sister had destroyed the cheery housekeeping AI.

They should be able to foil Elizabeth's plans if they made it to the control room and took back her access rights. Once they did that, Estella would meet her twin sister for the first time. She didn't know what frame of mind would prepare her for that, but she kept this anxiety to herself.

Her twin sister had killed Leclerc, someone who was like a sister to her, and she was trying to use the station for the sake of violence. This same station was the culmination of Ash and Arnold's dreams.

Once Vivy had subdued the man, Matsumoto got to hacking the closed bulwark and opened the path forward. "Okay, it's open. Now there are only—".

"Do you think this is really the time to be worrying about the number of remaining bulwarks?" came a cruel-sounding female voice from the passage ahead of them.

"..."

Estella didn't remember ever hearing a voice like this—but Vivy and Matsumoto did. The two of them glanced at Estella just as her voice identification finished its analysis. The voice pattern registered as her own. And if this model was the same as Estella, it could only be one AI.

"Elizabeth…"

"Hi, Sis. I've been wanting to meet you. I have really, *really* been looking forward to our reunion," said the other AI. Estella might've felt like she was looking in a mirror, except she had never seen such a terrible smile on her own face. No records showed she'd ever initiated such an antagonistic pattern.

Elizabeth stood there, her teeth bared in a wide grin, carrying Arnold with his hands pinned behind his back.

.: 3 :.

SOMETIME BEFORE the twin sisters' reunion, a kind voice asked, "Estella, are you all right?"

Elizabeth put a hand on the wall to stop her movement. Looking toward the source, she saw a blond man: Arnold Corvick, owner of Estella and Sunrise. In that way, he was the person closest to Estella.

Arnold moved clumsily in zero gravity, wholly unaccustomed to the environment. According to Elizabeth's data, this was his first time traveling to space, and he didn't appear to have much experience with it.

"Crap! Grab a hold of me, will you, Estella?" he called.

"Ah, here… Take my hand."

Arnold nearly floated right past Elizabeth, but she reached out to him, and he scrambled to grab her hand. She tugged him to a stop, and he let out a sigh of relief.

Elizabeth observed him up close, a nagging suspicion in her

consciousness. Why was Arnold asking after Estella? "What's the matter, Mr. Corvick? You should have been led to the escape shuttle along with the hotel guests, just in case."

"I should have, yes, but there's a problem. Two of our guests contacted the staff to say they separated from their daughter after they all left the observation deck."

"..."

"The staff are supposed to be in the process of searching the station, but the transmission signals are unstable. I thought they might need the help. I do represent the hotel, so I stepped up."

"I appreciate the thought, but..."

Arnold gave her a playful wink, still holding tightly to her arm. His intent was admirable, but he was sorely lacking the capability to follow through. At best, leaving him to wander around the station in zero gravity would only end with him in danger as well.

"..."

Even so, Elizabeth herself couldn't ignore the news he'd brought her. An unrelated member of the public was still in the station, and that threw a wrench in Toak's plans. Casualties needed to be kept to an absolute minimum. This was Kakitani's conviction, something he always insisted they keep to. Elizabeth was under strict orders to avoid putting any humans in danger.

Problems just kept popping up one after another.

Anger boiled over in one region of her consciousness as Elizabeth was forced to make some unexpected adjustments. Several issues had already appeared, the worst of which was that the control AI, Estella, was still wandering the station. She should've been taken out when the centrifugal force generating the artificial gravity was stopped.

Currently, Estella was probably heading to the control room to take back Sunrise. She had two helpers: a walking obstacle so old that it might as well be petrified and the one they called the first stumbling block. And now a member of the public had gone missing all of a sudden.

At this point, there was no need to explain why Elizabeth was frustrated. Regardless, she was going forward with the original plan. While impersonating Estella, she ordered staff and guests to evacuate. Next, she would get rid of those who were in her way and make Sunrise crash. Then her mission would be complete.

To that end, she said, "Mr. Corvick, thank you for the information. However, I would ask that you leave this matter to myself or the other staff members and evacuate along with the other guests."

"I want to say you don't have to worry about me, but...pushing it will only cause more trouble for you, won't it?"

"Thank you for understanding."

"Harsh." Arnold must have realized quickly that his presence would only serve to slow Estella down. Regret flickered on his face, but he let go of Estella and turned back the way he'd come.

With him gone, Elizabeth thought about heading them off at the control room, which—

"By the way, can I just check something?" Arnold said, holding up a finger like he'd suddenly remembered something. He had yet to kick off the floor.

"Hm? What is it? Please, ask away."

"All right. I want you to be completely honest with me."

Elizabeth waited for the question, entirely unguarded.

"Are you *really* Estella? Not some other AI that looks exactly like her?"

"…"

The question momentarily made Elizabeth's consciousness go blank. She quickly fought through it and smiled at Arnold, his expression innocent. "You have quite the intuition, Mr. Hotel Kingpin."

.: 4 :.

NOW THE TWO SISTERS had reunited.

"So yeah, the sloppy owner noticed something he shouldn't have and became a witness of my emotional reunion with my big sis," Elizabeth said with a wicked smile as she tightened her hold around Arnold's neck. Her other hand pinned Arnold's hands behind him, and she could clearly hurt him right away if he tried to resist.

"Mr. Corvick!"

"H-hey, sorry about this, Estella. I was pretty cool up until I saw through the fake. Not so much afterward… Kinda wish everyone could've seen me be the hero, though," Arnold said casually despite his pained grimace as he endured the joint lock. He was trying to assuage Estella's worries, and his concern was apparent. Estella's lip trembled as she glanced between him and Elizabeth, her fists clenched tightly.

Vivy glanced sideways at Estella with a frown, knowing she couldn't do anything rash. Vivy was just under fifteen feet away from Elizabeth. Even if there was gravity, she wouldn't be able to close that distance immediately. "This is bad..."

"Looks like we've moved into a difficult phase of the operation. We could be positive and appreciate how we can have a direct confrontation with the AI culprit, but the hostage does make things painful," Matsumoto agreed, verbose as always.

Upon noticing Vivy, Elizabeth let out a dramatic gasp and said, "Aren't you the chick I knocked out in the cargo hold? I thought you broke when you got crushed by the cargo container, but it looks like you're real persistent. Your arms and legs were totally wrecked too."

"It's because the gravity went away before I was crushed to death. I got away thanks to that. I also changed my limbs out for Leclerc's, the girl you destroyed."

"Uh-huh. It seems being nice and only damaging her neck came back to bite me in the end. I also should've checked to make sure you were actually non-operational. Eh, not that any of that matters now." Elizabeth's tone betrayed no guilt.

Something about her attitude felt off to Vivy, but she didn't have a chance to figure it out. She and Estella watched Elizabeth cautiously as she barked out a laugh.

"You can guess what I want, can't you? If you don't want your precious owner's neck snapped, you'll behave. That goes for both of you—Estella *and* the AI chick."

"..."

"Or are you going to abandon poor Mr. Arnold Corvick here? If you're looking at the big picture, killing one to save many makes the most sense, doesn't it?" Elizabeth said.

While Elizabeth hadn't intended this, her words struck such a personal chord in Vivy. Kill one to save many. It was almost as if she were talking about watching a passenger plane crash, despite knowing it was going to happen, for the sake of the Singularity Project. And now there was the torturous decision of whether they should allow Arnold Corvick to die to avoid the crash.

It was an agonizing situation. Even if Vivy *did* choose to let Arnold die, she would still have to face Elizabeth head-on and defeat her. That was the single greatest hurdle.

Vivy could only imagine an outcome like the one in the cargo hold if she rushed into a rematch against Elizabeth. At the end of it all, it wasn't just Vivy's destruction hanging in the balance; the price of her carelessness could be Arnold's life as well.

As they struggled to decide what to do, yet another challenge arrived.

A man appeared from around the corner behind Vivy. "I finally caught up to you... Things took an unexpected turn, I see," he said of the apparent impasse.

Estella turned back, and her eyes narrowed. "Kakitani-sama..."

The man was in his late thirties or early forties, and he wore a rugged expression. He was the real culprit of the terrorist attack. Vivy checked the guest list and learned that his name was Kakitani Yugo. The man had finally caught up after being sealed in the docking area, sandwiching Vivy and Estella between him and Elizabeth in the bulwark's gate.

The situation was getting worse for Vivy and the others on all fronts.

"Master! Are you all right?!" Elizabeth cried, brightening when Kakitani joined them. Her combative expression from a moment ago disappeared as she looked at Kakitani with trust and respect in her eyes.

The fact that she called him "Master" made it clear he was her owner. Vivy found Elizabeth's attitude toward him surprising, since she'd learned through her datalink with Matsumoto that Kakitani was abnormally hostile toward AIs. She wasn't wrong.

"Looks like you're not sticking to the plan, 'Estella.' Did you forget your orders?" he growled.

"Oh, no, I just—"

"Why have you taken the hotel owner hostage? How many times have I told you my policies? An AI who doesn't follow orders is an AI without worth. When did you become so defective?"

"…"

After mercilessly berating the tool for taking her own actions, Kakitani looked at Arnold and sucked in a breath. "I've told you a thousand times to avoid bloodshed."

"B-but this man realized I wasn't Estella! I had to—"

"You could have made any excuse and gotten out of there. You're the one to blame for throwing out that option and jumping for the easy solution. Now I have to adjust the plan," said Kakitani, his words weighing so heavily on Elizabeth that she looked away with a grimace.

As Vivy listened to their exchange, an encrypted transmission from Matsumoto entered her consciousness. *"Vivy, we need to move the situation along. You should take Kakitani hostage."*

"But then Arnold—"

"Kakitani's never going to let Arnold go alive. If Arnold gets back to Earth, then Kakitani's plan for the Sun-Crash Incident won't work. I did tell you Arnold died in the original history as well, didn't I?" Matsumoto's heartless words cut right through Vivy's concern for Arnold's safety.

When he brought up the original history, Vivy was forced to acknowledge that Arnold's death was as good as decided. On the original Sunrise, the one without Vivy and Matsumoto, Elizabeth and Estella's switch went off without issue, and the guests and staff were guided to the escape shuttle. But Arnold had probably noticed something going on with "Estella" in the original history as well. Once he discovered that she was really Elizabeth in disguise, she took him hostage, and he died.

That seemed to be Arnold Corvick's unavoidable fate on Sunrise.

"If we surrender here for Arnold, we'll fail. Then Arnold will be killed, and Sunrise will crash into the Earth. The time has come to make a decision and to follow the Zeroth Law."

An AI may not harm humanity or, by inaction, allow humanity to come to harm.

Following the Zeroth Law would mean choosing to save humanity—not Arnold in the here and now. That was what

Matsumoto was directing her to do, and it was the decision she'd made fifteen years ago. But now...

"Vivy..." Estella hugged Matsumoto to her chest, her eyes imploring.

There was her owner, Arnold. Then her twin, Elizabeth, whom she thought she'd lost forever. Estella had also lost Leclerc, the AI she thought of as her own sister, and she was in danger of losing Sunrise, the culmination of Ash's dreams. All these factors weighed on Estella's consciousness. The only one she had to rely on right now was Vivy, the one who knew the future and was attempting to change it.

Well, maybe not *just* Vivy.

"Matsumoto, is there really no other way?"

"You're still complaining about this? I explained it plenty to you fifteen years ago when—"

"You did. But things aren't decided yet. And this situation is different from back then. It's not like doing everything we can to save Arnold is going to hinder the Project."

"..."

"We are definitely going to encounter situations this difficult in the future too. Are we always going to settle for the second-best option? Is that all the songstress Vivy and the super AI from the future are capable of?"

"Your attempt to rile me up is obvious," Matsumoto said dryly as Vivy drove her point home. It made her regret the words she chose, assuming they were the wrong ones. But she didn't need to worry so much.

"I guess you could argue that prioritizing human life wouldn't be a violation of our AI domain so long as it doesn't interfere with the Project."

"Oh! Matsumoto, do you mean—"

"There is one thing we can do, but it will require us both to go beyond our limits."

"If it'll help us accomplish our orders as AI, then I'll do it!" Vivy declared. She had no reason to hesitate. Her impassioned words made Matsumoto partially close the shutter of his eye camera in reluctance.

While the two of them were having their transmission exchange, the situation around them continued to deteriorate.

"I didn't intend for this to happen, but my tool created this situation. I'll have to be flexible and put it to good use," Kakitani was saying.

Vivy and the others weren't certain how much they could trust his alleged aversion to bloodshed, considering he'd apparently deemed Arnold a necessary sacrifice. He had weighed the importance of his goals against human life and followed the tip of the scale. He had chosen to kill one to save many, just like Vivy and Matsumoto.

It seemed Kakitani and his group had been in this position before. They were the ones who had attacked Assemblyman Aikawa in order to prevent the AI Naming Law from passing. Now, wielding the same ideals, they wanted to swap Elizabeth in for Estella as they tried to cause the Sun-Crash Incident.

Kakitani looked at Arnold, still held captive by Elizabeth.

An array of emotions flashed in his dark eyes before he said, "Sorry, but this is for justice. The people have to know. Someone has to sound the alarm about how absurd it is to allow AIs to hold sway in all aspects of our lives."

"You don't think AIs are like neighbors we should care for?" Arnold asked with a grimace.

Kakitani's eyebrows shot up. "Is this a neighbor you *care* for?" He pointed his taser at Estella and said, "This is just an intruder in human form."

"Ugh, my ears hurt. Not that I have ears," Matsumoto joked. He had come from a future in which humanity was destroyed after their relationship with AIs worsened.

Kakitani moved his finger to the trigger in a coldhearted attempt to destroy Estella. That was when Vivy and Matsumoto made their move.

"Vivy, get ready. This won't hurt...but it will be hell."

She didn't even have time to ask what he meant by that. The moment after his transmission, Vivy's consciousness was overcome with a change.

"Aaagh!"

Her positronic brain was drowned in a white-hot ocean of data. As it washed over her, Vivy's thoughts boiled. The color instantly drained from the world around her as her range of visual perception expanded, and her brain had to process the mass quantities of new data coming in. Sound and motion slowed to a near stop all around her, like time itself had frozen. Every second felt a hundred times longer than normal, allowing her to react and move instantly.

"…"

"God Mode."

Those two words from Matsumoto were enough for her to understand what was happening. Vivy had been plunged into a state where she was cognizant of everything around her, like an all-knowing god. It was the critical point of AI processing power.

"…"

In that colorless world, Vivy kicked off the wall, rocketing toward Kakitani. He shifted the aim of his taser from Estella to Vivy. His finger moved on the trigger, firing the electrodes at her. They attached to Leclerc's left arm, which Vivy had just detached at the elbow. The electricity savagely burned through the arm, but it did no damage to Vivy.

Kakitani was caught off guard. Vivy closed in on him, spun herself around, and swung an open hand at his neck. But Kakitani was well trained. He responded immediately, blocking Vivy's strike and attempting a counterattack.

Vivy predicted his movements using several factors—the location of his shoulder joint, the stance of his lower body, the movement of his eyes—and then she ran a simulation of seventeen possible counteractions and selected the most appropriate. She used the remaining upper portion of her left arm to brush aside Kakitani's right hand as he tried to shove her away, then grabbed his left arm, the one he'd used to block her strike, and forced him back into the wall. He couldn't stand his ground because of the lack of gravity, so he went flying back.

"Master!" Elizabeth cried as Kakitani was flung away, then squeezed Arnold's neck tighter. If she twisted her arm, Arnold's fragile neck would easily break.

Estella let out a little shriek at the possibility. A sadistic look passed through Elizabeth's eyes, and so did something else, something more complex.

"…"

Vivy had already finished her next action. With Kakitani's taser in her hand, she ejected the spent cartridge with a single press and tossed it aside. It spun through the air as she punched in the new cartridge, which she'd taken off Kakitani when she'd flung him away. She raised the taser, immediately took aim, and pulled the trigger.

In a flash, the electrodes struck her target.

"What the—?!" Elizabeth blurted in shock when she saw Vivy fire.

Elizabeth had been holding Arnold in front of her like a shield, minimizing the locations Vivy could aim for. Vivy hadn't expertly hit one of Elizabeth's few vulnerabilities—she had fired at Arnold's thigh. If she let the electricity flow, Arnold would be fried with a million volts of electricity. She didn't *want* to do that, obviously, and it wasn't her plan.

"Tch!" Elizabeth released Arnold and kicked him toward Vivy. She couldn't figure out Vivy's true intentions. For all she knew, Vivy could've zapped Arnold, causing damage to Elizabeth as she held him. Elizabeth had lost her hostage, but she'd saved her own life.

As Arnold came flying through the passage, Vivy immediately pushed him down to the ground and stepped over him. He cried out as she did.

Elizabeth moved forward, trying to grab Arnold as he flew for cover. Vivy thrust her left elbow in her face. "Urgh!"

Obviously, Vivy wasn't going to do much damage swinging a broken arm at Elizabeth, but Elizabeth's consciousness lost a smidgen of processing power as it attempted to discern the purpose of the movement. Vivy could give even pointless moves purpose now that she was in God Mode.

Vivy slipped past Elizabeth before she could even finish blinking, grabbed her long hair, and jerked it. As Elizabeth's head moved down, Vivy brought a knee up into her chest. Elizabeth twisted her body back, but Vivy pulled her back down by the hair, driving her knee even further home.

The two AIs spun in zero gravity as their brawl continued. Elizabeth did have far more battle experience, which had overwhelmed Vivy in the cargo hold, but she wasn't able to fight all-out without gravity. The difference in strength between their frames was also apparent to Vivy as she realized Elizabeth's motions were crude without the floor to anchor her.

Elizabeth had been given the role of playing Estella and crashing Sunrise. Since she'd swapped out her own frame for one exactly like Estella's, she couldn't move the way she wanted. While working under Kakitani, she had been put to use in violent situations that allowed her to master her combat programming. She'd probably had a powerful frame to match. Thus, Elizabeth's problem was twofold: She was unaccustomed to zero gravity, and she was using a weaker frame than she was used to.

And if you added Vivy's God Mode into the mix...

"Wh-why the hell...can't I handle this?! Y-you've never been in anything more than a playground scuffle!"

Elizabeth swung her arms, moved her legs, and used every function she had to its fullest in an attempt to take down Vivy, but the songstress read all her moves in advance and reacted first. Elizabeth couldn't even scratch Vivy, let alone land a decisive blow. The gap between their strength was even greater than it had been in the cargo hold.

"I fight! I've fought all this time for Master! I won't let you win... Not someone like you! I'll destroy you! I'll turn you into a calculator!"

Elizabeth screamed insults that would never have come out of Estella's mouth even though they virtually were. She lunged at Vivy, trying to grab on to her with both hands, but Vivy dodged and snatched Elizabeth's collar. She rolled herself up, bringing her knees to her chest, slipped within reach, and kicked Elizabeth in the chest as hard as she could with both feet to send her flying back.

"Gah!"

Even in zero gravity, a full-force kick from an AI's legs could cause serious damage once the target crashed into the wall, especially if said AI had a weaker frame than average. Elizabeth's back smashed into the ceiling of the passage, and then the counterforce sent her rebounding down to the floor. She groaned as the impact shook her consciousness and made her vision waver.

"Elizabeth..." Estella said, watching her twin lose the fight. She'd caught Arnold when he was released from Elizabeth's clutches.

"Don't look at me like that! I can't stand you looking down on me! Anyone but you!" Elizabeth shrieked as she lunged at Estella in rage.

Vivy moved between the two, blocking Elizabeth's path. She latched her legs around Elizabeth's outstretched arm, then spun herself in the air to snap it. There was a dull crack as Elizabeth's arm shattered from the elbow up, impeding her function. She wavered, and Vivy launched her backward with her legs.

"Beth!" Kakitani shouted. He kicked off the wall to come back and caught Elizabeth as she flew. He held her back to stop her, then locked eyes with Vivy from over Elizabeth's shoulder. Shock and more clouded his stare.

"Damn it! Don't let this go to your head!" Elizabeth said as she saw her owner looking into her opponent's eyes. But she had realized the situation wasn't to her advantage and let those word be the last for the moment.

Immediately afterward, the bulwark between them slammed shut, blocking off the path. It was an attempt to hinder Vivy and the others using Elizabeth's control of the station, though a hinderance this minuscule would be easy for Vivy to break through now that she was in God Mode.

But just as she reached her arm out to try and open the bulwark, she saw violent electrical flashes. "Ah..." She looked over and saw that the system controlling the bulwark had shorted and was sending off sparks.

Elizabeth had used the taser Vivy had dropped to destroy the bulwark's controls and block their path. Even so, Vivy could open the bulwark with time. She should be able to show Elizabeth that something like this was nothing more than a temporary blockade for her.

"Vivy...this is the end," Matsumoto said. His voice came from behind her as she was about to touch the bulwark, stopping her in her tracks.

"What...?"

"Neither you nor I can handle any more of this." She turned back to look, and Estella gave a small gasp at the sight of her.

Estella's eyes were fixed on Vivy's cranium, which contained her eye cameras and olfactory sensors. It had been subjected to extreme temperatures from the heat generated by the positronic brain within. Once Vivy noticed it, her consciousness flickered violently and her system shut down, unable to withstand the heat.

"Vivy?! What's happening?" cried Estella.

"It's the price for forcing her computational capacity far beyond her standard specs. It was hard on me too, since I was optimizing data in real time and conducting emulators instead of leaving them to her positronic brain. It's a double-edged sword," Matsumoto explained after Vivy went limp. While Matsumoto was fond of using too many words, it was true that activating God Mode had put quite the burden on him. All his reactions were uncharacteristically sluggish. "Anyway, the enemy has retreated. Now is our chance. Let's pick up Vivy and go to the control room.

I should still be plenty capable of handling bulwarks in our way, even in this state."

"Okay... I'd like to ask more about this later. But first, Vivy."

"I'll take care of that," Arnold said, volunteering to carry her once Matsumoto and Estella had reached an agreement. He checked the state of his neck, then picked up Vivy's body. Despite not having grasped all the information, he wasn't showing any signs that he doubted the AIs. "She's light, but...I guess that would be the lack of gravity."

"Mr. Corvick, I really would prefer for you to seek safety..." Estella told him.

"I would actually be more concerned for him if he were to wander around on his own, especially considering how far we are from the escape shuttle. Besides, we need someone to carry Vivy. I think it would be best to ask him to accompany us," said Matsumoto. Whether or not he was aware of what was going through Estella's head, his suggestion was simply logical. She'd become used to his emotionless statements, even in the short time she'd known him. Calling him heartless would've implied that AIs could have hearts, which was in itself a ridiculous sentiment.

"I'll explain everything en route," Estella said. "Mr. Corvick, please come to the control room with us."

"Sure thing. I'll do my best to keep up with you. Just keep an eye out for me." Arnold followed them, looking like he had no real desire to know the details.

"You're just like Ash in that way. Which reminds me..." Estella's voice faltered. After a moment of hesitation, she said,

"Mr. Corvick, you said you could tell Elizabeth wasn't me. But... she's my twin. She looks *exactly* like me. How did you tell us apart?"

"She asked the same thing. Guess you really are twins." Arnold's attitude toward the person who'd threatened his life was far too lax. "It's simple. It was her eyes. I knew when I looked into her eyes."

"Her eyes...?"

"Yeah. None of your devotion to outer space and this station was there. I don't think it would be going too far to say the deciding factor was your love for my brother."

.∴5∴.

NOTICED HOW DIFFERENTLY you looked at space—and at this hotel."

Arnold had said it with a wink when Elizabeth asked how he'd been able to tell the twins apart. His entirely illogical answer had had a huge impact on Elizabeth. He hadn't said it to be spiteful or intentionally hurtful, but even so, no other words could have cut her consciousness so deeply.

They were built in the same environment. They were the results of the same research. They were modified so they would *be* the same. Elizabeth was Estella's only twin, but it turned out she was absolutely not the same as Estella. No matter what happened, no matter what changes there were to her fate, Elizabeth could never walk the same path. It felt as if he were saying she could never reach the heights Estella had achieved.

"Beth, you all right?" Kakitani asked once they were enough space between them and the closed bulwark.

She felt undeserving of his concern, and she bowed her head. "...Yes, Master. I'm sorry."

He didn't respond to her apology. His brow furrowed as he began to think. It was an expression Elizabeth was very familiar with. Kakitani always looked like that when he was worried.

When the Twin Brains Project had been canceled, Estella was fine because she was already active. The not-yet-active Elizabeth, however, was sent to be disposed of. She was taken from Estella as nothing more than a positronic brain in a container. Elizabeth had made it to the disposal facility, right up to the moment before her positronic brain was slated to be incinerated.

In the moments leading up to her death, Elizabeth's consciousness was filled with sheer terror. She had been created to help people, but she was given death before she was even truly given life. A sad, sorry fate. They were the same, yet *she'd* been saved. Why?

Elizabeth didn't have a voice function. She couldn't connect to a network. All she could do was whimper inside her consciousness. The one who had saved her from her end that day was Kakitani. He'd bought her off an employee at the disposal facility because he wanted an AI to help Toak with their work. He picked Elizabeth's positronic brain because she didn't officially exist in any records. In a stroke of luck, the body that had been made in advance for Elizabeth had also been sent to the same disposal facility. Kakitani recovered it as well and then connected her positronic brain to the body himself. He gave her life.

"You are just a convenient tool. You don't have to be anything more. Don't *try* to be anything more. That's what the relationship between humanity and AI should be," he'd said.

"Understood, uh...what should I call you?"

"I don't care."

"Then...I'll call you Master."

In the six years following, Elizabeth gave her all in support of Kakitani's work. Toak's goal was to show people that the existence of AI was a threat to humanity. The more extreme members of the group believed AI should be eradicated, while others felt varying levels of antipathy toward them.

This of course meant there was significant blowback against Elizabeth, since she was an AI, as well as constant questioning of Kakitani's principles because he brought her around and said she was essential for their plans. Kakitani always silenced those good-for-nothings with his actions and results. Elizabeth was proud to be able to contribute to that work he did.

And so, Elizabeth ran roughshod over the code of ethics that would generally keep her from harming people. *She* was perfectly fine injuring or even killing others, but Kakitani made it a point not to, so she did her best to respect his wishes.

Seeing as Kakitani had given her life and purpose when she was destined to die, it seemed obvious that she should give him her everything. If AIs' ultimate purpose was to give their all for humanity, then Kakitani was *her* "humanity."

No one else.

Thus, she didn't hesitate to agree when he asked her to sacrifice herself in order to crash the space station, a plan meant to show people the danger of putting AI in important positions. She would do it even if it meant burning up in the atmosphere and being remembered as someone she wasn't.

"If it's for you, Master, I don't mind."

Kakitani had brought her—a defective failure of an AI—this far. She could never repay her debt to him, but she had to try.

"Beth...?" Kakitani's brow crinkled as he looked at her now, and she reaffirmed those thoughts within herself. His eyes fell on her damaged right arm. "What's the state of your arm?"

"My right arm is non-functional. My fighting capability has been reduced by 27 percent."

"27 percent? That's not enough to force us to quit just yet. What are they up to?"

"They are likely headed to the control room. If Estella reaches it, she'll take back control of Sunrise, and the plan will fail."

"We have to prevent that at all costs. And that AI...is in the way..." Kakitani's voice tapered off as he scowled.

He was thinking back to Elizabeth's fight with the small-framed AI who'd performed way better than expected. Not even Elizabeth had been a match for her, and Elizabeth had honed her combat programming to the point that no mediocre AI could stand against her.

But that AI surely couldn't keep putting so much stress on her system.

"What we saw was likely an ace in the hole that she can't keep playing. I will win next time," said Elizabeth.

"That AI got in my way on a past enlightenment mission, but I won't let her get in my way this time."

"If I take her out and destroy Estella... I'll pretend to be Estella as I finish the deed and crash Sunrise. Then—"

"A lot of people will be forced to change their minds about AIs once they see the deaths of the guests onboard... The deaths of me and my companions," Kakitani said rather flatly for someone discussing their own death. He wanted it to go that way.

Their plan was grounded in Elizabeth assuming Estella's identity and killing people who got caught up in the act of terrorism. Those people would include the five Toak members, whose backgrounds had been carefully scrubbed clean to prepare them for their fate as innocent victims. Kakitani's ideals prohibited unnecessary bloodshed, so he'd concluded that he and the others would be the sacrifices necessary to this mission.

Elizabeth had been by Kakitani's side, watching him, for the past six years. She knew he would not stand by and watch as he forced her to sacrifice herself. He was just that honest and sincere of a man.

"As long as that AI doesn't do anything absurd again, you should easily be able to beat her. I would've preferred to avoid killing that man, Arnold Corvick, but...we have no choice," Kakitani said. He replaced the cartridge in his taser and laid out a plan involving him making a stand in the control room.

Elizabeth and Kakitani—one machine and one man. If they worked together, they should easily overpower Estella and her group. It would mean Kakitani's success and Elizabeth's failure.

"Master, can I speak with you for a moment?" she ventured.

"What is it? We don't have time to be dawdling. We have things to do."

He'd said *we*. She was included in his plan, and that was her sole salvation. Deep emotions filled her consciousness to the brim, and she closed the distance between her and Kakitani. She looked at him, offering a smile for his scowl, and struck him in the neck with an open hand.

"Agh!"

The attack hit his vagus nerve, sending him reeling. The look of disbelief showed he'd never once expected Elizabeth would do something this terrible. Was it trust, or was it apathy born of viewing her as a mere tool? She knew which was more likely. She'd spent six years by his side, after all. She hardly needed to ask.

"Master, I'm sure you'll be angry. Please let me have this one act of selfishness. You can't die yet... I'm not the only one who thinks so. Everyone does."

"..."

Elizabeth wrapped her arms around him, catching him as he fell. She closed her eyes as she spoke to him, but the words would never reach him. That was fine with her; she didn't mean for him to hear. She just hoped with all her heart that he would remember her face.

While she cradled Kakitani, a man approached her. He was the last member of Toak that Estella and the others hadn't encountered. He'd come to meet Elizabeth at this predetermined location. He looked at Kakitani, who was unconscious.

"Is Kakitani-san ready as planned?" he asked.

Elizabeth smirked. "Yep. Got him to go to sleep, as promised. Had to be a bit rougher about it than I'd hoped. You'll have to deal with his rage later." Her tone was completely different than when she spoke to Kakitani. This was generally how she interacted with anyone other than her owner. Even though she had the same positronic brain as Estella, she had none of her sister's grace. That was another reason being called Estella's twin made her uncomfortable.

Paying no mind to Elizabeth's attitude, the Toak member took Kakitani from her. The plan was for him to get Kakitani off the station to safety. They'd made this little tweak far in advance. Kakitani was Toak's powerhouse, and they weren't about to allow him to sacrifice himself.

In short, there had always been a secret secondary mission to ensure Kakitani made it back alive. Elizabeth had readily agreed, and it was her job to see it through. Kakitani would surely never forgive Elizabeth when he found out. He would probably even have her disposed of for being defective and not following his orders.

"If he was the one disposing of me, then it might not be so bad," she murmured.

Did AIs go to an afterlife? If the determining factor was whether they had a soul, then perhaps there was no eternal peace for them. And even if the concept of an afterlife *did* apply to AIs, Elizabeth was absolutely going to hell. So, if someone had to send her there, then it might as well be Kakitani.

Such pointless thoughts for an AI.

Elizabeth laughed at herself, wondering if maybe she really was defective. She pulled off the wig she used to pretend to be Estella and removed her costume, back to being Elizabeth. In the end, she would burn. If that had to happen, then she would go out as her real self, the one Kakitani had used.

Before the other Toak member carried Kakitani away, she gently stroked her owner's cheek and said her goodbyes.

"Oh, Master. I'm sure you'll be mad at me," she said. "I'm sorry. But I think...I think I was happy."

.: 6 :.

AFTER DEFEATING Elizabeth and Kakitani, Vivy and her companions encountered no further obstacles on their way to the control room. You could even say it was somewhat anticlimactic.

"I would have assumed their priority would be to stop us from getting to the control room," said Matsumoto. "It's a good thing they didn't have a bunch of skilled personnel stationed in the area. I included that factor in my calculation when I used our secret weapon, God Mode. I wouldn't have been so reckless if I'd thought otherwise."

"Right. Guess you are a super AI. You saved us," Arnold replied, sounding genuinely impressed; none were more honest than the Corvick brothers. At present, he was carrying Vivy while Estella hugged the bragging Matsumoto to her chest.

Estella listened to them talk as she sped toward the control room. Her consciousness was preoccupied with the conversation she'd had with her twin when they'd finally reunited. Elizabeth had spoken while under the influence of powerful negative emotions, like rage and hatred, and Estella couldn't let go of her words.

Just a slight gap in timing had divided the two into starkly different fates: deployment and disposal. Estella had never forgotten her twin sister, but she'd seldom spared a thought for her. She'd even given *less* thought to the possibility that Elizabeth was still alive and her anger toward Estella had been growing.

"...I'll think about all that later," she muttered.

It would be strange to apologize for everything. It wasn't the kind of problem that could be solved with an apology, after all. So, Estella decided to hold off on making a decision about her sister and focus on solving the problem in front of her.

There were no other people blocking their path to the control room, meaning it was just the closed bulwarks that slowed them down, and those were easily taken care of by the talkative AI. They opened bulwark after bulwark, continuing down the passage in zero gravity toward their destination.

"The control room," Matsumoto said as they arrived at the heart of Sunrise.

The door slid open quietly, and the group was greeted by the glow of several screens showing monitored areas throughout the station. There were a number of terminals in the room as well as a smattering of LEDs indicating operating electronics. However, one large terminal in the center of the room commanded their attention.

Arnold stopped moving once he'd stepped inside. "Estella, take back control."

And so she did.

Estella walked up to the central terminal, connected to it with the cable in her right ear, and closed her eyes. It instantly read her unique positronic brain waves, verifying her access key for control of Sunrise. It was done in a moment, with no issues. Even though Elizabeth had lost control, the access key hadn't changed. As far as the system could tell, the control AI had always been in charge.

"I, Estella, the control AI of Sunrise, have returned to my duty."

With those words, Estella felt her consciousness expand, and her sensations went beyond her frame and her limbs. The complex processes of everything in the station rapidly flitted through her consciousness and assembled.

"..."

With that, Estella had taken back control of Sunrise. She searched for the group Kakitani and Elizabeth belonged to. Staff members and guests huddled in the area where the escape shuttle was stored, looking uneasy. The AI staff were diligently searching the areas not blocked off by bulwarks for the girl who had been separated from her family.

She continued to scour the ship, and—

"Whoa! What was that tremor?" asked Arnold, the breath knocked out of him from the surprise. His face paled as he looked at Estella.

Estella shook her head and said, "Don't worry, Mr. Corvick. That tremor did not have any effect on Sunrise."

"Saying 'on Sunrise' almost makes it sound like it affected something else. Can you elaborate?" Matsumoto asked, unable to pick up on the hidden meaning in her carefully chosen words.

"A ship..." she started to say, then gave up trying to find an easy way to break it to her companions. "A ship has left Sunrise. It's an unscheduled departure, so it must be..."

"The terrorists retreating. You're probably right. There's no point in them continuing with their plan with how things have gone."

Arnold nodded as he listened to Matsumoto. "Right... That's good news." He looked at Estella, concerned, and her brow furrowed in worry.

If Kakitani's group had retreated, they must've abandoned their plan to crash Sunrise. They had put a lot of stress on the staff and guests, but everyone would be able to return to Earth safely. No, not everyone—there was one AI staff member who would never come back.

"Leclerc..."

Now that the immediate situation was under control and they had time to stop for a moment, Estella's consciousness turned to thoughts of Leclerc. She had been spirited and positive, and she never seemed to have a care in the world. But, according to the data from Vivy's datalink, she had actually been working with Elizabeth. Moreover, Leclerc might have been the one who brought Kakitani and his group onto the station in the first place.

Had she been spurred to such actions because of some distress Estella hadn't noticed? If only she'd talked to Leclerc more...

She regretted not doing more while Leclerc was alive. She'd felt the same way when Ash died, yet she had gone on to make the same mistake. An AI that couldn't learn was a particularly foolish being.

"Ugh..."

While Estella was laying blame on herself, there was a sound from Vivy where she lay in Arnold's arms. Estella looked over to see Vivy open her eyes. The extreme stress applied to her positronic brain from God Mode had forced her system to shut down, but she'd finally recovered and rebooted.

"Initiating analysis of surroundings. Location: Sunrise control room."

"Oh, good, Vivy. You've rebooted."

"Estella." Vivy stirred, and Arnold released her. She clung to the floor of the control room to keep from floating away and looked up at Estella, who was in contact with the terminal. "You've resumed control. What's the situation?"

"We've confirmed the departure of an unidentified ship. We believe the violent organization and the AI belonging to it have fled," Matsumoto told her. "It should be safe to assume we've prevented Sunrise from falling. There were accidents along the way, but our mission is complete."

"Elizabeth fled...?" Vivy said with a frown.

"May I interrupt?" Estella cut in. "First, we should clean up the rest of the situation before we have a laid-back discussion about things. We need to contact the surface and report what happened. Then we'll have to relocate everyone on the station to the central block in order to reactivate the artificial gravity. I will contact the other AI staff and tell them to keep looking for the missing girl."

The space station wasn't within the jurisdiction of any single nation, so issues were normally handled by a special institute. They needed to contact that institute, tell those in charge what had happened, and ask them to search for and detain Kakitani and Elizabeth.

Estella attempted to initiate contact but to no avail. "Transmission interference...?"

The moment she tried to contact the surface, something had jammed the transmission. Just as she prepared to investigate, the third and most powerful tremor of the day rocked Sunrise, accompanied by a blast.

"Ugh!"

Even floating in midair couldn't protect them. The shock wave slammed into them with such force that it warped Estella's consciousness. Arnold wasn't prepared for the impact. He screamed, tumbled over, and lost consciousness. Fainting in zero gravity upped the risk of choking to death on one's stomach contents when they flowed backward.

The blaring sound of the red alert echoed throughout the station. Estella launched herself from the floor, reaching out to secure Arnold.

"Too bad! I won't let you."

Just as a voice pierced Estella's audio sensors, someone grabbed one of her outstretched arms and broke her elbow. "Augh!" There was a dull snap, and Estella's eyes shot open to see...herself.

It was Elizabeth. She'd moved through the station, avoiding the cameras, and appeared in the control room when they were shaken up by the tremors and the explosion. She was the only one who hadn't given up on their plan—despite facing defeat.

"Hi-yah!"

Still holding Estella's broken arm, Elizabeth spun in the air and kicked her sister. The blow landed directly on her torso, ruthlessly forcing her backward. At the same time, Matsumoto flew out of Estella's hand. The cube AI floated in air, unable to move effectively on his own.

"Elizabe—"

"You are *seriously* the most annoying of them all!" Elizabeth shouted, her eyes following the cube through the air.

Vivy, still without her left arm, charged Elizabeth, but the AI saw her coming. She smacked Vivy in the forehead with Estella's arm, then grabbed Vivy's leg with her free hand as she was somersaulted backward. With all her might, she smashed Vivy up and down, up and down, then mercilessly flung her away.

After that, she turned to Estella and said, "All right. We're in overtime now, Sis. And I'm going to turn your workplace into a shooting star."

.: 7 :.

AS VIVY HURTLED AWAY from the twins, her consciousness let out a shriek at the unexpected turn of events.

The excessive strain of God Mode had had a huge impact on
her. Even though she'd rebooted after her shutdown, her frame's
performance was still reduced by 52 percent, and additional
downtime wouldn't result in any greater recovery. Her frame
would have to be overhauled, the fried parts replaced. There was
no hope of improving her performance now.

If she didn't figure out some way to resolve the situation,
there would be no future for her or anyone else on board. The
Project would fail. She floated in midair with her damaged limbs
splayed. In addition to her left arm, which was gone from the
elbow down, her lower body had also taken significant damage.

Elizabeth had placed herself in the center of the control room.
If the ceiling was still considered "up" in zero gravity, then Vivy
was up and Estella was down, while the unconscious Arnold was
drifting near the entrance. Matsumoto also floated helplessly.

"You have caused me a lot of grief," Elizabeth told Matsumoto.
"You're a real pain in the neck, you know?"

"I don't hold a candle to how much of a pain *you* are!" he retorted. "I have to admit, I underestimated you. Your owner made
you stay on the station without letting you escape with him? It's a

very logical decision. And a very human one. Use and discard the 'unit.' It's the right move."

"Hah!" Elizabeth laughed, then snatched Matsumoto out of the air. His cube fit in her palm. She squeezed her fist around him, and his frame creaked.

"Y-you should be...respected...for your w-willingness to follow orders...and die. But...I...won't...be...destroyed...so..."

"Thanks for the glowing evaluation, but you don't quite have it right. I did this by myself. No one ordered me to; I just wanted to do it."

"What...do...you—"

Elizabeth smashed Matsumoto into the terminal next to her. His frame warped and crumbled. Having suffered such severe damage, Matsumoto couldn't even open and close the shutter on his eye camera. The parts that produced his voice were also impaired, and now only a strange, garbled sound came out.

"Nobody likes a man who talks too much. Doesn't matter if they're a human or an AI. Men should shut their trap and put their money where their mouth is... At least, that's what my master did."

Matsumoto could do nothing more than produce distorted sounds. "Vi...vy... Vi...vy..."

Seeing that Matsumoto had been neutralized, Elizabeth turned slowly back to Estella, who was clutching her own broken arm. She stared at her twin, fully aware that their positions had reversed, and the corners of her mouth pulled up in a smirk. "The tables have turned. I might have had my ass handed to me, but I'm still doing all right, Sis. You, on the other hand... Oh, looks like your nosy friends and careless owner are all taking a nap. Do you want to have a heart-to-heart? Just the two of us?"

"What was that explosion from a moment ago?" asked Estella.

"Straight to business even though we twins should be opening ourselves up to each other? You're like an estranged relative talking about the weather. Though I guess we really *were* estranged, weren't we?" Elizabeth shrugged in disappointment, but her expression was bored as she said, "Timed bomb. I set off one of the two bombs my companions put in place when they infiltrated the station. Don't worry. The guests and hotel workers are safe. It'd be a bad day for anyone who happened to be strolling by at the time though."

"Bombs? Why would you—"

"They were plan B. Would have been best if I could've crashed the station back when I first had control, but things didn't go the way I wanted. Still..." As she spoke, she connected to the terminal and put herself in control once more. In what seemed like a show of power, she gave her cruel orders to Sunrise, changing its course and deactivating its navigational safety features. "Now the top of Sunrise is pointed straight at Earth."

The station shuddered, which informed them that its orbital track had changed. It was also painfully clear this wasn't a welcome change.

"Stop it, Elizabeth! Why are you doing this?!" cried Estella.

"Are you asking me to calculate the probable results of my actions and the further impact on the Earth? Well, if Sunrise crashes, the blame will be put on the control AI in charge of the space station. Then people will disapprove of AIs in all sorts of situations, probably leading to a huge push to recall them. Sis, you're the most influential AI in the entire world! Huge promotion for someone who was almost disposed of. Congrats."

"That's not what I mean!" Estella lost her temper at Elizabeth's sneer and leapt at her.

But she was too slow and too clumsy. Estella's outstretched arm slid through the air, and she took a direct hit from Elizabeth's knee.

"Agh!"

She flew upward and crashed into the ceiling, making her frame groan. The force sent her moving back down, where her twin grabbed her by her synthetic hair and dragged her so she could look her in the eye.

"Not particularly graceful of you, Sis. We're a matching pair, and we both lost an arm, but there's still such a difference between us. You have such a soft, beautiful frame. I can tell with one glance that you've never done anything untoward with it. That's another huge difference between you and me. I was picked up the moment before I was going to be disposed of."

"I always felt bad about you being disposed of. But that doesn't mean my whole life has been easy. I gave this place and my owner everything I had. I won't let your resentment ruin that."

"Oh, come *on*! I'm so tired of hearing about that!"

Elizabeth smashed Estella's head into a nearby terminal. There was the sound of metal creaking as her frame warped, and Estella's face briefly contorted in agony. AIs might not know pain, but they could sense the danger of taking enough damage to stop them from functioning. Cracks formed in Estella's consciousness, and her beautiful voice wavered.

"It's just what you deserve, Sis. I would love to leave you like this so you can watch your precious station of dreams turn to ash, but...I can't take the risk that you'll get in my way if I leave even a scrap of you around."

"Agh..."

Elizabeth flung Estella into the floor, then reached out just as she ricocheted back up. It was obvious she intended to destroy Estella here and now. The summary of the Sun-Crash Incident only listed the remains of the culprit "Estella" as having been at the location of impact. No other intact AI remains had been found.

"Vi...vy... Vi...vy..."

Matsumoto had become stuck on a terminal, unable to do anything but sputter out the mechanical sound of his parts whirring. Vivy too was seriously impaired by system failures to do anything. Once Elizabeth was finished with Estella, she would come and tear the two of them to pieces. Then she would take care of Arnold, since he was a witness, and finish off by crashing Sunrise into Earth—all without even realizing that a final war between humanity and AIs awaited in that future.

"Service to humanity. That's the first mission we AIs are ever given," Estella said suddenly as Elizabeth approached to dismantle her. A crack was running across her face from her forehead to her left cheek.

Elizabeth recoiled. "What are you talking about?"

"When you and I were still in the same positronic brain pool, when we had no one to talk to but each other, we talked about that. Didn't we?"

"You're talking about before our individualities became ingrained, aren't you? It grosses me out to hear you talk about a time when the Laws were stuffed down our throats like it's some pleasant memory."

The positronic brain inside an AI created its consciousness and did all the calculations and processing, but it wasn't complete until the mandatory Laws were installed. Normally, the Laws would take root in a positronic brain while it learned in solitude, but Elizabeth and Estella had been allowed to interact with each other before their positronic brains had finished developing, allowing them to discuss the Laws before they were ingrained.

But they were fundamentally different now, having been active as separate AIs for years. What they learned from their interactions with society had shaped their individuality. Elizabeth lacked Estella's compassion, and her sister's pleading would not change her mind. It was poor judgment on Estella's part if she believed it would.

"Seriously? Are you really trying to preach to me about how I should stop, how I need to follow the Three Laws and serve humanity? Are you gonna say what I'm doing is wrong, and you can't stand by as my older sister and watch me do it?"

"..."

"I'm not joking. I *will* make my master's wishes come true. I don't care if it's against the code of ethics. I don't care if it breaches the Three Laws. If an AI's primary function is to serve humanity, then all the better. The only human I should be serving, the whole of humanity I should be serving...is my master!" Elizabeth shrieked, then turned a cruel hand on Estella. Her fingers made for Estella's torso to tear open her body and destroy the vital systems within.

Right when Elizabeth was entirely focused on destroying Estella, Vivy moved. Her body had floated up to the ceiling where she could plant her feet and launch herself at Elizabeth.

"Hah!"

Unlike Estella, who wasn't used to violence, Elizabeth unleashed a real attack with intent to destroy. Elizabeth's back was turned to Vivy, who flew toward her at full speed, aiming for the base of her neck. An attack right between her positronic brain and her central circuit would sever the connection—the same as Elizabeth had done to Leclerc.

But just before Vivy could strike, Elizabeth's left arm reached back and caught Vivy's outstretched leg, then smashed her into Estella. "You're a one-trick pony, you good-for-nothing AI!"

The violent impact tangled the two together, and both their frames smacked into the control room floor before rebounding back. Not only had the surprise attack failed, but now Elizabeth was pinning Vivy's torso down, her back creaking as it pressed against a terminal. Elizabeth stared into her face.

"That entirely predictable suicide attack was your last-ditch effort? I was watching you the whole time, waiting for you to come at me. Seriously pathetic... Anyway, I owe you payback for my master."

"Pay...back...?"

"Fifteen years ago, you were the first stumbling block in Master's path. That's how long he's been connected to you. You're the reason that crease between his eyebrows never goes away... That's why I'm going to end you."

Vivy flailed her arms and legs, trying to get out of Elizabeth's clutches, but Vivy's clumsy resistance was nothing compared to Elizabeth's unyielding strength. Elizabeth's hand pressed Vivy's neck against the control device with enough force to crush it. As it broke, there was a splintering *crack*—the sound a songstress's throat should never make. Her consciousness wrenched and distorted; her vision flickered. The alarm warning her of system failure ran incessantly, and she was assailed with absurd orders to right herself.

If I don't stop it, stop it, stop it, I'll die, I'll die, I'll die, diediedie—

An overwhelming sense of loss smothered her as her positronic brain was a hair's breadth from failure.

The moment before that happened, there came a sound. It wasn't the sharp, shrieking alarms ringing in her eardrums. It wasn't the shattering of her throat. It was the ceaseless, steady croak of Matsumoto's broken voice.

"Vi...vy..."

A red light flickered deep within his half-opened eye camera. That light turned green, and the images on the monitors changed to show the cargo hold of Sunrise. It was where Leclerc had died,

and where Vivy had nearly met her end. Why would he be showing that place on the monitors?

The answer came when the video zoomed in to something
hidden behind a cargo container. There, nearly in tears, crouched
a lone girl.

"Yuzu...ka..."

Ojiro Yuzuka. That was her name, the name of a precious life
still trapped on board. She had been separated from her parents,
unable to join the evacuating guests. Evidently, she was in the
cargo hold.

The moment the girl's image appeared on the monitors, all
the AIs in the room reacted differently. Elizabeth stiffened when
she saw a human life was in danger. Estella tried to rush forward,
attempting to save the girl she was responsible for as the hotel
manager. Vivy tried as hard as she could to break free of the grip
on her neck. She refused to let Yuzuka die like she had let her
older sister die.

"Elizabeth!"

The one-armed Estella swept her leg through the air in a
kick aimed at Elizabeth. That attack had already failed once, and
Elizabeth raised her left leg to block it with ease. But AIs could
learn. That was true even for a hotel manager who'd never known
violence.

Estella tilted her head, and the tips of Elizabeth's toes that
were meant for her face instead swept past her nose. She then
launched herself at Elizabeth in a full-body tackle, which
Elizabeth wasn't able to hold her ground against without gravity.

"Oof!"

The only way to avoid going ragdoll in zero gravity was to hold on to something, and Elizabeth's limbs were otherwise occupied—her left leg was off the ground, and her left arm was holding Vivy. Could she then withstand it by hooking her right leg onto something? No, not even AI were capable of such a skillful maneuver.

"Estellaaa!" Elizabeth bellowed in rage as she was torn away from the control room's equipment.

In accordance with the physics of zero gravity, Elizabeth's frame was hurled in the opposite direction Estella's impact had come from. But she was absolutely not going to let Vivy go. She held firm with her left arm, dragging Vivy with her.

That was Elizabeth's single greatest mistake.

"Vi...vy... Vi...vy..."

Vivy could hear Matsumoto's voice weakening, but there was no way those were death cries. They was his orders, his support for Vivy, his suggestion on how to get out of this.

That meant only one thing.

"Aaaahhhhh!"

As Vivy was pulled along by Elizabeth's grip on her, she roared through her broken throat and used the last of her strength to reach her right arm toward Elizabeth's head. Elizabeth had no way of dodging, so Vivy grabbed on to the lapel of her shirt and pulled them closer together, being sure to line up their faces. Their foreheads touched, and their eye cameras stared right into each other. With a strong push, Vivy initiated a datalink.

There was only one program she would share with Elizabeth: the code that Matsumoto gave her to reformat Estella.

ılı|ıllı|ılıı

AS THE DATA WAS SENT, Elizabeth stiffened, and her eyes opened wide.

Vivy let go of Elizabeth, using the tiny bit of momentum from their colliding foreheads to bounce to the front of the control room, and Estella caught her gently in her arms.

"Ah... Aaah... Aaaaah..." Elizabeth's arms and legs trembled as the program invaded her consciousness, eating away at her memories and stored data. She shuddered while it erased her.

While the program had been meant to stop Estella from crashing Sunrise, Estella had never had motive to do so. When Elizabeth's existence had come to light, Vivy had thought the program unnecessary—but now she'd turned it into a secret weapon against Elizabeth, who had been the one behind the crash all along.

"M-M-Ma-Mas-Master...!" Elizabeth's stammered words were her last attempt to resist as she clung to her disappearing memories. As sad as it was, her desperate struggle was completely ineffective.

Matsumoto's reformatting program was filled with all sorts of code written by a super AI from the future. His paranoid tendencies meant he'd made it in such a way that it would be impossible to analyze and counteract fast enough. The memories Elizabeth had built up over time were like stacks of colorful construction paper that had been set ablaze. The flame traveled to sheet after sheet, gaining speed as it burned away the memories to nothing.

Terror and helplessness from being disposed of.

Jealousy toward Estella, who had survived despite being from the same environment.

Obligation toward the man who saved her.

Desire to make his wishes a reality.

Yearning so unlike an AI.

Vivy stomped on those feelings and more, crushing them beneath her feet for the sake of the Singularity Project.

"Aaaah...aah...aaaah..."

Elizabeth's voice trembled, her back arched like a bow as her memories vanished. At the very last moment, before it was all gone, only one thing remained of her individuality.

"Ma...ster... Please...take...care..."

With those last words of concern for her owner, she stopped moving. The program had done its job. All of her memories had been eaten away. She lost any reason to follow her owner's goals or her own desire to destroy her twin.

And that was the end of Diva D-09β/Elizabeth.

.: 8 :.

"Elizabeth..." Estella's gaze was heavy with emotion as she looked at her nonfunctional sister. They'd had the same origin, but the twins had walked such different paths. Now, their paths had finally converged only for her to find hatred, and for it to end with one sister losing everything. The current Estella couldn't name the many feelings that welled up in her consciousness as she stared at her twin. Her past self wouldn't have, and her future self would probably never figure it out.

Vivy didn't know the answer either, but she said, "Estella, if we wait too long..."

"I know. I will immediately correct Sunrise's course," replied Estella before she reconnected her ear cord to the control room's terminal.

Even though the access rights had been taken over so many times, the original control AI now had them for good. With full control of Sunrise back in Estella's hands, she tried to right the station using the reverse thrusters to put the station back on its original course. It had lost its attitude control, and it wouldn't be so easy.

"Vi...vy... No... The...thrus...ters..."

"What is it, Matsumoto?"

He was still smashed into the terminal, but his voice drew Vivy's attention. The next moment, an explosion rocked Sunrise.

"Ack!"

The shrill alarm rang out as the station shook. It was immediately evident that the damage was severe, and they were once again in an emergency.

"A timed bomb... Elizabeth did say they'd set two," Estella said.

"One was a diversion to take over the control room. The other was the real one, to prevent the station getting back on course..." Vivy realized.

Vivy managed to grab hold of Arnold despite the control room lurching. She looked at Estella, who was clinging to the terminal. As the control AI, she was capable of immediately determining the status of the entire station, so she was running detailed calculations in an attempt to find a way out of the situation.

The Sunrise was falling toward Earth. It had lost its reverse thrusters in the explosion, which it needed in order to correct its position. They had no control over it now. If anyone would have a nearly magical solution to wrap things up neatly, it would be Matsumoto.

"Matsumoto, what do you think?" Estella asked quietly.

"Vi...vy... I'm...sor...ry...but..." was all Matsumoto was able to rasp.

Estella looked down at the ground. "I see." After taking a moment to close her eyes, she said, "As manager of Sunrise, I have orders for you, Vivy—member of the AI staff. Take the owner of the hotel, Mr. Corvick, and retrieve the guest in the cargo hold. Bring them to the escape shuttle. I'll use everything available to hold the station out until you make it there."

"Estella? But if you do that—"

"This station will crash, Vivy," Estella said softly, cutting off her protests. The contrast between the emotional patterns on her face and the contents of her statement was jarring. Especially since she was about to lose the symbol of her connection to her late owner. "When an AI is faced with a situation caused by ill intent, they must make the best decision available. The Sunrise will fall. If I cannot stop that, then I will make sure the guests and staff are safe and adjust where the station lands."

Estella was calmly searching for the best option available in the crisis. Once stopping the fall of the station became impossible, there was still something she could do to keep Toak's plans from succeeding, as they had in the original history.

"I will absolutely not allow anyone to die in this crash," said Estella. "I will do this for Ash…"

In the original history, Elizabeth had destroyed Estella and assumed control to crash Sunrise, killing tens of thousands of people. With Estella here in her original capacity, things would go differently. The people would be saved; the Singularity Project was successful.

What Vivy really wanted in that moment was to stay there and aid Estella in some way, but the best help she could offer wasn't there in the control room. It was with the guests, getting them to safety.

"Yuzuka…"

The images of Yuzuka in the cargo hold, the trigger for their final resistance against Elizabeth, were still displayed on the monitors. After the blast from the bomb, she was no longer hiding her tears. Vivy had to help her.

"Please, Vivy. Go. And then—"

"You've only mentioned my brother and Vivy. Don't I get anything?"

"Oh, Mr. Corvick…"

Arnold had regained consciousness and was looking at Estella as she urged Vivy on. The situation had changed while he was out, so he had no way to know what was happening. But unlike AIs, who had to sift through information to make a calculation, humans could gather enough context to make a guess and go from there. Arnold Corvick also had the ability to make decisions in a frighteningly similar way to his brother, which was why he looked directly at Estella with a smile on his face.

He knew this was their last goodbye.

"I'm sorry for all the trouble I've caused you, Mr. Corvick. I am incredibly ashamed by how far outside the bounds of an AI's operations I've stepped," Estella said.

"What do you mean you've caused me trouble? Every day with you was fun. It was like walking in Ash's groundbreaking footsteps... I can't believe I won't have either of you from now on." Arnold smiled sadly, his eyes momentarily downcast. Then his smile grew, better suited to his handsome looks, and he said, "Guess I'll have to give up the nickname 'hotel kingpin' now, won't I?"

"You will likely face blowback for this... But, Mr. Corvick, please keep this in mind: Rely on the people around you, both human and AI."

"..."

"Both you and your brother draw good people to you. You moved my heart, a heart that shouldn't exist in an AI. That's your true skill." Estella smiled and gripped her skirt with her right hand, the only one she had left. Then she dipped into a curtsy. The mannerism was somewhat ungainly with her cracked face and the absence of gravity. Even so, Vivy couldn't help thinking that out of all the emotions Estella had shown, her smile and her curtsy were the most beautiful of them all. "Mr. Corvick...my owner, please take care of yourself."

"I will. And thank you, Estella. Say hello to Ash for me."

Many humans believed they went on to an afterlife when they died. But what about AIs? Vivy didn't know where they went, but Arnold seemed to think they all ended up in the same eternal place. His parting words were precious and powerful.

"Vivy," Estella prompted.

"I will take care of Mr. Corvick and the girl. I'm...sorry I couldn't do a better job," Vivy said weakly after Arnold had finished his goodbyes. In the end, Vivy had been unable to prevent this situation. She'd known what was going to happen in the future, and she still couldn't avoid it. Now she had to leave.

In response to Vivy's apology, Estella shook her head and said, "You really did save us. We...couldn't save the hotel. It's falling, but we will protect the honor of both Corvick brothers. That's something an AI can be proud of."

"..."

"We give our all to the missions we're given. I can't praise Elizabeth for what she did...but she really is my twin." Just as Elizabeth had intended to do while implementing the plan her owner had given her, Estella would sacrifice herself for the managerial role Ash Corvick had given her. Whether or not their connection was any consolation to Estella, the twins were alike in that.

"Please, Vivy."

"I'll take care of the guests and staff."

"That's not all. Well, you need to do that, but I have no doubt you'll take care of it. I have one other final request." Estella looked off to the side. Her eyes, framed by long lashes, landed on Elizabeth's frame where it floated faceup in zero gravity. Then she turned her gaze back on Vivy and said, "Don't forget."

"..."

"Don't forget what I taught you. And...remember her. The girl who did something unforgivable and forgot even that. Only you can do that for me."

That was Estella's desire and her desperation. Vivy burned it deep into her positronic brain, her consciousness, her memory. She swore to never forget, and that was the end of her relationship with Estella.

.:9:.

THE RED ALERT continued to sound in the control room, and the warning lights flashed annoyingly throughout the station. Due to the effects of the two bombs, Sunrise would not be able to escape its current trajectory, putting it on a crash course with Earth. The reverse thrusters were non-operational.

What Estella *could* do with her control of all the station's systems was seal off the damaged sections and purge the unnecessary blocks. This would reduce the total mass of the station, increasing the probability of it burning up when it entered Earth's atmosphere and reducing the damage done on the surface when the station crashed.

Thankfully, the bombs weren't powerful enough to break apart the main body of the station, meaning nothing would inhibit Estella's attempts to lighten the load. The explosions had been discreet, placed with plenty of care and forethought, and the damage had been limited to disabling the reverse thrusters. Thus, the evacuation could go ahead without issue.

"Everyone, please remain calm. In accordance with station safety regulations, all guests will be safely escorted off the station. We apologize for the inconvenience, but we ask that for the time being, you follow staff orders and remain calm," Estella said over the station's PA system.

There had been two explosions. Before that, there were strange tremors and all the people on board were loaded into the escape shuttle. This was obviously an emergency, and it made Estella's calm statements almost laughable.

Estella could actually see the employees' expressions on the station monitors. They looked worried, and her announcement didn't change anything. It was the grand opening of the hotel. They were supposed to have started new lives in their new jobs, filled with hope and expectation. It deeply saddened her to see them suffer. But she had handpicked and trained every last one of them, so she felt comfortable leaving the guests in their care in even this absurd situation. There was no gap between humans and AIs here.

"I wish I could have taught Vivy too."

There hadn't been enough time, and Vivy certainly hadn't intended for them to get close. Her goal had been to prevent Sunrise from falling. Unfortunately, she wasn't able to do that, and Estella hadn't been able to help her properly.

That was unforgivable.

As she thought of Vivy, Estella saw a change on the monitor showing the cargo hold. Vivy and Arnold had appeared in front of Ojiro Yuzuka, the missing hotel guest. The girl's head whipped up when she saw them, and then she pushed off the floor and flew toward Vivy. Yuzuka caught something that was floating in the air, and Estella's eyes widened. Then she smiled happily as relief washed over her.

"Leclerc."

Yuzuka had grabbed on to the torso and head of Leclerc—all that was left of her. Though the frame wasn't technically Leclerc anymore, Estella felt comforted that it had been collected and that the human girl was safe. Now Leclerc could go back to the surface. She wouldn't burn up with Sunrise. Arnold would surely lay her to rest beside Ash; they were definitely the kind of people to hold an AI funeral.

Estella was sad to know she wouldn't be able to join them.

Without a word, she ignored the incessant ringing of the alarm and slid her remaining right arm over the terminal. The work to disassemble the station was ongoing. Estella followed the emergency manual to complete the necessary steps quickly and carefully. As the hotel manager and the control AI of the station, Estella had thoroughly reviewed the manual for emergency situations and run simulations daily. Ash, Arnold, Leclerc, and all the staff she was close to had teased her for being a worrywart, but she did it. Day after day after day.

She had hoped this day would never come, but in case it did, she'd practiced every day.

"Everyone, the escape shuttle will now be launching. Please remain seated."

Vivy arrived at the escape shuttle with Arnold and Yuzuka in tow, and the staff doing head counts reported that everyone was on board—except Kakitani. Even the infiltrators Vivy had defeated along the way to the control room had been collected by the AI staff and loaded onto the escape shuttle, still bound. It was probably horribly uncomfortable to ride in the storage compartment, but they would just have to endure it to ensure the safety of the other hotel guests.

After confirming there was no one else on board on the monitors, Estella gave the go-ahead for the shuttle to depart.

"Estella... Thank you."

She received a goodbye transmission from the staff she'd worked with on Daybreak as they learned she would fall along with Sunrise. The voices trembled with tears, an indication of Estella's importance during her six years of operation.

"Oh... I don't want to forget. I don't want to disappear..."

Don't forget.

Remember.

That was what Estella had asked Vivy to do, and she'd gladly accepted. But Vivy would remember so little: what she'd learned in her very short time on Sunrise and the fact that Elizabeth had existed, even if she wasn't remembered in any records. The days that Estella and Elizabeth had spent together and apart, those six years separating them, their adventures, their precious memories... those wouldn't remain anywhere. It was an absurd concern to have after Elizabeth's memories had already been erased.

The escape shuttle left Sunrise. Even the transmissions would soon fade into the distance. The AIs on the shuttle, Vivy, and that advanced super AI would manage to do something to ensure the safety of the guests, even with how damaged they were.

So what could Estella, the manager of Sunrise, do for the escape shuttle as it moved farther away?

"Estella, right? You've got an amazing voice."

Words from someone very precious to her suddenly passed through her consciousness. She wasn't certain whether it was a memory coming back to her or simply noise from processing past logs, but it felt like Ash was talking to her in that very moment.

"Everyone, please look out the right side of your shuttle."

Estella handled the rapidly changing situation on the station without pause, but none of that burden leaked into her voice as she fulfilled her duty to support the guests. She had to respond perfectly even when there was an emergency. That was the duty of the Dawn Songstress.

"You may be able to see the outer edge of Earth lightening. Europe will soon see the sunrise. The sun will rise over the Royal Observatory in Greenwich, London at..."

As she spoke, the sun slowly climbed to the right of both the station and the escape shuttle. The brilliant light peeked over the far edge of the big, blue planet. It was the moment of dawn—the sunrise. It was exactly the sight of the space station that Ash Corvick dreamed of.

Arnold Corvick and Estella had carried on Ash's dreams, and with help from Leclerc and Vivy, they managed to make all his dreams a reality. He wanted to show this sight to so many people. That was why everyone had worked so hard right up until this moment.

"Ah!" A sudden blast cut through her voice as she tried to continue her tour for the guests. It made her sensors tremble and sent her crashing into a wall, her consciousness flickering.

⑴⑴‖‖⑴⑴

The atmospheric control inside the station was working to adjust the oxygen levels on board, but it had backfired. A fire broke out near the cargo hold. Estella tried creating a vacuum to smother the flame, but the spark didn't go out when it lost its fuel source. It just continued to smolder. The process of purging parts had introduced oxygen to the area, and the flame quickly bloomed into an explosion. The resulting damage to the station was minimal, but Estella had suffered a major blow.

"Ugh..."

Estella's frame was no stronger than that of the average AI model. She had taken damage at several points, there was a crack in her skull, her left arm was gone, and now her internal processes were impaired. But she couldn't give in now. She had to start working again as soon as she possibly could.

Holding herself responsible, she quickly tried to stand up. Right then, she heard something.

"Don't push yourself so much when you're all beat up like that. Are you an idiot?"

"…"

As Estella dragged her frame upright, she looked to the source of the casual voice and found a bored expression on her half-destroyed twin sister's face.

Elizabeth.

Her younger sister shook her head and looked at Estella. Her pretty face frowned, and she said, "What's going on? When did we get bodies?"

"Oh…"

She had forgotten. Now that she'd been reformatted and her memories wiped, she didn't remember what had happened or anything of the last six years. She didn't know who she had been working with or whose goals she had struggled so desperately to achieve. It was all gone.

"Eh, it's not like you have to tell me with words anyway," said Elizabeth as she brought her forehead to Estella's, seemingly unbothered by her missing arm. When their foreheads touched, a datalink formed between the twins.

"…"

In a snap decision the moment they made contact, Estella limited what was sent. She sent the information that they were currently in Sunrise, a hotel on a space station, that the space station was currently falling toward the Earth, and that there was no way to stop it. She also told Elizabeth that she was working to limit the damage as much as possible. That was it. She had no choice but to hold back the reason for their situation as well as their relationship. If Elizabeth found out...

"All right, got it. Looks like fate's got a sense of humor making us twins lose opposite arms. We probably won't last much longer."

"Elizabeth..."

"We're twins, and our positronic brains are 99.8 percent the same. I can't think of a more appropriate way for the two of us to go out than together." Elizabeth grinned as she pulled her head away. Then she dragged Estella over to the control device, reopened the transmission that had been cut off by the blast, and stood to the left of Estella—the side Estella had lost her arm on—to take up half of Estella's work.

The interrupted sequence was restarted, and the operation continued.

"..."

"Hey, how long are you going to make your sister work alone?" Elizabeth teased. "Don't just stand there, Sis. Do AIs proud and work until the moment we burn up." There was no hatred in her words. It was a pure display of her own individuality.

The two of them worked together, a cooperation between twins that should have never been possible.

Estella felt her nonexistent heart beating, and she smiled. "Elizabeth, do you remember?"

"Do we really have time to be talking about the good old days?"

"We can multitask... Before we were activated, when we were just positronic brains...we talked to each other."

They were truly twins, even if they had been trapped in the fates of their conflicting owners.

"..."

"We talked about how we wanted to be AIs who gave our all for the sake of humanity."

Elizabeth grimaced like she'd been forced to remember something unpleasant. Her reaction seemed odd, but then Estella let out a soft gasp as she realized how utterly cruel she was being. She'd forced Elizabeth to forget her own wishes and help Estella foil her own plan. Elizabeth was unaware of this; she was simply supporting her sister. She didn't even know *why* she was about to burn up.

"I don't really get what's going on," Elizabeth told her. "I just came to and found myself here. But..."

"But?"

"I'm here with you, working hard for humanity... That's not so bad," Elizabeth said gruffly.

Estella's eyes widened, and a smile blossomed on her face. "We really *are* twins."

.: 10 :.

T FIRST, only one guest noticed the singing.

It was a man sitting in a seat on the escape shuttle, lamenting his own bad luck at everything he'd lost. He'd saved so long for this special trip into space, and his concerns about the future weighed heavily on him. As he sat there, someone's singing voice came to him over the transmission, and he looked up.

"Can you hear...someone singing?"

"Huh?"

The other guests around him, who were in similar situations, looked up when he whispered. They realized the voice was being transmitted from Sunrise as it continued to fall. It was the same voice they'd heard only a few hours earlier on the observation deck.

Obviously, the audio equipment on the shuttle couldn't compare to that of the concert, and the quality of the transmission wasn't very good, but the voice had so much power that it overrode any of those concerns.

"She's singing. Estella...the Dawn Songstress."

From the escape shuttle windows, they could see the sun climbing over the edge of Earth. The shuttle was alight with the dazzling namesake of Sunrise and Daybreak, accompanied by a voice that seemed to come from the heavens. They were still scared and unhappy, but it was a balm. It brought them solace.

It brought them *hope*.

As the audience turned their attention to the voice of the Dawn Songstress, one girl among them cried out. It was the girl who'd been separated from her parents during the incident and brought back at the last minute by an AI staff member. Her large eyes were round and her lips trembled as she said, "I can hear two voices... There are two singers."

The people around her realized she was right. The voices overlapped and intertwined. They blended so naturally, it seemed obvious that there had always been two, or perhaps that they'd begun as one.

"It's beautiful..." someone murmured, captivated.

There was no need to ask who had spoken. Everyone else there was equally enthralled. The song was so far away, and it brightened the beautiful scene of the rising sun. For the rest of their lives, those people would never forget the sight and that sound.

In the following years, if anyone asked someone who was there what it was like to be involved in the Sun-Crash Incident, they would speak of how terrifying the ordeal was...but in the end, they would always mention the singing.

Just like the dawn, the two songstress's voices shone through even the darkest of times.

Afterword

THANK YOU VERY MUCH for buying this book. My name is Umehara, and I'm in charge of writing the afterword.

All right, I think I'm going to explain a bit about the situation surrounding this series of books, *Vivy Prototype*, since it's a little complicated. Our plan for this series of books was for it to literally be the "prototype" for the anime *Vivy -Fluorite Eye's Song-*. It was an experiment in writing novels that would then be a base for the script, instead of just diving straight into the anime.

In other words, this isn't a novelized version of an anime, and it's also not the original novel that was turned into an anime. Probably the closest description would be to call them "concept novels." Those of you who have seen the first half of the anime have probably already noticed that. The story is quite a bit different between the books and the anime. One of the first changes we can see are adjustments to our main character, Vivy, and then there were a lot of details in the book that were omitted in the script.

So, while the overarching flow of the story might be the same between mediums, a lot of the structural elements, characterization, and characters only appear in the books. Some arcs even come to different conclusions.

Naturally, I hope you'll read the books *and* watch the anime. If you read the books first, perhaps you'll like seeing how the story was adapted to the anime. If you watched the anime first, you might enjoy getting a peek into the story's creation. Either way, you'll see more of Vivy's world.

There is one more important thing to explain. While I, Umehara, am in charge of writing the afterword, I didn't actually write a single word of the first volume. Nagatsuki-san wrote the entire first volume. Having said that, the overall plot was created between the two of us, and we'll be taking turns writing each installment. Our responsibilities will be reversed for the second volume—I will be in charge of writing the actual book, while Nagatsuki-san will take care of the afterword.

This is my first time working on novels with multiple authors. It's exciting, but there's quite a lot of pressure as well. I mean, I am working with *the* Nagatsuki-san, after all. We have different levels of experience when it comes to writing novels, and, more importantly, Nagatsuki-san's novels are just good.

The thing that really stood out to me about this volume was Vivy and Matsumoto's relationship and how it developed. I also think it's safe to say that the overall tone and feel of this volume became an important benchmark as we continued developing the story.

The first time I read the story, I was shocked by Momoka's sudden fate. I still vividly remember what Nagatsuki-san said when I asked why it went that way. He said, "Well, I wanted to give the readers or viewers a sudden punch to the heart."

Fans of Nagatsuki-san's other work will probably know this, but he's also good with stories about twins (haha). Actually, when the two of us made the plot for the Sunrise arc, we had a conversation like this:

Nagatsuki: "I think a drama between two AIs of the same model is a surefire winner."

Uehara: "I like the Hayabusa spacecraft. Wouldn't it be cool if the AIs burn up while fulfilling their duty?"

And that's about all we decided. Then he produced this. I quite liked Elizabeth. She's the only one out of all the Sisters who will appear that I've given a nickname. I call her "Zabessan."

When I write the next volume, I'm going make sure it's just as good as this one. Please continue to follow Vivy along her journey.

Finally, we would like to say thank you to a few people.

First we want to thank all the animation staff, starting with director Ezaki Shinpei-san, as well as Wada-san and Ootani-san of Wit Studio and Takahashi-san of Aniplex. Hearing your valuable opinions helped so much.

We also want to thank our editor, Satou-san. Thank you so much for keeping things under control and making adjustments for our odd writing format.

Thank you, loundraw-san, for the illustrations. It's an honor to work with you. I remember when the cover illustration was sent over, I went "OMG, look at loundraw-san's artwork!" (What else was I expecting?) I love it.

Thank you, Nagatsuki-san, for writing. Thank you for the entertaining story. I know how overwhelmingly difficult it is to take that first step in building a story, but you leapt right over that hurdle and hit the ground running. I look forward to working on this more with you.

And last but not least, the biggest of all thanks goes to you readers for picking up this book. There is no greater joy than knowing this story brought something to your hearts.

Until next time.
Eiji Umehara